The Woman Who Owned The Shadows

D1533866

E'me haah kosha si'ano Kawaike
Shrai ' ena schat-chen-ni-ni Sti'its'tsi-naku
E'me haah kosha si'ano Kawaike

(For I am born Kawaike
Let this little writing go to Thought Woman
For I am born Kawaike)

The Woman Who Owned The Shadows

PAULA GUNN ALLEN

aunt lute books
SAN FRANCISCO

First Edition
20 19 18 17 16 15 14 13 12 11

Aunt Lute Books
PO Box 410687
San Francisco, CA 94141

Parts of this work in somewhat different form have appeared in the following publications:
>Shantih (vol. II, #2, 1979)
>Ikon (spring 1983)
>New Lesbian Writing (Grey Fox Press, 1983)
>That's What She Said (Indiana Univ. Press 1983)

Originally published by Spinsters, Ink, 1983.

Cover art: © Helen Hardin 1983, Hohokam Shadows, acrylic
Cover photo: © Cradoc Bagshaw 1992
Cover design: Pamela Wilson Design Studio
Text design: Linda Jupiter, Sherry Thomas, Jean Swallow
Typesetting: Community Press, San Francisco

Printed in the U.S.A. on acid-free paper.

The publication of this book was originally made possible, in part, with public funds from the Literature Panel of the New York State Council on the Arts and The National Endowment for the Arts.

Library of Congress Cataloging-in-Publication Data

Allen, Paula Gunn.
The woman who owned the shadows / Paula Gunn Allen.
213 P. :22cm.
ISBN 1-879960-18-4 (pbk.) : $10.95

1. Indians of North America—Fiction. I. Title.
PS3551.L397W6   1994   94-5839
813'.54—dc20   CIP

ACKNOWLEDGEMENTS

So many have helped, supported and encouraged me in the writing of this book over the fourteen years it was in the works. I am especially indebted to Mary Tall Mountain and Paul Vane for letting me know that the book was worth the effort it took to write it, to Marcia Allarie for her unfailing support and confidence in me.

I want to acknowledge the importance of my mother's confidence in my work, which she has shown in so many ways over all these years. She has kept it safe on her shelves, read it, talked to me about it, showed it to family and friends, and let me know in countless ways that she believes in my ability and in the usefulness of my work. So often, knowing she thinks I can do it has kept me writing however tired or discouraged I got.

I am particularly indebted to my loving companion Judy Grahn for the time she has spent proofreading and questioning this book, for her insistence that good stories are about real-life people, and for pushing me to reach far beyond what I thought was possible.

I am also grateful to the women and men who read drafts of the novel with sympathy and gave clear and generous responses to it: Karen Sjoholm, Nancy Angelo, Gloria Anzaldua, Carol Lee Sanchez, Lynn Andrews, Elaine Jahner, Linda Hogan, Geary Hobson, A. LaVonne Ruoff, Tim Jacobs, Bill Vartnaw, and Charlotte Sheedy. Special thanks go to Judith McDaniel and Maureen Brady for their excitement and commitment to the novel and their clear-eyed understanding of its intent and to Sherry Thomas, whose caring, trust, and courtesy as my publisher have meant a great deal to me.

Thanks go to Brian Swann and Roberta Hill for publishing the first chapter of this novel (in somewhat different form) in *Shantih* (Native American Issue, II:2, 1979); Susan Sherman, for publishing several sections of it in *Ikon* (New York: Spring/Summer, 1983); Margaret Cruikshank, for including several sections in her forthcoming anthology, *New Lesbian Writing*, (San Francisco, Grey Fox Press, 1983); and Rayna Green, for excerpt in *That's What She Said*, an anthology of American Indian Women's writings (Bloomington: Indiana University Press, 1983); to the University of California Regents for support in the form of a post-doctoral fellowship that in part made it possible to finish the novel, and to the National Endowment for the Arts whose grant in 1978 helped free to write portions of the first draft.

Without the encouragement and good cheer of feminist audiences who welcomed portions of the manuscript at readings so enthusiastically, I'm certain I wouldn't have had the courage to finish it, and I want to thank all who contributed energy to the endeavor in that way, and in the vision of a strong woman's culture they create and recreate so powerfully in their work and lives. Here too, go thanks to Gertrude Stein and Mary Daly whose ways with words have taught me much.

Finally, deepest gratitude goes to N. Scott Momaday, whose genius and persistence has made all my work possible, and to my American Indian people, whose traditions, vision, history, and power to endure with tenacity, grace and humor in the face of overwhelming destruction are the guide and motivation of both my work and my life. And to my parents who taught me that balance, honor and courage are always possible.

Nos Vemos.

This book is dedicated with gratitude to
my great grandmother, Meta Atseye Gunn.

To Naiya Iyatiku.

And to Spider Grandmother, Thought Woman,
who thinks the stories I write down.

"To be an Indian in modern American society
is in a very real sense to be unreal and
ahistorical."

Vine Deloria Jr.
Custer Died For Your Sins

SHINASHA

(Navajo Song sung when the Navajo returned
from exile at Ft. Sumner, New Mexico)

Shinasha   Shinasha
       Shinasha La de ho zho la
He ye   He ne ya
       A ly A ly   Ko ny sha
       A ly A ly   Ko ny sha

I am Walking, Alive
Where I am is beautiful

I am still alive,
Walking, lonely.

PART I

PROLOGUE

In the beginning was the Spider. She divided the world. She made it. Thinking thus she made the world. She drew lines that crossed each other. Thus were the directions. Thus the powers. Thus were the quadrants. Thus the solstices. Thus were the seasons. Thus was woman. Within these lines placed she two small medicine bundles. Singing, she placed them. In the sacred way she played them. There were no others then but the Spider who sang.

In the center of the universe she sang. In the midst of the waters she sang. In the midst of heaven she sang. In the center she sang. Her singing made all the worlds. The worlds of the spirits. The worlds of the people. The worlds of the creatures. The worlds of the gods. In this way she separated the quarters. Singing, she separated. Upon the face of heaven she placed her song. Upon the face of water she placed her song. Thus she placed her song. Thus she placed her will. Thus wove she her design. Thus sang the Spider. Thus she thought.

Within the pouches, the sacred identical pouches she had placed the seeds that would bear the woman who was her own twin. Uretsete and Naotsete she would name them, double woman would she name them, from whose baskets would come all that lives. In the northwest placed she one. Placed she one in the northeast.

And as she sang, as the Spider sang, the pouches swelling, dancing, gave forth the seed, the women. Thus have the women of our people ever reverenced the seeds, and saved them. Thus have we given honor to them. Thus are the seeds eaten, thus they remind us of our generation, thus they sit on the altar of power, thus are they planted in the ground, thus are they kept ever with us.

And the sisters awoke, those two, they who would give human form to the spirit which was the people. Singing they awoke in the darkness that is below in the place of the Spider, in the firmament that is the place of the Spider. Singing they awoke and sat near the Spider, the Grandmother, who sang.

1

And the Spider sang. She thought to name the twain. Long she thought, singing. And she knew one was She Who Matters and the other was She Who Remembers. So she named them Uretsete and Naotsete. The women who made all that lives on earth. Who made the world. Who formed matter from thought, singing.

And as they sat with the Spider, alongside the Grandmother, they took up their work, the work of the sisters, the women, the double women who would bear the world.

And they said, "We will name. We will think." Thus they said. Thus they did. Singing, chanting in the way of the people, made they the languages, all the tongues of the earth. Thus finished they everything. In beauty finished they. All the names. All the tongues. Thus was everything made, and made different.

Shaking, Uretsete named them. Shaking, Naotsete thought about them. Thus made they the sun. The stars. Singing they made the elements, the rains, the thunders, the winds, the snows. Shaking, they were singing. Shaping the katsina and the spirits, the game and the mountains. Singing, chanting, shaking, crooning, they named everything. Thus made they everything ready for their children.

And Uretsete made the division of the waters and the land, shaking. Saying the water and the land have become good. Only the earth will be ripe, said she. Upon the earth will live the people. Thus she said.

Thus they sent their thought into the void. Singing, chanting sent they their thought, the thought of the Spider, out into the void. Thus finished they everything and set everything in place.

Her Name Was A Stranger

In opening the door let the dingy light pass through, as if on its way to a quiet dark place. The sun was gray that morning. The color of bored conversation. Inevitably. The winter insinuated itself into every corner. Dreamlike. Would not be completely banished no matter how many fires tended. How many wines drunk slowly beside their glow. The time of quiet, of rest. She could see how the house, its people settled in, grew subdued. As gray as the light that came through the door. The old blue wooden door she had just opened. Ancient sign of entering. Springing a dream momentarily free. For her to look at. But she let it slip away. Distracted by the cold.

Her children were gone then. Staying at her mother's in the village, Guadalupe. She didn't have even them to keep her still. Connected to time. To place.

Four o'clock. The brass handle was cold in her hand. They'll be here pretty soon. The others. She thought. She crossed the room, smoothing her disorderly black hair as she again walked toward the door. No, they just left. I thought I heard them talking, coming up the walk. She turned again, pulling the door shut behind, vagueness hunching her round shoulders, her round brown arms raising to circle her for warmth. Slowly she sat in the nearest bright orange chair. What time is it?

Ephanie. Too stange a name, deranging her from the time she first understood its strangeness. Her body, choppy and short, sturdy, was at odds with her name. Ephanie was for someone tall and serene. Someone filled with grace. But like her it was a split name, a name half of this and half of that: Epiphany. Effie. An almost name. An almost event. Proper at that for her, a halfblood. A halfbreed. Which was the source of her derangement. Ranging despair. Disarrangement.

But she wasn't deranged just now. Only distracted. It seemed so late, so early, so indeterminate when she got up. But there are people coming today, or did they come and now they're gone. Why they went so early. She began to dig, habitually. Down into herself. Trying to find a point that would give her the time. Clocks evaded her. When she looked at one she

3

forgot to register what it said. Resistance. Digging, brown hands clasped, she went carefully over what had happened that day. When the people had come. What they had done. What said, how gone. She knew that much of what had gone before was missing.

"Jump. No. Get out here in the open where you have freedom to move. Jump. No. Here. You're too tense. It doesn't work that way. Remember what I said about expectations. Open your hands. That's right. Now. Close your eyes. Breathe. You are the tree at the edge of this field. Tall. Quiet. The wind moves you. You are alive. Unimpressed by it. Relax your legs. Let your arms free. Quiet. Quiet. Begin to soar. Don't try to move your body yet. Just soar in your mind. Get the feel of soaring clearly in you, in your muscles, in your breath. Now. Jump. Don't open your eyes. Again. Open your hands. Jump. Soar."

She Is Remembering

Empty spaces. A room of long shadows, climbing into night. Sun that is simply there.

"I never assume. What is past is an illusion. You make up. It probably is." She said.

He said, "Remember that you, like the air, are a complex of molecules. Let yourself know it. Know that anything can pass through you. Don't make yourself into a net to trap things. Time, as you feel it, is an illusion. Delusional. The reality is molecular. A thread. Imagine a moment as you know it. Think how a molecule would know the same thing. Consciousness is the essential lie. I think therefore I am? No. You are, so you think. But being is not thinking about it. It is imaginary, being is. An image. A hallucination. To be awake. Really. Aware. Is to know nothing. Moment by moment, breath by breath. To hold nothing. Alive. The last superstition built into memory is that you exist as you think you do. Mama gave it to you with her milk. Nothing only is alive. You can hold it, if you hold it lightly. Like sunrise. Only if you let go of everything else. There isn't room for two in your heart."

4

She sat beside him, understanding nothing. Unable to say so. His words, the sounds themselves, were lulling, letting her slip away into safety. From the puzzlement of torture. Let him go on and I will sit. Pretend to listen. She thought. The sun is cold.

"The sun isn't cold," he said. He took her hand, held it, warming. "You're cold. the sun's temperature is constant." Smiled.

"I am cold," she said. "I close my eyes. I rest. You hold my hand. I do not pull away. The sun shines. What are you doing here?"

She opened her eyes then and looked at him, refusing to look away. Seeing if she could read his answer from his look. He reached back, long, did not answer except to close his hand more tightly on hers. She watched him. Long enough to be sure he wouldn't speak, long enough to be certain she couldn't decode the look he gave her. The tightening hand. Then she closed her eyes again. "I dreamed I could fly." She said.

"You didn't dream. You remembered the field yesterday. You flew then, but you didn't know it. Mind. The lie-builder. Let it go, Déjalo. It is better. Be the wind out here, el viento. The birds you saw flying, falling through the sky. Be the birds. It will snow soon." He let go of her hand. Got up from the step they sat on. Left.

Don't finish the paragraph until the next day. Always stop where you can start again. Memory leads to completion eventually. You should never expect yourself to face emptiness. He said all that and she knew he must be right because he had always finished. Was finished now. But to hold the thought, as if it were a meal half-eaten. Left over for the next day. The sentence half-written. The unutterable pose. She could feel hysteria building crazily in her. She saw herself movable. Tinker-toy. Falling to pieces on the floor. Stephen. Estebanito. Amigo. My friend. She looked around her and saw dust lying. Thick on everything. Nobody was ever here. I didn't have that conversation with Stephen. I wonder if I can speak at all. To anyone. It is always so quiet. She wrapped her arms around herself tightly like the women wrap their shawls and started walking, aimless,

5

around the room, sniffing, looking dogwise for some clue. Or else he left and I didn't hear him go.

She had dreamed the dream of years. Of her whole life. That dream of herself with Elena, amiga, tiny girls running in frantic circles around her grandmother's house, screaming. Being chased by a long circle of animals: coyotes and wolves, bear and deer, antelope and jackrabbits, goats and lizards, snakes. Running forever with no way to escape while the others—mother and aunts, sisters and grandmother stood, watched, slouching familiarly with each other, laughing and pointing. Unconcerned.

Shaking, She Makes It Matter

Fear. Bloody fingers pressing her temples. Her breastbone. Her gut. I will not be afraid. Fear, the destroyer. Even I know there is nothing really frightening here. The red carpet. The stereo. Dusty records. Table, dark brown. The sun in the window. Going out. The lamps. Coming on. Turning them on, Ephanie. It will be all right. Be quiet now, Ephanie, my beloved, don't think. Ephanie. Any other way is dangerous. Stephen will be back. Maybe this evening. Maybe tommorrow. You couldn't have imagined him. You didn't make him up.

She walked through the tiny quiet house. Turning on lights, turning out lights, picking things up, carrying them awhile, putting them down. Among the litter of my own things, she kept thinking. Grew angry at herself for thinking it over and over. As though it was a prayer, a ritual, a rite. Among. Pick up the robe. The litter. Walk with it. Of my. Put it down. Own things. Turn out the bedroom light. (Among.) Turn on the hall light. (The litter.) Go downstairs. (Of my.) And begin again. (Own things.)

She knew one thing. She was alone. There was no one in the house with her, to see the last sun go, to see the darkness crawl into the room, to see the fire brighten in front of her eyes. There is something else I know. It is dark. But is it night? Dark comes early now. I wonder if it is really night. How long do I have to wait until I can expect someone to come. (He said not to expect.

6

He must be right. He knows about this. He's sure.) Or did he say it, Stephen. Or did I read it. Somewhere. Or did I make it up. It seems true. But I want to know who. Said that. Maybe everyone. Like one writer wrote all the books. Like the Spider thought everything. But if only one writer wrote the Bible and Shakespeare and Alice in Wonderland and the Bobbsey Twins. Maybe no one writes anything. Maybe there's no books after all. Maybe I just think I read. Pretending. Maybe a witch makes me think there are books. To make me afraid. To steal my mind. Or maybe I'm really asleep. Dreaming. Maybe I make them all up in my sleep. Who am I that I can make up everything?

Or maybe it's a conspiracy of the streetlights. The lamps inside. Maybe they beam their own dream thought into my mind. Everyone's minds. And we all think we read them somewhere. All in the same books. They have names. And the lamps and the streetlights get us to believe there are books and type and paper and writer's names. Dreams can be so real sometimes. How would anyone know? I've had dreams that were very real.

She could feel the fingers, more insistent. She began to laugh. Wildly. Felt the streetlights pull at her eyes. She began shaking. Humming a tuneless song. "They aren't real," she said. "You aren't real. You can't write books. You can only stand there and shed light. All night. You can't even keep the murderers away. I write the books. I do. Myself." She wanted to cry. To scream. To shriek like a crazy wind. She picked up the lamp that looked at her, unconcerned, smug. She smashed it against the table edge. Smashed the window with the unbroken shaft that was left. Threw it at the streetlight. She knew she was losing control. Was scaring herself. But the lights seemed so alive. So evil. Those unalive manmade things seemed too alive. Even if they were not to be feared, she feared them. And couldn't convince herself otherwise. The streetlights don't let me sleep right.

In The Shadows, She Is Shaking

How Stephen had gotten into her. Life. Mind. Skin. Her skin his medicine bundle. Bone and hair. Intrusion. Extrusion. Never minding. That. How Stephen, her Indian cousin, friend, dear as a brother. Who was as she could not be. Bright. Pale eyes. Tawny skin. Lion hair. That glinted in the light. His ever present sun.

Starlight. Candlelight. Flame. Against her shadows, sharp. Pointed he was. Keen. Slicing through the fogs that shuddered her. Through her. Through her. A flicker of light. Of fire.

All her life he had been there. In Guadalupe. Walking along the road. Looking over at her. Smiling, enigmatic, serene. In the store. Her father's store, Stephen, hermano, she remembered. She never remembered without remembering him. How strong, secure he was. Slim hands, brown and gold in the depths of the store, the merchandise spilling over rough-hewn shelves: shirts, levis, bright-colored shawls. Tins of food glinting high. Medicines. Candy. Bins of flour, sugar, beans. Stephen there. And beneath the blooming boughs of the apple tree. Kneeling at the spring cupping the sweet pure water in his palm. Drinking. In forever sunlight, soft and sweet. A cry within, bright, piercing. A light. And though they weren't by blood related, he was as close to her as her flesh, her bones. When she was an infant, a child, growing up. And later. After the cruel marriage to the man who left one night, late, into the rain slanting down around him, his small-brimmed stetson pulled tight over his skull, brim protecting naked face from cold, from rain. Who had gone into the darkness, the water. Who had not ever come home. Who had gone then. Left. Her. And the babies. Agnes, quick and sinewy, even then. Ben, tiny and silent, so serious in his deep owl eyes. Her, Ephanie. Who would not be anything other than an opening, a shadowed place. Who she didn't want to think about ever again.

And Stephen coming then. Staying silent and still. Sitting day through day in her living room, taking her to her mother's house, to the store to buy food, to buy some bright new blouse, something for the kids. Coming up her drive in the battered truck he drove, coming to a stop just outside her door. Coming in. Arms full of food. Presents, his presence, coming to sit and stay with her in her fear, in her despair.

And when that other thing began. She did not know. Only that the fear left her, transformed into something she kept beneath her bed. A shadowed thing. A bundle of hair and memory. Bone and rage. Tight knotted in black string, blackened with the oil of her hands, the candle's smoke. Chanting she had made it, knotted the thread tight around the small bundle of things. That had been her life. And Stephen patient, telling her how. To do that. To put her rage and despair to good use.

A picture of the husband that she had taken. She tore it carefully. She spit upon it. She burned it, chanting the words Stephen had taught her. She placed it in the growing bundle. Binding. Where he had gone, her husband. Where he would not ever ever return. And with his ashes, her spit. With his hair, her blood. With his memory, her core. She added to that mixture a kernal of corn. A pipe. These she bundled, chanting. These she knotted with black and red yard. Singing. Shaking with rage and bewildered, she cursed, murmuring. Goddamn sonofabitch. Goddamn sonofabitch. Cabrón. Pendejo. Rotten lousy bastard nogood sonofabitch. She had said. Bleeding. From her womb, from her slashed bleeding palm, from her chest. He'll never do it to anyone else. She vowed. She swore.

And for days vomited. Ate nothing. Huddled over herself in pain. Cramping and cramping. Wanting, needing to die. And Stephen feeding her. Something. She did not remember. Stephen taking the babies to her mother. Saying "It's better this way. You can't take care of them now. You need me to take care of you." Saying, "You be still now, Ephanie. Now you rest. Now you let me take care of you. I'll take care of you." Saying, "You know you need me to. You are so weak, now. I will take care of you, little one, sister. I will take care of you."

And now in the darkness of terror that had longsince turned to quiet everpresent dread, she understood that he had kept his vow. He had taken care of her. Surely, he had. That without his presence that never asked, never raised its voice, so quiet, so sure, so in command, she would surely have died.

Then why her fear? Why did she incessantly long for him,

9

his presence when he was not there? Wish with all her shadowed heavy burdened being that he be gone when he was there? And why did she not get stronger? Why did she no longer even care?

I hate him, I hate him, she would weep, find herself weeping. On her knees. Pleading. To an empty room. To the shadows that stood, mute along the floor and walls, alongside the door. And realizing her words, contrite, would deny. No, no. I need him. He is so good to me. He is the only one who cares. He tells me so. Over and over. He tells me so. I must believe that. Him. Or I will die.

And did not realize that it was he who told her often, every day, more, that she would surely die without him to secure her, to make her safe. She was helpless, he said. The blow to her. The mothering. She could not do. He said it. She silent, sick and exhausted, believed.

Stephen, coming in. Going out. Over the stove, stirring, tasting, mixing, blending. Over steaming pots, frowning, seasoning. He was judicious. Careful. And in his sweeping, makingbeds. In his boiling the wash. Carefully. Cautious. Wiping the baby's face, setting him down. Sending him off to play. Tending to the fires, the hearth. Stephen, carefully tending while she watched, wrapped securely in the shawl he had brought her one day. She sitting in the shadowed places, the corners of the rooms. Her eyes only lighting sometimes, glowing taut and raging, maybe unseen.

He would come sometimes to sit with her. To take one of her hands. To hold it between his two. Talking soft, low, to her. To her empty face. To her contorted mouth. To her tightscrewed eyes, glinting. Once he came from the kitchen where the light slanted into the other room where she sat alone, huddled in the dark. He came then, holding the paring knife he had been chopping onions with. He put the knife, slim and sharp, in her hand, closed her fingers around it. He told her it was hers. To keep. His eyes looking into hers. Probing. Commanding. Bland. No light coming from them. Absorbing all the light in that dim dim room.

She sitting, dumb. Unable to speak. To comprehend. Knowing somehow in the shadows of her mind that he was trying to give her something. To tell her something. That she did not

10

understand. She dropped her head, hair falling over her forehead, into her eyes. Looking dully at the blade protruding from between thumb and palm where it emerged from her limp grasp. She held it because he had put it there. Because he had curled her fingers around the smooth wooden handle. Because she had not the will to let go. To undo what he had done.

And she remembered the tears that had come from some hidden river in her eyes. Had fallen on her hand, on her lap, on the knife. Silent, they had coursed, beyond her willing, beyond her power to start or to stop. And Stephen, hermano, closing his soft hand over hers, comforting. An almost smile somewhere lurking on his face. In his words. "There, little one," he said, low, almost so she did not hear. "I have given you something you can use. You hold this power. This little knife. You must learn to use it. To slice very deep."

And low, so low, she had finally managed to say. "Stephen. I want." Pausing then. For a beat. One beat the length of one single word. Then finishing. "To go away." She did not say that one, that crucial word. "You. I want you to go away." Nor did he hear. What the tiny pause, that silence was intended, inarticulate, to say.

She Is Always Dreaming Something

She slept then, seeing orange. Flowers. Roses. Something with large petals. She had colored them with green borders of forest. Of summer lawns. Telling Stephen about it after he had gone. "My brother kept using a machine that finished his pictures perfectly, and because of his selfishness we started to fight. He wouldn't finish a picture completely so I could use the coloring machine. He just kept starting over on new pictures. One large rose, colored just like mine. One big rose on every page. He just ignored the others on the page, and the trees and fences too, so he could start again and say he wasn't finished. That way he would never finish. It would never be my turn. Besides, he was copying me, and I was sure he would get the praise for what I had done. So I told him he wasn't fair, that I knew what he was doing. And I started crying because he didn't pay any attention to me. He wouldn't give me the book back, or the machine."

It was true that there was in her that streak, as in everyone she knew. That they were going to steal everything. That someone would take it all away. In her case she had been aware of that particular turning inward, of shutting off what was painfully outside since earliest memory. Something to do with her mother. Needing her love. Touching. Concern that seemed to go to others. Always.

Stand up for your rights, they had told her, she had told herself, someone was always telling someone. Sometimes she did. Stand up. Stand out. But that was frightening. Her mother had insisted on it. Saying, "Stand up to them." Pinching her leg, her arm. Insistent. Sometimes she stood up. Surely she did. Othertimes she just dissolved. Trying to become one with the shadows. With the silences, with the dark. Like now as she sat, weeks and months, trying to discover the source of the fear that voiceless coursed and surged through her muscles and her bones.

She thought about what she remembered, trying to make memories match events. Trying to separate her memories from her dreams. The time the white stranger came and called to her. Friendly, he called, persuasive. And she wouldn't come out to meet him but lay, huddled in the farthest corner beneath the big bed in her mother's room, trying to be invisible. She didn't want him near her. She was afraid. She never knew, never remembered why. He was her doctor. He had taken her tonsils out. He was her father's friend. And her mother's friend. He and his wife were their friends. Because he had taken her tonsils out. She knew she was supposed to like him. But she was afraid.

She remembered taking her own children to him years later. Certain she should trust him. Taking strong, bright Agnes. Taking silent, stalwart Ben. Remaining in the examining room with them. Seeing him touch them between the legs. Wondering at the stiffness that came over her muscles then. Her wish to flee. To hide her eyes in shame. Something more than shame. To snatch her children and take them far away. Or hide with them under some safe huge bed. In memory that threatened to break through the barriers, she wondered. She didn't know why she was fearful and ashamed, but she wondered about it for years.

The stiffness might have been in imitation of the nun at boarding school who had averted her pious eyes stiffly when Ephanie had been sick and the doctor had come. She remembered that. Lying in the narrow iron-steaded bed, helpless, quiet, as he used his stethascope to listen to her lungs, her pajama top opened, the nun, pale face ringed by black hood, body safely covered except for hands and face, standing at the door with eyes carefully turned upward, away. Her mouth held in that certain expression of disgust that only white women ever wore, almost always wore.

She had wanted to stand up then and run. She had wanted to make him go away then. She had wanted to tell the nun to go away. But she didn't have those kinds of words to put on the feelings that rose in her, hot with confusion and rage, shame, redcheeked tightness. He kept telling her to breathe. She kept concentrating on the air in front of her, on not letting them see her feeling anything like Grandma had said for her to do. She concentrated on not remembering her own fever, her helplessness cornered and open there. She concentrated on making them seem far away. As if they were not there. As if she weren't there. Were anywhere else. She thought herself under the bed. Hid and huddled there. Beyond his stare. Beyond the nun's unconcerned, averted gaze.

What had been taken then? Nothing, surely. That hadn't already been lost or stolen. At that time she couldn't have been more than nine years old. But still. Whatever she had of hope and joy. Of sturdy self and defiant reason. Of exuberant faith in the safe sweetness of her own rejoicing self had fled long before. Long before that helpless day when Elena had repeated what the nun had said. That evil made Ephanie and Elena play dirty things. That the sister had said they must stop playing with each other like that. They should be ashamed. They should be afraid. They would have to go to confession about it if they kept on playing like that, between each other's legs when they were one or two years older and could sin.

13

He Was Her Twin

He was her teacher. Her friend. From a long time. From ever since they were small. She remembered something. About a time so long before. Stephen, almost grown. Coming by her house. Saying, "Let's go with me. We'll go to the hills. On a journey."

He was like that. Her guide on journeys. Patient. He taught her so much that she knew. Would always know, even when she forgot. That she knew. What she knew.

And she had gone, happy. Proud he had chosen her to go. To take. What fine thing he would show her. Would help her learn. To leap over dizzying crevices. Over the shadows, in the sun. To hold her body, limbs, torso, eyes, just so. Allowing no flicker of light, of shadow, to deflect her thrust. Across the emptiness, to land safe on the so far other side.

How she would tell Elena, later. That he had come for her and she had gone. What marvelous feat she had done. How she would show her small friend. How she would glow in triumph at what she had learned.

She remembered something. That had no words. That had no pictures. About Stephen, the light. The heat of that July day. The sun blazing, hurting her head, stupifying her brain. The numbing sun. The fire. A shadow coming down over her. A hand. A mouth. A feeling of suffocation. On her chest heavy. Knowing that she would surely die. Wanted to. But that she could not remember. Could only in her body know, its humming, its buzzing, the sound of static like on their radio, that sound within her now, that sound she could not abide, would on hearing it become senseless, enranged, a buzzing angry like bees, like wasps, like hornets, in her brain just behind her eyes, near the top of her head, in her skull, in her eyes, in her throat shutting off words, in her chest, tight in her chest, a buzzing like static so that she would not breathe.

So long before and unthinkable even now. The sun blazing down. Was it in that shadowed place, the one beneath the huge rock, the sacred cave he said, that they should not go into, the one they would be killed for entering, but just this once, he had

14

said, they must be brave. Was it there or somewhere else. How would she ever know. How crazy she must be. To ever think she could remember such a thing. That made no sense at all. Stephen, hermano, her teacher, her guide, her loving friend, her strength, towering, quietly knowing, serene.

And now remembering rose in her body, in its muscles and in its bones. And with it from somewhere far off, from beyond the shattering heat and the buzz of shade, of humming silence, of suffocation, there came, thin and wailing, unhuman in its wail, a long moaning rising scream.

All is very still. There is sky leading everywhere. Or nowhere. And the woman in a beige dress is telling Ephanie she is too meek. That she lets them run over her. That she must take charge. And Ephanie tries to make the woman see that it isn't true anymore. Didn't she refuse to let him get away with it? "He was so crafty, so sly," she says, "thinking he could twist the rules to his will. But I told him I knew what he was doing. I told him. But he didn't listen. Didn't stop. And you don't listen either. You just keep telling me I was wrong. No matter what I say."

If dreams order what happens, in other words, they may be real. The self may so interpret what is real to itself. Mind contemplating what is real on its own terms.

Ephanie sat the afternoon pondering the window, its light. The reflection of the yellowed tree. Branches standing as if on the threshold of awareness. Throwing light at the sky. Fall now, winter soon. Time a floating crap game.

If She Remembers, She'll Know The Time

"Now get this straight, friend. I tried it once and once only, and that is all."

This memory. Nightmare. So true she shudders, wide awake. Shakes herself to be rid of it. The reality of it. "Is dreaming when you're awake a prophecy or a hallucination?"

"You are so old. Who are you? I never saw you before. But I remember you. How you pressed the dry sweetish folds of your dead flesh against me. Why?"

She holds her hands carefully still in her lap, eyes looking neither in or out. Quiet. Why is it so quiet here? She wants night. To hide the tree and its shivering temptation. She keeps seeing herself hanging from it. Swinging. Swaying. Quiet. The sun slanting on her head makes an ache.

"The dreams don't seem to stop. Whether I'm asleep or awake," she tells him, Hermano, Stephen, Esteban. "Querido, I am so afraid. Why don't the dreams stop?"

He has no response, or none that she can remember. He just looks at her, eyes empty, eyes clear. "Don't you know how to dream?" He asks. He looks at her. He looks away.

At night it is raining, the grass wet and slippery, the logs too, bark almost glistening in the headlights. But there is something strange in the light. A strangeness there. A stranger. It is sepia like a film made to remind you of memory. The lighter areas are pale, almost tan. The shadow spaces brown/red. Not too deep. The rain oscillates between the two. She is running. The stranger in her beige dress.

"What is she doing, running in the rain?"

"I must wake up completely." Ephanie sat up. Her eyes were huge in the halflight. "I've been asleep for years." And knew with certainty that this was so, even if he tried to make her think it wasn't.

Light was coming in the east window, high above her head. She looked at it, uncomprehending, for several minutes before being able to say inside her head, "I am awake. It is dawn." The streetlight had gone out. Or maybe its light was unnoticeable beside the light of growing day. She turned over in the bed, eyes wide, and waited for sleep.

Stephen would understand. He would tell her what was happening to her. He would make her see.

She thought about how it was long ago. Trying to keep attention on the slender thread that snaked silently through this year and that, curving. Bringing them together somehow, like the Spider and the fly, the woman and her son, the gnome who always accompanied the Lady in Ephanie's dreams and disappeared with her into the sky.

"I want to be able to tell you how it was for me so you can understand." She said. "I want to know why everything is so strange to me now. I don't know what I feel, what name to call my feelings by. Reaching back into myself, into my memory, doesn't explain anything that happens to me now. I have to keep renaming everything, Stephen, as though it were new. As if I were new."

"You are," he said. "You are new, Ephanie. I have remade you." He smiled, calm and certain. She saw how her hands shook.

"If this was rebirth wouldn't I feel happy, ecstatic?" She looked at her hands twisting together in her lap. She lit a cigarette to keep him from seeing that. She lit a cigarette with hands that shook. She felt tears spring to her eyes. She squinted. Like smoke burned them.

He took her hand. Took her cigarette. Put it out. Put her hands down at her side. Looked calm and unconcerned into her eyes. "Death and rebirth are the same thing, Ephanie, beloved, hermana."

She wanted her daughter and her son. With her. She was terrified. At what he was saying. At what she knew he meant. She wanted her babies, but she didn't dare bring them here.

Ephanie looked at Stephen. She felt abandoned seeing his face empty and intent. Then she forgot what she was looking for in his face and continued to look, as though he had been anything at all in the direction of her gaze. She thought of something strange. She said, "Dying is good then, isn't it, Hermano? I could grow a dying tree in my background, couldn't I?" And felt elated to think herself beautiful, alive, with that thought. She saw a blooming happy apple tree that would grow dying into sweet, tart apples. Dying of birth. She laughed. She stood and skipped around the room. She clapped her hands.

Stephen watched her for a time. He nodded his head. Gravely. He left. When he had closed the door behind himself she was surprised to discover that the room was no emptier, no more silent than before. She picked up a cloth lying beside her and began to dust the room, intently. She hummed a very quiet song. Stephen is not able to help her

17

She Thought She Was Related To Someone

Dear Stephen,

   I seem to have been lost forever, my mind seeming to recount rememberances as though they had meaning beyond their simplest existence. Hot quicksand. Desert surmises. Sunrises. Empty as the sky just after the sun has set. Welcoming memories? I am not old enough for that. I imagine a single lilac, blooming in impossible desolation, like those my grandmother grew in Guadalupe. Nothing surrounding. Not one cloud tied in.

   I know all of this that happens to me is exactly that sort of impossibility, yet I can't seem to make it stop. Perhaps the spring of my being dried up so long ago that I have forgotten how to pray for water.

   There is a question in all of it. I feel it, but I can't locate it, or its coordinates in my—I started to say "my heart," but that's too imprecise—a term lost at the edges of the nineteenth century. Modern people have hearts that pump blood and get clogged with the leftovers of rotten food and last night's dreams. That is all. Can't locate the question in my mind then. There are always thoughts there, flowing over thoughts flowing into memories, flowing into dreams, real and made up. Or all made up. How can I tell the difference? There isn't any way to, not since they raised the curtains of Absolute to reveal an empty stage, vast and silent. No actors. No script. Not one single character to measure myself beside. Everyone the audience, not one listening soul among. Everyone their own Shakespeare. Is this what it was all for? Everything relative, nothing related?

   There's a book in front of me filled with pictures of silent tombs and chipped statues and jungles. Like live and dead ideas trapped in a senseless time warp. No wonder jungle people hate the pictures of their worlds. Here and there the faces of Mexican and Central American Indians look out at me. I think I see a sense of knowing on their faces and, of course, resignation. And a nagging sort of shrewd understanding, like Grandma used to have when she told me a story or made supper or helped Grandpa take off his boots. Do they know something I don't? They seem to, and I feel troubled by that look. I peer at it as if I could also know if only I could look hard enough, see clearly, clear my head. If I could remember something. Forget something. Figure something out.

I look again at the pyramids and statues, what's left of them. I read the text that describes the intricately carved walls, those temples of the Ancient Sun.

On the beach near Malibu I once saw their brothers, the new sun worshippers. I found myself studying as intently their bronzed faces, gestures, looks. There is no reason that I can see for that irritating knowingness on the Indian peasants' faces to be found on the others here.

Sun worshippers?

Heliotrope.

My thoughts pause, bound, questions rise to silence and pollute my mind. What in me can possibly meet memories without renewal, can ever disperse the original wind of that mind built into me by my people and my time? Thoughts of broken gods don't lead anywhere. They only tell a tale bound to questions. They leave me restless, stupid, unsatisfied, longing for a good stiff drink.

Oblivion.

Ephanie

Long before, they had taken everything away. And they were still afraid for what they know the thieving meant. They had stolen whatever mattered. Were always still stealing it. Hope. Faith. Dreams. Laughter. Love. All that they hadn't stolen was her life, she thought. And they were trying to steal that too. To take control of her very breath. To tell her when and how to breathe. He was.

Often she decided to let them have whatever they wanted from her. What's the point of fighting about it, she had thought. They always get it anyway. Even now she had to decide again and again. To let them have their way so they would leave her alone. With her thoughts and her dust and books and imaginings. They can't steal what's given to them, she reasoned. And somehow felt empowered by that idea. Not a poor helpless creature after all. But a willing partner in the theft of her own soul.

What's the point of fighting?

19

Other times she was not so sure. Maybe she was too willing to give them freely her mind. Then she would talk as little as she could. She would evade their look or their words. She would shrink away from their presence. Close herself into a tiny corner of her mind where they couldn't follow. And she would refuse to come out for the longest time. Saying all the while to herself, "No no no you can't take that no no no I won't let you." Thinking they could hear her. Thinking she could refuse.

Sometimes even she went out to fight the thievery. To face it. Head on. To tell them what they were doing. To break windows and smash doors. To make them stop. Sometimes it even worked. They did stop for the time being, until her attention was elsewhere. Until she felt safe and certain. Until she looked the other way. Until she was vulnerable because of something—a thought, a feeling, a face through the window, in the mirror, on the street. A conversation. Then they would move in and take it anyway. Whatever it was she was saving. For herself. It always happened that way. She had never learned how to make it not.

Constant vigilance is the price. Of freedom. They said that. And they knew a lot about it because they had never been free except when they stole someone's soul, its freedom, and took it for themselves. They were experts in freedom. Because they were free to do anything they wanted to somebody else. To her. They could do what they pleased with her mind. Her breath. Her longing. Her grief. "I am not vigilant enough," she would think. And resolve again to let them have whatever they wanted. They'd get it anyway.

The Arapaho say death is a hill. The side of the living is separated from the side of the dead by a barbed wire fence, at least since the whites came. Before, it was separated by what they knew about boundaries. Or by the sky. Both those left on the living side and the children who play on the death side call the person who is dying.

"Come here." They call.
"Stay here." They sing.
"Come."
"Stay."

It is the same for a man or a woman, if he dies in battle or she in childbirth. It is the same. It is the competence of the Arapaho not to judge.

She thought of those other years. Those so far behind memory and so easily confused with dream. After twenty years to enter in memory the house where her grandmother used to sit during Feast and receive and feed all who entered as was the custom. And after so long for the house to be the same as Ephanie remembered dreaming about it, so long before.

Still clear the center of cool that frightens those who do not know the streets of now, that place of solitude and silence possessed of its own deep light. And I, Ephanie, know it is the place that the earthbound call the dark. Yellow and red is the light there. The dance is like that of petal fall. The way there is by the self-extruded thread of beckoning Old Spider, she who is the guardian of my life, who takes me into memory, into mind. I will not betray that beckoning, whatever it means.

Old Spider

In The Shadows Singing She Remembered

It had been the apple tree. The long spring days there. With the girl. They had watched the village going. They had watched the clouds. When they thirsted they climbed down from the branches and walked to the nearby spring. Took a long sweet drink.

Elena had taught Ephanie about the weeds. Which to eat. When they had gathered prickly pears in the summer, brushing carefully the tiny spines from the fruit before they ate. They had wandered the mesas and climbed the nearer peaks. Together they had dreamed. Sharing. They never talked about growing up. What that would mean.

They had ridden horses, pretending to be ranchers, chasing the village cattle around the town, they suffered scoldings for it. They learned to be trick riders. Roy Rogers and Hopalong Cassidy. Maybe they could be stunt men in Hollywood if they got good enough at it, if they could learn to jump from the rooftop onto the horse's back. They had chased the clouds.

Or lying, dreaming, had watched them, tracing faces and glorious beast shapes in the piling, billowing thunderheads. On July mornings they had gone out from their separate homes, laughing, feet bare and joyful in the road's early dust. The early wind cool and fresh, the bright sunlight making promises it would never keep. They had lain together in the alfalfa field of Elena's father, quiet, at peace.

They were children and there was much they did not know.

In their seasons they grew. Walking the road between their houses, lying langorous and innocent in the blooming boughs of the apple tree. Amid the fruiting limbs. And had known themselves and their surroundings in terms of each other's eyes. Though their lives were very different, their identity was such that the differences were never strange. They had secret names for each other, half joking, half descriptive, Snow White and Rose Red, they named themselves, in recognition of the fairness of Elena, the duskyness of Ephanie. In recognition also of the closeness they shared, those friends.

The events that measured their shared lives were counted in the places that they roamed, and Ephanie always remembered her childhood that way. The river, the waterfall, the graveyard, the valley, the mesas, the peaks. Each crevice they leaped over. Each danger they challenged, each stone, each blade of grass. A particularity that would shape her life.

They had especially loved the shadows. Where they grew, lavender, violet, purple, or where those shadows would recede on the mountain's slopes and closer by, beneath the shading trees. And the blue enfolding distance surrounding the world that meant the farthest peaks. Shared between them in their eyes, in their stories, but where, together, they had never been.

All those years, in spite of distance, in spite of difference, in spite of change, they understood the exact measure of their relationship, the twining, the twinning. There were photographs of them from that time. Because Elena's gold-tinged hair looked dark in the photograph's light, no one could say which was Elena, which Ephanie. With each other they were each one doubled. They were thus complete.

22

Jump.

Fall.

Remember you are flying. Say you are a bird.

She had said that, Ephanie. Had urged Elena to leap the great crevices that lay between the huge sandstone formations that shaped the mesas they roamed. Some of the leaps were wide and the ground far below. She had always done the leading. Elena, devoted, did what Ephanie decided. Or it seemed that way.

Ephanie didn't want to remember it that way. Wanted the fact to be that Elena had gone on her own windings, ones not of Ephanie's making. And in some cases, that was true. There were some things that no matter how Ephanie urged them, Elena would not do. Some ways in which she remained safe within her own keeping. Sometimes, when she had adamantly refused, Ephanie would give up and go back to her own home. And it also went, sometimes, the other way.

They did not argue. They did not fight. Elena would do what was of her own wanting. And while it seemed that the dark girl was leading, the fair one did the guiding. And in her quiet, unargumentative, unobtrusive way, Elena kept them both safe within the limits of their youthful abilities, gave the lessons and boundaries that encompassed their lives.

Kept them safe. Or almost so. Except for that one time that she hadn't kept them safe. Had missed some signal. Had turned aside in some way, away or toward, a split second too soon, too late. Had not known in time not to speak. Had not known what her words, in time, in consequence, would create.

Perhaps it had been the shadows that betrayed her. The certain angle of light that somehow disoriented her. Perhaps so accustomed to being safe, she did not know the danger, any danger that might tear the web of their being. Shredding. Shattering. Splintering.

Or maybe it was the sun. The bright, the pitiless, the un-wavering sun.

But whatever had disturbed her knowing, her keeping in time with the turns and twists of their sharing, their lives, in that splitting second everyone had abandoned Ephanie. Everything had gone away.

23

She Didn't Know At The Time

It was on a certain day. They went hiking. Exploring. They went walking. It was an adventure. One they had planned for a long time. Ever since they were small. They planned to walk to Picacho, the peak that rose, igneous formation, straight up from the surrounding plain. The arid floor of the semidesert of their homeland.

They wanted to climb the peak. To go to the top. To see. Elena said you could see the next village. The one that was invisible from where they lived. She told Ephanie the story, one she had recounted before. Much of what Ephanie knew about the people and land around them she learned from Elena. She didn't hear much that others told her. Not for many years.

Not that others had not spoken. Had not told her stories, had not given ideas, opinions, methods. They had. Some part of Ephanie recorded what they told her. What they said. But she did not acknowledge it until later. Not for many years. She did not understand how that had happened. But it did.

They had planned very well in the last days before their journey. Deciding what to take. What would not be too heavy to carry. What would not get in their way. What to wear, for comfort and protection, in the heat, against the stone. Which shirts, which length pants, which shoes. They knew they would get thirsty. It was July.

They wore tennis shoes and jeans. Usually they went barefoot from spring well into fall. Every chance they got. But this journey was special. It signified accomplishing. That they were grown. That they knew something, could put it into use.

They took oranges. For the juice. They knew how to use them, slit the rind with a toughened thumbnail, in a circle. Peel the small circle of rind away from the flesh. Press finger into the fruit, firmly, gently. So as not to lose too much juice. The juice was precious. It would sustain them. Then put the opening thus made to their mouths. Sucking. When all the juice was thus taken, they would split open the fruit and eat the pulp. And the white furry lining of the rind. Elena said it was sweet. That it was healthy.

Ephanie never ate an orange that way later. It didn't seem right. She didn't know why she wouldn't. Like her dislike of spiders. Which made no sense either. She remembered how it had gone, that journey, and why they had learned to eat oranges that particular way. She didn't understand her unwillingness to follow that childhood ritual. Not for a long time. And she found the lining bitter. Peeled it carefully away from the fruit all of her adult life. Threw it away.

But she loved the smell of oranges. The orange oil that clung to her hands when she was done. Its fragrance. Its echoing almost remembered pain. She would sniff it, dreaming, empty in thought, empty in mind, on her way to the faucet to wash it off her hands. And in the flood of water and soap she would banish what she did not know. Averting. Avoiding. Voiding. Pain.

They met in the early morning. While the cool wind blew down from the mountain. The way they were going was into the wind. The earth sparkled. The leaves. The sun was just getting started. Like a light from elsewhere it touched their eyes, their hands. They shivered slightly, shaking. They began to walk. Taking the road that curved upward. Upward and out. They were leaving. They knew that. They knew they would never return.

They didn't talk about that intuition, but walked, silent, amiable, close. They listened to the soft padding of their footfall on the dusty road, watched their shadows move, silent, along-side of them. Elena told Ephanie how high the peak was. Much taller than it looked. They speculated about climbing it. Ephanie was afraid of heights that had no branches to hold on to, but she never let on. She had never let on.

The great isolate rock rose maybe a hundred feet from the ground. Its top was slender, precarious. It stood alone, gray and silent, reaching into the sky. It was a proud rock. A formation. It brooded there on the plain between the villages. It guarded the road to the mountain. Sentinel.

The story it bore was an old one. Familiar. Everywhere. They remembered the old tale as they watched the rock grow larger, approaching it. About the woman who had a lover. Who had died in a war. She was pregnant. Lonely, desperate, she went to Picacho, climbed to the top, jumped to her death. That was one version, the one Elena's Chicano people told.

There was another version, one that Ephanie's Guadalupe people told. The woman was in love with a youth she was forbidden to marry. He was a stranger, and she had fallen in love with him somehow. Maybe he was a Navajo. Maybe he was a Ute. But her love was hopeless from the start. Then the people found out that she was seeing the youth secretly. They were very angry. They scolded her. Said the things that would happen to the people because of her actions. Shamed her. Hurt and angry, she had gone to Picacho. Climbed to the top. Jumped to her death.

Ephanie imagined that climb. The woman finding places to put her hands. Her feet. Tentative, climbing. Tentative but sure. Shaking. She climbed to the place where the rock was narrowest. Where the drop was straight and steep. Dizzy she had stood there, thinking perhaps, of her anguish, of her rage, of her grief. Wondering, maybe, if whether what she contemplated was wise. No one knew what she had been thinking. They must have wondered about it. They must have told themselves stories about what had gone through her mind as she stood, wavering, just on the edge of the narrow rock bridge that connected the two slightly taller peaks of the formation.

From there she could have seen the wide sweep of the land, barren, hungry, powerful as it raised itself slow and serene toward the lower slopes of the mountains to the north beyond Picacho and was there lost to the wilderness of tabletop hills, soaring slopes, green grasses, flowers, shadows, springs, cliffs, and above them the treeless towering peak. Where it became wilderness. Where it came home.

She could have seen that, looking northward. Where the mountain called Tse'pin'a, Woman Veiled in Clouds, waited, brooding, majestic, almost monstrously powerful. Or she could look southward, eastward, towards the lands the people tended, that held and nurtured them. But probably she had not looked outward. Had not seen the sky, the piling, moving thunderheads. The gold in them. The purpling blue. The dazzling, eye-splitting white. The bellies of them pregnant, ripe with rain about to be born. The living promise of their towering strength. For if she had seen them, would she have jumped?

She Is Swept Away

End of Eph. & Elena's friendship

By the time they got to the foot of the peak it was late morning. The sun was high and the earth around them looked flat. Sunbitten. The shadows had retreated to cooler places for the long day. Ephanie, slender, sturdy, brown, and Elena, slender, sturdy, hair tinged with gold, lightly olive skin deepened almost brown by the summer sun. They sat down to rest amid the grey boulders that lay in piles at the base of the peak. They ate their oranges. Looked at the climb that faced them, uneasy. The grey rock soared above their heads, almost smooth. Ephanie looked at Elena for reassurance, thinking how beautiful her friend was, sweating, laughing. Wanted to reach out and touch her face. To hold her hand, brown and sturdy like her own. Reached and touched the smooth brown skin, brushed tenderly back the gold-streaked hair.

"When we get home," she said, "let's go to the apple tree and cool off."

"I can't," Elena said. "I have to go with my mother to town. We're going to stay a few days at my sister's." She looked away from Ephanie. Looked at the ground. Ephanie felt uneasiness crawling around in her stomach. She shifted her weight away from Elena. She didn't know why she felt that way. "Let's go on up," she said.

They climbed. Elena went first. Finding places to put hands and feet. They pretended they were mountain climbers climbing Mt. Everest. They didn't have ropes, but they knew about testing rock and brush before trusting weight to them. They climbed over the boulders and up the first stage of the climb. That part was fairly easy. It was steep, but there was a broad abutment that circled most of the igneous peak, as though supporting its slender, massive skyward thrust. The abutment

27

was composed of hardpacked dirt, light sandstone, and the same grey volcanic rock that formed Picacho.

They camed to a resting place, high above the valley floor. It was very hot. They sat and looked around them. Behind them rose the peak, at the other end of a narrow pathlike ribbon of rock that lay between them and the end of their journey. A sheer drop on either side. Dizzy. Can we cross that? They looked into each other's eyes. Daring. Testing. Their old familiar way. "I don't think I can get across that. It makes me dizzy," Ephanie said. Elena said, since Ephanie had admitted her fear, "Just crawl across it. That's what I'm going to do. I'm not going to try and walk across. We can crawl. It's not far." And she began crawling across the smooth sand that lay over the rock bridge that stretched between them and the smooth curving roundness of the farther peak. "Look down," Elena said. "It's really far."

Ephanie, on hands and knees, crept behind Elena. Feeling foolish, scared. Foolish in her fearfulness. Shaking. She did look down. It was a long way to the ground. She imagined falling. Smashing herself on the rocks below. How Elena would manage. Going home to tell them she had fallen. How the woman long ago had fallen. From here.

They got across the narrow bridge, stood up and clung to the grey rock of the highest point that rose some three feet above their feet. They climbed up on it, scooting their bodies up and then turning to lie stomach-down on the flat peak. They looked down, over the back side of the peak. Saw the mountain a few miles beyond. "Let's stand up," one of them said. They stood, trembling slightly, and looked around. They saw the villages, one north of them, the other just beyond it to the west.

They rested for awhile, wishing they hadn't left the rest of the oranges down below. They realized they still had to climb back down. The part they were always forgetting. As they examined the descent, Elena said, "Ephanie there's something I have to tell you." She didn't look at her friend. She looked at her hands. Sweating and lightly streaked where the sweat had washed some of the dust of their climb away. "I can't come over to your place anymore. Not ever. My mother says I can't see you at all."

The sun was blazing down on them, unconcerned. It was so hot. Ephanie looked at Elena's hands intently. She didn't speak for a long time. She couldn't swallow. She couldn't breathe. For some reason her chest hurt. Aching. She didn't know why. Anything.

She tried to think, to understand. They had been together all their lives. What did Elena mean? She wondered if it was because she had more. Of everything. Dresses, boarding school, a bigger house. A store-owner for a father. A trader.

Elena's father had a small cantina that he owned. But he didn't make a lot of money at it. He drove a school bus to make ends meet.

Elena's house had three rooms. Besides the kitchen. They were all used for sleeping. One of them they used as a livingroom too. One of them was very small, hardly large enough for the tiny iron bedstead it held. Five or six people lived there, depending on whether her brothers were both there or not. They didn't have running water, and their toilet was outdoors. Ephanie thought maybe that was what was the matter. That they were growing up. That now that they were near adulthood, such things mattered. Were seen in some way that caused anger, caused shame.

When Ephanie didn't say anything for so long, Elena said, "It's because my mother thinks we spend too much time with each other." She looked at Ephanie, eyes shut against her. Open, not closed, but nothing of herself coming through them. Nothing in them taking her in. Ephanie sat, thinking she was dreaming. This didn't make any sense. What could be wrong? How could she not see Elena? Be with her. Who would she be with then, if not Elena?

She put out her hand. Took hold of Elena's arm. Held it, tightly. Swaying. She looked over the side of the peak and thought about flying. Dropping off. She thought of going to sleep.

She moved so that she could put her hand on Elena's arm. Held her like that, staring. Trying to speak. Not being able to. There were no words. Only too many thoughts feelings, churn-

29

ing in her like the whirlwind, chindi, dust-devils on the valley floor below. "What are you talking about," she finally said. Her voice sounded strange in her ears, her question sounding flat, uninflected like a declaration.

Elena tried to back away, get loose from Ephanie's hand. Pulled away, but not completely. She looked at Ephanie. Her face was wet. Beads of sweat had formed along her upper lip. She wiped them away with the back of her hand. Her eyes looked flat, gave off no light. Her light brown eyes that were flecked with gold. Her brown face had a few freckles scattered over it. They stood out now, sharp.

"You know," she said, her voice low. "The way we've been lately. Hugging and giggling. You know." She looked down at her hands, twisting against themselves in her lap. "I asked the sister about that, after school. She said it was the devil. That I mustn't do anything like that. That it was a sin. And she told my mother. She says I can't come over any more."

Ephanie sat. Stunned. Mind empty. Stomach a cold cold stone. The hot sun blazed on her head. She felt sick. She felt herself shrinking within. Understood, wordlessly, exactly what Elena was saying. How she could understand what Ephanie had not understood. That they were becoming lovers. That they were in love. That their loving had to stop. To end. That she was falling. Had fallen. Would not recover from the fall, smashing, the rocks. That they were in her, not on the ground.

She finally remembered to take her hand off of Elena's arm. To put it in her pocket. She stood up again. Almost lost her balance. How will we ever get down. She couldn't see very well. She realized her eyes were blurred with tears. "Why did you do that." She said. "How could you tell anyone? How did you know, what made you ask? Why didn't you ask me." And realized the futility of her words. The enormity of the abyss she was falling into. The endless, endless depth of the void.

"I was scared. I thought it was wrong. It is." Elena looked at Ephanie, eyes defiant, flat and hard, closed.

"Then why did we come today? Why get me all the way up here and then tell me?" Ephanie felt her face begin to crumble, to give way. Like the arroyo bank gave way in the summer rains.

She didn't want Elena to see her like that, giving in to anguish, to weakness, to tears.

"I'm sorry." That was all Elena would say.

They got down from the peak the way they had come, using lifelong habits of caution and practice to guide them. In silence they walked the long way back to the village. Elena went inside when they came to her house. Ephanie went the rest of the way, not so far however long it seemed, alone. She went to the apple tree and climbed up into it. Hid her face in the leaves. She sat there, hiding, for a very long time.

She Didn't Understand That The Spiders Sent The Dreams

Jump.

Fall.

"You are a petal that has seen the stars" he said, siamut, hermano. She said (beloved Anciena, Old Woman) that Ephanie should never betray herself to them. "Don't let them know it matters. Don't cry. Don't change the smile on your mouth." And how she pinched Ephanie's arm. And how Ephanie didn't cry.

Seen then and then on that tidal pull returned. Riding high on the memory, the force of a lost living room (sneaking glances at a half-hidden door). "A person like her must be lonely," she had heard someone say. And that was half the problem. The other half was secret, hidden dark in the half light of a star.

"Night knows no enemy stronger. This is what purity is, and what I must explain, Stephen." She said one day not long after the last Feast Day she went to. But he was distant that day and full of noise. He could only say that the enemy of night is day. Unable to hear her fear or her need clear in the chalice of its own perspicuity.

Not simple, she thought suddenly. Suddenly clear in her sober understanding. I am not simple. So he will not hear. And she reached out, briefly, making a futile loop with her hands. And put them to rest in her frozen lap.

Like a strange food I might gag on if I swallow. Oyster on the half shell. She laughed abruptly. Abruptly pushed her chair back with a harsh grating. Abruptly she stood and left the room blue behind her as though pine smoke had veiled his eyes.

"If I could simulate Venus rising. If I were Fortran in three dimensional tones. To be duplicated only symbolically, a half turn executed, a dance that betrays the expectation blooming in my hermano's eye. If only I could be as certain as whatever caused Her creation. And things didn't disappear while I looked at them."

Yes, that was half the problem, she thought. And her name. Ephanie. That stood before her like the emblem of a delphi that in this world could not exist.

"Oh, am I bored with ideas of destiny," she said out loud. "It fills my mouth with the taste of dust. I'm going to get my kids."

He won't leave me now, she thought, carrying in it the tone of black, a buzz. Because he won't know that I've gone. She left off depending on him. For anything. To help her. He couldn't help her. Couldn't make anything right. That she knew. But he wouldn't know she had changed her mind. About him. About what he could do. She wouldn't let him know. She would get the children, bring them here. She could manage that now. Be happy and with them. Stay alive.

She went out, got in the battered old pickup she drove and headed out of the city toward Guadalupe. She took the freeway north out of town, and after a time left it for a blacktop road that wound through some orchards and tall rocks into the village of Guadalupe where she was raised. Her mother was outside when she drove up. She had slowed when she passed the old apple tree near her mother's house, just a stone's throw away from the yard. The yard was hard-packed earth. Some wild roses grew there, and some hollyhocks. "Hi," Ephanie said to her mother as she got out of the pickup. "I've come to get the kids."

Aqui. Aqui está la ventana. Drinking through endless night. Day and uncertainty to cloud her eyes. She learning to distinguish between confusion and the light. Unwilling yet to betray in any movement the half forgotten message of her mind.

32

Knowing only that if she should walk the unseen path below she would be courting disaster, as when somebody unprotected walked near Old Spider, The Woman's house. But she did not quite believe that disaster could hide behind those dream awakened enchanted eyes.

She sat long in her yard, watching the leaves turn and fall from the cottonwood tree. She thought about Elena. The years gone by. Elena and she walking. Lying on the grass making stories out of clouds. Climbing the endless mesas of her home. Talking for hours safe in the welcoming branches of the apple tree. Holding hands. She thought about how she was lonely. She thought she needed a friend. After all these years without one. Yes, she thought, I need a new friend.

And went out. To bars and to coffee shops. To meetings and dinners. To centers and gatherings. To the dances in her pretty fringed shawl. Keeping her eyes open. Trying to make a new friend. Who would be like Elena. A friend she could be safe and sure with. A friend who was like home.

She looked and never noticed how she looked for a certain shade of eyes. A certain small round brown hand. A certain cast of hair. A certain tenuous smile. A kind of ease and acceptance. She didn't notice that. Or that it meant years. She forgot about all the years it took to know Elena. And all the years since that time.

And she found women smiling. Women to talk with endlessly to gossip over cups of coffee and ashtraysfull of cigarettes. To shake her head with, and to cluck her tongue. She found women to dance with, going round and round as the drum went round, as the voices went, over and over, chanting. She found friends, but not the friend she looked for. She found women to cry over and to cry with. Women with babies like her own. Women who had their own Stephen in their livingrooms or bedrooms or bars.

And returned to the simple dust of her house, as though forever knowing that no one would live there for a long time. Maybe when the kids grow up, she would tell herself. Maybe then I'll believe that something is real. Knowing that wasn't true. Was why she was always sending them away.

33

Starlight. Evening bell. And after that to the east a cloud soaring like myth over the mountain just as afternoon gave way to rain. Remembering that anguish in terms of the huge cloud. So strangely brooding two and a half miles above the city.

A strange thing to see, she knew. And wondered what it meant. The children came in from playing. Dirty and tired. Quarreling. To the livingroom to turn on the t.v. Noise filling up the spaces she had carefully spun. Wondering about the omen that cupped itself over the mountain and hung there, white and curving like a shell, she sat alone in the growing kitchen dark.

"This house is always dusty. And spiders live in every fold of wood and shelf and corner of this house. I don't appreciate spiders the way I should," she said. Not so anyone could hear.

And taking the broom and the dustrag she began methodically to clean.

"Grandma says not to kill the spiders," Agnes and Ben were peering over their shoulders at her. "She says they make a house a home. Or just take them outside."

"I know," Ephanie grinned and nodded vigorously at them. "She told me that too." Then she got out the vacuum cleaner and vacuumed up the webs, spiders and all.

She Tries To Make Something

She went through her days then almost functioning. Half-minded, half-remembering. Doubt and uncertainty were beyond her ability to take care of. She dreamed of dreaming marbled halls, like the story said. She wandered through the days like the seasons wandered through her yard, a gift of shadows, wings, dropped suddenly after each hesitation of shadow into shocking clarity. This sustenance, this madness, she countered by turning backwards in the light at evening and speaking to Stephen through half-closed eyes. She made of every yesterday a motif, unconscious of this arrangement. But in this way she turned telephones and unmade beds to her advantage. Not exactly a shriek, a terrified scream, but going always in that direction, never hurried, never sure, going as the clock goes, because it has been set that way, a circle. So she tried to make sense out of her days, significance out of her nights. To learn to tell time.

Stephen would come sometimes to sit beside her, wanting, as she could see in the half-perceived corners of his thought, to bring her into a focus he could understand. "He wants," she said to one of her friends, "a peg to hang me on." Wishing she could give him one. Or someone could. But she eluded his examining gaze, hands vague and tenuously forming invisible shapes in the air, making melodies that she only half understood.

Sometimes he would press on her, press against her thought with his thought, a beam that pushed against her skull. "This way, I can lead you into certainty," he seemed to say. He drove her ever further into waking dreams. Her own elusiveness remained unseen. To her and to him. Put carefully away behind cautious, innocent eyes, if glimpsed.

The children grew silent in the house. Ben haunted her like a constant shadow. He slept badly, and at night Agnes wept and sometimes screamed. Ben made fires in dangerous places. He was often found sharpening his small knife intently. They avoided Stephen. They avoided Ephanie as long as Stephen was there, daring to come out only after he was gone, home or somewhere. Then they would quarrel with each other and joke with Ephanie. Then Agnes would comb her mother's hair. They would sit at the table in the kitchen and eat cookies and drink coffee, chattering with their mother, badgering her for permissions, doing their childish best to make her smile and laugh and tell them stories in the light.

But Stephen slowly gained in force. As each day paragraphed its way into her mind, he penetrated the cover she had put over her thought. His thought swirled like unseen chindis, dustdevils, into her eye in a way that forbade seeing. She would look at him and almost see a blue smoke veil on the air between them. She wondered what he saw when he looked at her. A short woman. Held tightly within herself. Huge wide spaced eyes, slanted upward slightly at the outside edge. Was she fragile to him or strong? Did he see behind her habitual bland smile? Did he see what she covered with that blank look, the

35

expression she wore like a blanket of snow, a shawl? Covering. Pretty. Hiding danger. Aloof. Enticing. Gone. Her light-absorbing thick black hair. Shadow woman, she called herself, thinking of what he must see. And of what he must not see.

And she would picture other lives. Not those she had known but had imagined, read about. If someone else were sitting in that chair. If there were no fire behind his head. If shadows did not play with the light in quite that way. Or in another place.

She wanted him gone. To leave her to her shadows. She was afraid of what would happen to her if he did go.

So sometimes she went instead. She would leave Agnes and Ben with her mother. Then for days she would spend all her time talking to people she believed were in control of their lives. Who she imagined were confident, competent, free. She would imitate their gestures, their words. Their expressions, their thoughts. She would practice thinking like they did. Reading the books they read. Seeing the movies they saw. Watching the television they watched. Going to the places they frequented. Trying on their lives. Trying to make them fit hers. How desperately she wanted to be like she imagined these tall, cool white women, rich, reserved, intelligent, educated, self-assured, to be. Cool. Safe. Hidden from Stephen's oppressive, arrogant eyes.

But her desperate attempts to free herself from the frightening entanglement were futile. Stephen ignored them. He would still come to her house, doggedly enter it and sit in the place that he called his chair. He would do all the things he did for all the hours and days she would be gone. A comfortable arrangement, seemingly, unaware of its fearfulness to her new-grown eyes when, stoned or drunk, high on borrowed knowledge of how things were in the world of reason and sophisticated understanding, she would return home to find him there asleep or half dreaming in the lamplight that illuminated his hair, turning it almost gold in that light.

"Stephen." She would say. "You're here." And holding his hands in hers would see in her mind how softly the turquoise rings she wore gleamed in the light.

She did not say how sorry she was to see him.

inertia

She Remembers Something

Too tired. Too much. Like corn-filled pottery bowls she could hold on her head like books when she was a girl. Always probing for the single thread that ran along her days. A bobbin. Not seen but holding secure what had been torn asunder.

"If a person dreams of Thunder, he is secure and safe. Assurance will bind him then like leggings bind the legs of a warrior. That's what the Cheyenne say." Stephen said one night.

They were sitting in the livingroom. In the small light one lamp gave. Across from one another, reading, talking. She was glad he was preoccupied. He had been around a lot lately. She had been home a lot too. She was feeling restless, irritable. She knew she should go out more, but somehow she couldn't find the strength. Getting dressed was almost beyond her. She longed for the children. But her pickup wasn't working. She couldn't get it to the garage. She didn't think she could take care of Agnes and Ben anyway. Leave them with mom, she thought. It's better that way. Stephen's here so much. They don't do well when he's coming around. Her inertia was almost complete. She was almost paralyzed. She didn't know why, but she suspected Stephen. What he was doing.

She looked up at him, smoothing her face to look blank. Blanketing her thoughts with irrelevancies. In all honesty do this day declare. "Thunder is the power of the light?" she said out loud.

"Or flint." He put away the book he had been holding and his eyes that looked blinding at her pushed her beyond her modesty, her resolution, her fear.

"You don't understand the finer points of keeping in psychic disequilibrium." She said. Thinking this would reveal to him what many months, movement, silence, had hidden. "I've seen the Thunders," she said. "And they were gold. Their dwelling is the hollowed sky. I saw their chariot. I mix my metaphors with care. Take care to listen to me." Not knowing that what she said made no sense. Filled suddenly with rage that went beyond her fear. Knowing that what she had seen was true.

And left him standing there. Not caring if something happened next. Anger making her shake. Almost breaking through. Shaking.

She understood then the fall taken by the ancient one, Sky Woman, Grandmother, in a way far beyond the hints contained in the puzzling manuscripts that lined her walls.

Anciena. Ck'oy'u, Old Woman. Ephanie named her that, in memory of what she had forgotten, in place of what she understood. She understood this naming, this fall, as her limbs understood autumn. A fall unlike evening. Like a star anciently displaced in the sky. Earth, refugee, poor one. Falling into the void like a dream. Ephanie thought everything was alive. As the old women of the village had taught her to think. She thought that made her crazy, what they had taught. She lived mostly among people who thought everything was dead.

According to legend a woman had spoken to her dead father. He had told her to marry the sachem in the village downstream, who then put her to a series of unusual and cruel tests that proved her power greater than his. After they were married, she dwelt with him, because his customs were different from hers. During that period he got sick. Now this sachem was renowned for the beautiful tree that grew outside his lodge. Its blossoms were white and shone brighter than the sun at midday. The tree had been hung with the flesh of his previous wife, and that was why it gave light.

When the sachem became sick, his advisors had told him that the cause of his sickness was the woman he had married. They advised him to rid himself of her by uprooting the tree of light and exposing the abyss. Then, they said, he should invite her to look over the side, and when she did he was to push her into the void. This he did, and she fell into the void, falling forever, it seemed. She fell through the darkness. Then she fell through the place where all was blue light. Then she saw something. She didn't know it was water. She fell and fell until some waterfowl saw her falling and they made a secure blanket of their wings and caught her, stopping her fall. Then they placed her on turtle grandmother's back and brought mud up from beneath the waters. They died doing this, for the waters

38

were very deep. They put the mud on Turtle's back, spreading it all over her carapace. In this way the earth began to grow around Sky Woman and she was safe.

Now, though she had never lain with the sachem, she was pregnant. She gave birth to a daughter there on Turtle's back, far away from the lodge of her mother and far, far away from the devastated tree of light. It was a death tree, or so Ephanie always believed.

She Plants a Dying Tree

By day Ephanie dreamed of roses and yellow leaves. She smelled crisp smells that were not always in the room with her, but part of her life. She saw the garden as held in the hollow of the hand of rain. Immanently. Could nearly see how the rain-smell would circle roses like a wall. And that the avenues of sensing she wandered in had no counterpart in the books that walled her. They merely offered possibility by negation: the null hypothesis. Too well read for her hands or comprehension, she uttered strange sounds. Pretended to be bird calls and jungle light. Bright pain and unutterable wish. In early winter the sunset was dark. The bird people slept early. They were very quiet.

Some days she went to Guadalupe to take her children to visit her parents. She would sometimes leave Ben and Agnes there for a few days. Sometimes she would stay out there too, and smell the snow in the air, the woodsmoke from the stoves. She would talk long to her mother then, working beside her in the kitchen. Or in the other room sit with her father and her grandfather, listen to them talk. Her grandmother had been dead for several years and her grandfather was still forlorn. But he took life in his quiet way. Always with a smile for her. Sometimes he would walk up the road to the store and return with cigarettes for her. Sometimes he would tell her stories about time before memory. Usually he went out to sit with other old men along the walls in the sun, or on very cold days in the store around the stove. She loved him quietly. Like he loved her.

And she would return to her little house in the city, curved into the arm of the bosque, the cottonwood forest that sheltered the river's length. At such times Stephen would watch her. "What's wrong, Ephanie," he would say then. "The lamplight on your hair doesn't enter it. No brightness do I see."

Because she fell, Ephanie replied now in silence. Because she's gone. And smiled at the distance between them. "Because I'm dark," she would say.

"Ephanie, oh Ephanie," he said once. "You could be brightness I could be through." He didn't smile then exactly, but Stephen knew what he had said.

"You'll have to be by yourself," she replied. "I can't go with you now. Winter is for quiet. Walk softly when the Mother sleeps." She smiled at him then, on her way out of the room. She thought about Hummingbird Man. Mee'tchu'tse. How he grew fat while the people starved in the drought. The famine that came. When they asked him how it was that he was so sleek and fat he had replied, "I go back to Shipap. To the mother. There I eat."

"It's the sense of loss, of the futility of things." She said now, her hands a shadow of the snow that fell at her window. "Such stupidity. Each change so blind, like this corpse I try to embrace with my thought. But thought can't hacer the impossible." She stopped then, surprised that she had chosen in her intent a not-English term. Had become lost searching for the English sister to it. "Hace, it makes. Or does. Or fashions." And gave up the attempt as futile. So once again her hands rose and fell, fingers opening and closing as again she echoed sunrise and snow.

And in the long shade of winter she too saw her own death. "How earth pulls at us. Makes mockery of attempts to move beyond." She saw the resemblance and the significance and the futility of that realization.

The Tree Had Been Split By Lightning

One afternoon they had buried her grandfather. He was very old. All his friends had been dead a long time. He had lived mostly alone for years. He wouldn't speak English in those last years. He spoke Spanish instead, defiantly. She had thought of him as her friend. He had planted the apple tree near her house years before she was born. She had spent hours in it all summer long. She and Elena. Who was also gone.

The tree was almost dead. She had noticed that this past summer when she went home. It had been split by lightning. Most of it just lay on its side, leafless in the summer heat. Only one branch had bloomed and leafed, and it bore no fruit. Near it someone had piled old tires and discarded butane tanks.

They buried the old man in the graveyard in the city near the graves of his mother, his father and his wife. He wasn't Indian. But he had spent his life with the people, working. Ephanie didn't know how such people blended together. What a squawman understood.

She had always known about the division that made her life and her mind, light and shade of herself. They had lived together, all of them, meeting at weddings and funerals, baptisms and confirmations, parties and feasts. Had danced and laughed with each other. Worked with each other. Shared food, shared anger, shared joy, shared grief. Shared life and shared death with each other. They had hated and cherished one another somehow. Nobody talked much about the rest of it. They never talked about division. Thinking maybe that in not talking of it, it would not matter, would not harm. Or maybe it was hard to know what to say. Or maybe their bonds had been more important than their differences. ¿Quien sabe? Who knows?

She had stood next to her mother at the grave, holding Ben and Agnes' hands in hers. They stared, wise eyed. They understood. Her mother had seemed smaller somehow, as though she had contracted into herself. Nobody cried much. Just a few tears. Ephanie had driven Ben and Agnes back out to her mother's after the funeral and the gathering afterward. Then she went, alone, to her house. She stood by the window for a long time, watching the frost grow on the grass. She knew that it would snow again tomorrow.

They Were Swept Away

Help me, hermano, I'm dying. I feel myself disappearing. Entering the shadows. I can't seem to make myself real. Bright. Sharp. I'm sliding away. It's so quiet.

It was not what she could say out loud, so she looked it in his direction. Hoping he would comprehend. Hoping he wouldn't. And turned away, shoulders hunched, hands tightly in control so that way she could keep from showing herself the inexorable truth.

She knew she was frightened. And somewhere, like off in the vast snowy distance, that she was ashamed.

She said, "Would you like some coffee? A drink? I have some wine. Stephen. Make a fire and I'll get it and we could sit and be together awhile, couldn't we?"

She didn't hear his reply but recorded his willingness to join her in this simple ploy. His assent and, not exactly gratitude or joy, but amiable enough agreement. He built a fire and took the wine she offered him and drank it and looked at the color in the firelight. And was pleased.

She could fool him. She could be cunning, sly. She didn't have to seem like she was afraid. Could keep her hands near the fire so he wouldn't know how cold they were. They would never get warm.

So she smiled and talked about her day. About what she had been reading. Thinking about. And though she hurt somewhere inside her ribs and wanted to cry, she kept her face warm and smiling. Knowing that to reveal the intensity of her pain would be a mistake, out of harmony with the firelightamiable wine, maybe dangerous.

So she talked instead. Relentlessly. Making Stephen smile. "Life is a simile. A simile is a correspondence that uses like as the term of comparison. I like you, Stephen, mi hermano, siamut. Does that make us a simile?"

"Our relationship."

"Yes, our relationship is a simile. For what? I wonder what a simile for our relationship might be."

"What the words suggests, I imagine." He said, looking at her as though he was amused by something. "You like me. You like snow. Your hands are like falling snow when you move them. And they are like the snow so cold. Ephanie, make love to me. I would very much like to make love to the snow."

She heard him but could not make sense of his words. The terms of the thing. She thought that sex was like clocks. It evaded her. Or like that corpse they had laid to rest this afternoon, planting it before the snow. Besides, one doesn't make love to similes. So instead of answering him directly, she laughed and said, "Oh, Stephen. That wouldn't work. You can't possess snow. It moves around so much when it's falling. And it melts when it gets warm. And when it's on the ground, well, that's not the same. Ask any Eskimo. Snow is to die on."

Stephen took her glass away from her and set it down carefully. He took her hands and held them and looked at her for a long time. "Ephanie, you can't fuck the snow. That's true. Or exactly hold a simile where you can catalog it. Define, articulate, dissect and possess it. That's true. But Ephanie, there are only words between our hands now. Eventually, words run out."

And he stood, and took her in his assurance to bed.

However bright that sunrise might have been, however splendid Evening Star might rise above the peak west of her bedroom, Ephanie couldn't shake the impression of something wrong. Not that he had betrayed her, split her in two, but that he had emphasized the split that had too long been on her mind. Something was out of time, off-paced, as though her heartbeat had developed a trick of beating that echoed itself. Perhaps his eyes did not meet hers directly. Perhaps he ducked his head a fraction of a second sooner than he should. Flying is not what he wanted, she thought. She shrugged and made coffee do for warmth.

43

"Never let expecting get in your way," he said. Suddenly. Pages of quiet preceding his words. She saw him then. Stephen, brother. Seeing her in that one way that once had let her believe in wholeness. That she did exist. Was something real.

"You expected something you didn't get," he said, eyes intent, toward her, toward the light in the window behind her, away. He said that. Put down his cup. Picked up his jacket and put it on. Pick up the jacket, Stephen, she thought. Put it on.

At the door he turned. Looked at her . His face tight. Eyes going in her direction but not quite regarding her. "Maybe you should go to Guadalupe and get the kids."

She knew he was leaving. Knew she needed to tell him what she wanted from him. Knew she would seem to herself whining. Defensive. Felt the need to be defended. To make something clear, anything clear. Stood and watched him go out and close the door behind himself. How the bright sun came suddenly into the room, as suddenly left it in shadow, dim.

She put his cup in the sink, refilled hers, sat down in her chair looking toward the small window across the room and its small light. She thought about what he'd said. Thought about her children. The night. "I didn't expect something I did get," she said to the spider meditating in the corner near her chair. She nodded to the tree outside, repeating it. She said, "He was wrong."

What the Spider Sang

Circles, circles, described on air, beginningless, endless but definitely, each singing its own song, humming its own tune. Stephen did not see the necessity for this rambling, circular, through eddies and swirls of time, politics, astronomy, the moon, all patterned perfectly she knew, though inexpressibly. And listening to that voice, Ephanie understood the ancient nightmares, felt the great slab lowered on witches to unbend their maniacal minds. Longed for such a stone pressing on her own chest, to stop the ache centered there, longed for the certain recognition of her own death in that condemnation. Objective

44

events. Mythic reality. Pied Piper and Buffalo gone to the same place, left only as legendary tracings of other times, less ordered than these, less closed. And maybe still the buffalo would return with the circles hidden now in the sacred secret cave of the four winds somewhere on the eastern plains.

Blindly, then, the object had been to die quietly on the snow. She could understand the necessity of that, but not of Estebanito's refusal to regard her real.

She thought of her body, pictured it painted with the waxen blue of death, of the west where that blue lived. Of blue itself. Sky. Song. Veins. Death. And of cold. How snow shone blue in shadow. And knew the melody of blue. Of wax. Of a body lying inert on the mind of snow. Of how snow took over everything. Possessing with a quiet finality. A certainty. An assurance that was not quite allowed in her own life.

I should go west for awhile. Toward the blue. To live with it and come to peace that way. Or to some understanding of the body I knew so clearly in the snow, friend, brother, twin, life that is an echo right now. My life is its own echo. I can't find the source of the sound.

She finally got out of the chair that was at an angle from Stephen's accustomed chair. Got dressed. Went out. This time she locked the door.

She drove to Guadalupe. Past the apple tree. Turned off to the yard of her mother's house. Went in and stayed for awhile. Told her mother she was going, but nothing about why. Could she keep the kids. "I have to get away." If her mother wondered, she did not ask. It was not her way. Of course the kids could stay.

She Was Shaking, But She Made It

Owl song. Night falling into earth. Reaching up in flames to be embraced. Romantic image of some kind of truth. The kind in popular music that she played on the radio. Driving herself away.

Mesas flinging themselves in studied abandon skyward. Gasping at the thought of missing union this time. Coyote disappearing over crested hills. Reappearing on the next rise suddenly as the last breath of day tumbled into the embrace of night.

Ephanie drove nightward, aimlessly, turned as the east-mountain dimmed, turned on her headlights. Settled in for a long drive. Tomorrow she would be in San Francisco. Would feel the fog cling soft in benediction on her face. Watch monstrous half shapes rising out of the predawn waves. Or she would stay near the great peak rising beside Flagstaff and climb to the top and ask the katsina there to answer her. She knew they were there because it was there that the last of the clean air on the continent had hovered and disappeared.

She could go somewhere tonight. Tomorrow. The next day. At least those three days she could know were planned. She would go somewhere filled, dustless, blue, light not so brutal, sun dulled by water. Somewhere west of where she lived. Somewhere west of yesterday. Of last night. Of this morning. Of this new understanding. She did not want yet to touch just what she understood. So she fled. And watched day become lost to darkness, wondering.

Half light filled her mind. Lights of the dashboard sang their being to her as she drove, tires swishing, singing to the pavement as though they were wood, her lamps, the tree outside her door.

Night half spent she stopped for coffee and speed, swallowing both dutifully, there's a good girl, returned to the car and drove on, mesmerized by the machine swift mating of the drive.

Dawn, Kingman and food behind her, driving onto the great desert, cactus blooming, ground vaguely green. As though winter knew enough to stay away from here. Mountains too far away for contemplation, huge psychic hulks falling away behind as she drove. They were all in desolation of stone in the bright morning light. Barstow. Dirty air. Eyes red from pills and smog and driving. She stopped to sleep so she could go up the valley in the dark. So she would not be able to see how many people marred her dream, her union with sky, night, sound, half buried thought, heart, lonely in a locked house far behind.

46

She slept in a rest area near the road, possessed by the thought of the desert and the high mountains between her and her home. And woke. Got out to watch sunrise. Sensing little difference between the mountains she had left and the place she stood. Got in the car and drove on to the north.

Locked. Lost in the folds of valleys. Lost. Continent mourning her dead forests, dying lakes. Sky meditating above the glare of headlights. All moving. Omnipotentis.

In the last days they painted their faces black and shuffled circlewise, hands locking. The longing in it swelling in the crests of voices and breaking on the heads of anguish. They fell on the ground. They went home. They saw the ones they had lost and were comforted for awhile. Eating pemmican. Rose, danced again. Soot blackened faces howling toward the sky. And lost again. Were lost. Blood frozen in the snow. Finality. He said a dream had died there. He was not wrong.

She drove off the highway toward some lights. Coffee, gas. Then a short way to San Francisco. Maybe she could really rest. There. Stopping she got out of the car. Told the attendant to fill the tank. Unaware that she spoke. Or how. Moved toward the john. Her eyes were shocked by the empty glare that echoed sight. She reached for more pills. Looked into the small water-stained mirror.

I don't need any more pills. I don't even know how many I've taken so far. I wonder where I am. Realizing herself awake, conscious, aware of the hum of the fluorescent light, the stained toilet, the bathroom smells, for the first time in miles, weeks perhaps. Awake.

Then opened the door and stepped out into fog smell and night. The being of water that they mocked, the whitemen. Said could not exist. Did not. Would not. Ever. The sailors haven't found that water being, their eyes tightly shut to fear, determination, no recourse.

But Water lived. Here.

She remembered an old story. A line from it. If you don't see that orange, does it mean the orange isn't. No, it was hermano, Stephen, and he'd said, "That orange doesn't see you. Do you exist?"

But not that.

She didn't want to think about that. It made her dizzy. Stupid. Crazy. Crazy Indian. Crazy halfbreed. Get it right.

The Waterthing lived here. Just at the tip of her extended foot.

She stopped and sniffed the air and felt herself grow outward to reach the tiny particles that flowed around her skin. And in the expansions felt her need to hide. To contract. To wither and blow across parched hills. Mute testimony to a history, a meaning beyond her. Beyond understanding.

She turned and went toward the car smiling automatically at the attendant. Not looking at him. Signed the slip. Got into the car and slid away.

But not that easily. If she could slide away gentle into the fog mocking her headlights. Get beyond the tip of the vanishing point, where everything was the opposite, the obverse, the converse, the convection of here. Where the buffalo were. And the children who were danced mysteriously away. Where she could see water. Step into the underworld, undeclared world, or whatever passes for it in this humourless time. And though carandbodyandfeelinglights moved north and west, she was stopped with foot extended on the edge of reaching, of flowing into the fog, Water being just beyond release.

And suddenly exhausted by this perverted sense of life, she jammed her foot down on the accelerator. The other one on the brake. Stopped. Tumbled into void. Oh, Ephanie, beloved, eucalyptus tree. And jarred, looked stupid, blindly, at her face in the mirror, white, carlight dimming pallor, eyes huge as a hunger distended belly. Comfort here. Then.

Not in a way like warm or soft things but comfort still. Trees understanding and giving in the wind. Dreams haunted the air of her mind. And she rolled the window down. Leaned over the side and threw up. Then sitting herself into position she started the car and joined the lines of taillights disappearing into the fog.

PART II

PROLOGUE

Rite of Exorcism: (The Spruce Dress)

[Sundown: the patient comes into the healing place. She is garlanded with loops of spruce branches that signify the chains of her sickness. The War Twins, Ma'se'we and O'yo'yo'we enter. The singer sings:]

In the land of the spirits, he comes. In a land of the spirits, he comes. Ma'se'we walks here now. In the land of the spirits, he walks.

In the land of the supernaturals, he goes. In a land of the supernaturals, he goes. O'yo'yo'we walks here now. In the valleys and among the lowlying hills, he walks. In the land of the supernaturals, he goes.

The enemy of alien gods I am now. She who bears the sun rises with me. She comes up and travels with me. Together we travel in the valleys and the plains. She dwells with me.

Child of water am I. Eme haa kosha si'ano Kawaike. Eme haa kosha si'ano Kawaike. She who bears the moon comes up with me. She rises and travels with me. She goes into the valleys and the plains with me. She dwells with me.

I am the one who slays alien gods. Wherever I travel white forests are swept before me. The lightning sweeps away the forests. The wind sweeps away the forests. But it is I who do the sweeping. Eme haa Kawaike. Child of Water am I. Wherever I travel white waters are swept before me. The storm clouds sweep over the white waters, but it is I who do the sweeping.

sweeping

51

[The gods vanish. The singer brushes pine needles from the loops and scatters them over and around the patient. He makes sweeping motions with a grass broom, sweeping away the sickness, sweeping it out through the door of the healing place. The singer sings:]

The corn grows tall, the rain falls. I sweep it off, I sweep it off.
The rain falls, the corn grows tall. I sweep it away, I sweep it away.
The corn grows tall, the rain falls. I sweep it off, I sweep it off.
The rain falls, the corn grows tall. I sweep it away, I sweep it away.

The corn comes, the rain comes down. I sweep it up, I sweep it up.
The rain comes down, the corn comes. I sweep it up, I sweep it up.
The corn comes, the rain comes down. I sweep it up, I sweep it up.
The corn comes, the rain comes down. I sweep it up, I sweep it up.

Shaking, She Was In The Northwest

The noise outside her window was almost intolerable. She was accustomed to large silences, great spaces in time. The city grumbled and shrieked at her, tightening like a net around a struggling fish. She would look curiously at the people around her to see if they minded it, but they seemed not to hear the agony of the streets, nor to care. She imagined the streets were endowed with power, so that they could allow only the chosen to enter awareness.

Dear Stephen,

In my mind I run away endlessly away, a charge of energy, a pulse neither thing nor process, but going somewhere always, never getting anywhere, like the ocean, I suppose, like the wind. A sailor told me that when you're on the water, out in the middle of the ocean, the horizon seems like it curves upward like a bowl. The water appears to be about to fall on you. Terrifying. A case of the mind, illusion, as you call it. Based on a certain sense of things on land. Where if the land rises above you, you at least know it doesn't move, won't fall on you. The sky is another bowl. Holds the water away. Sometimes, he said, the water's edge and the edge of the sky are colored exactly the same, like a meeting, a marriage of sky and water that gives birth to strange creatures, like the old stories say. That's how it is with me.

Remember the story about the cacique who went to the land of the dead just before he was to take office? He went into a coma or something and a couple of spirit people came and took him on a journey to see the mother, to see Iyatiku. He went through all sorts of weird places, seeing those who had died after a life of evil or laziness. They were in terrible shape, as I remember. A lot like stories about hell, but there wasn't any fire or anything like that, just endless painful tasks and a sense of despair hanging over it all. And Iyatiku told him, after he got to her place, that he would be like those he saw if he wasn't careful. She told him also that it was his obligation to take care that none of the people were driven to end like that. That he must guard and provide for them, so they would be happy and at peace in their hearts.

53

I especially remember the two-hearts, the divided ones who used magic to harm others, and the ugliness of them that showed there in that shadowed place. That was a demonstration for his benefit. As I remember he was really dead, and he could choose to go back to the village if he wanted to risk what he was risking. He decided to go back, sobered, no doubt, by what he had seen. I don't know why the story has been in my mind lately. Maybe because I'm north in this weird place, and the pall of despair is everywhere.

You asked when I'm coming home. Maybe never, I don't know. I have to get something clear in my mind. Besides, the kids like it here. They're doing okay. We go to powwows and they dance. They're getting good. Ben won a prize last month and Agnes just finished a fine new dance dress. She may get first place in the next powwow. Of course a lot of that's politics, and mine are no better than ever. And it costs money for their gear. But we have fun. You should come out and see them dance. You'd be proud.

Ephanie

They got to the Richmond powwow early. Only a few people were there yet, setting up their booths and settling in certain spots they had chosen for the evening. The Soucies were already there, and she went over to talk to them. Agnes headed for the ladies room with her gear. She had been fussing about which hair ties to wear, and she was in a bad mood. As usual before a powwow. She was going to enter the junior girls dance contest, and she wanted to win, but she thought Maxine Soucie would get first place because her mother had an important job at the Inter-Tribal Center and they had been around the Bay Area, involved in Indian things, for years.

"I know the judges will only look at Maxine," she had complained as she fussed with the cowrie shells on her new dress and knotted and unknotted the fringe on her newly finished shawl. "She thinks she's so important. Do you know she got the other girls to make fun of me last time because I didn't have the right leggings. They're so mean!"

Ephanie had done her best to soothe the girl, reminding her that she had a new outfit with good leggings. "You worked so hard on that dress," she had said. "You'll look really good tonight. And you've been practicing hard at class, so you know the dances cold. Just do your best and have a good time. No sense in getting all upset. Powwows are supposed to be fun."

Now, she looked after Agnes who was scowling her way across the gym toward the ladies room. She sighed and sat down by Mrs. Soucie who smiled at her and then looked away. Ephanie wanted a cigarette, but Mrs. Soucie didn't smoke and Ephanie was afraid to. Maybe Mrs. Soucie would scold her if she did. So she begun to pluck at the fringe of her dance shawl, remembering the first time she had come to a powwow. She had never been to one and she had been in culture shock. The dances at home were nothing like this. There they were doing serious business. Here everyone was preening and puffing, looking around to see who to score with, who to gossip about, who to snub, who to be sure to talk to.

The women kept a sharp eye on the goings on: they carefully checked out every stranger, eyeing them carefully to see if they knew how to conduct themselves, whether they were white tourists or hustlers, culture groupies, or Indian kids stoned or drunk. They took a very dim view of such, and were likely to see that they didn't hang around too much. They left the tourists alone, nodding politely sometimes, mostly ignoring them. The drunks they scolded off the floor. They avoided the militants' booths with a vengeance.

Ephanie had been terrified the whole time. She didn't know the dances, didn't know anyone there, didn't know where to sit or how to act. She had finally scored some mescaline from a man who had talked to her at one of the jewelry booths. He was from home, and she vaguely recognized him. When he had offered her the tablet she had at first declined. Then thinking better of it, considering her state of terror, she had taken it. The rest of the evening had gone better after that.

Since then she had learned some of the city ropes. She had worked at the Indian Center for awhile and had gotten to know a lot of the community. They were from everywhere. Sioux from

55

Dakotas; Navajos, Pimas, Chemahuevis from New Mexico and Arizona; Paiutes and Washoes from Nevada; Pomos, Hupas, Yuroks, Kamiai and Mohaves from California. Of course there were Cherokees, often too easily confused with whites, but there were also Kiowas, Creeks, Chocktaws, Chickasaws and even a Tonkawa from Oklahoma and some Athabascans from Alaska. And there were the Pueblos, some of them third generation in California because they had moved there years before to work for the railroad.

She had enrolled the kids in dancing classes so they could enjoy the fun and had put dance costumes together for them, buying some parts from local folks who made them, helping Ben and Agnes make the rest for themselves. She had spent hours beading Ben's armbands and their hairpieces. Now they came to the powwows in style, sort of, and they felt more or less at home. She had made herself a beautiful shawl, violet with deep purple fringe. The fine wool had cost a fortune, and the silk fringe had cost even more. On the wool she had carefully embroidered a rainbird design she had taken from a pot her mother had sent her. It was in the same deep purple as the fringe, and it was one of the nicest worn by any of the women. She was proud of it. Even Mrs. Soucie was impressed. She asked Ephanie now where she had gotten the design. "Did you have it made? It must have been expensive," she said.

"It was," Ephanie said with a bland expression on her face, she hoped. "The wool was six dollars a square yard, and I hate to think what the fringe cost."

"Oh, did you make it?" Mrs. Soucie looked at her intently for a second. Her brown features seemed to focus sharply, become more alert.

Ephanie looked down at her hands. The soft turquoise gleamed back at her, reassuringly. "Yes, I made it."

"Did you do the embroidery?" Mrs. Soucie sounded very skeptical about that.

"Yes, I did it." Ephanie found she was having trouble breathing. She wanted to say something nasty, like "Yeah, I made it you old bat," but she clenched her jaws and made a smile. "I found silk thread that matched the fringe perfectly. Wasn't that lucky?"

Mrs. Soucie turned away. She smoothed the bright yellow shawl next to her. "I always make my shawls and my daughters' too," she said. "Where did you get the material?"

"At the fabric store on twenty-fourth. It's near Army."

"Oh, yes. Do they have much of it?"

"I saw some other colors, but the wool wasn't as fine as this. I like a fine wool, because it gets too hot."

"Yes, it does," the older woman said. "But I get good wool in Oakland for a lot less. Did you make Agnes' shawl too?"

"I did part of it. She did the fringing. Did you make Maxine's?"

"I made the one she's wearing tonight. She's so busy these days. With her school work and all the time she spends helping out at the Inter-Tribal House. We don't see much of you around there," she said.

Ephanie felt herself getting hot. She thought Mrs. Soucie was baiting her about spending so much time away from the community. I don't care, she thought. I came to the coast to learn something about how the other half lives. And that's what I'm doing to do.

She got up. "I think I'll go see how Agnes is doing. And I have to find Ben and tell him to start getting ready."

"Tell Maxine to come here," Mrs. Soucie said. "And come back later. I brought some tamales I made. I want to give you some."

"Okay," Ephanie said. "If I see her I'll tell her you want her. And I'll come back after awhile." She went across the floor, grinning to herself. Oh boy, she thought. Tamales. She tried to ignore her excitement, her pleasure. But she knew something good had just happened. She was afraid to think about it, to put too much stock into it. Maybe it didn't mean anything more than that Mrs. Soucie just wanted to pick on her some more. But she hoped it meant that she had been accepted.

There Was A Shadow Place

Blackness and under the wind, pools of darkness that made doors to Shipap. Light somewhere, a vague haze, and the constant mutter of cars over the hills. Dingy corners holding secrets tight, curling in on themselves in the night. Fog covering houses like resolution in the city of St. Francis. Only shit on the sidewalk and ground-in spit and an occasional dark stain to remind her that the blood sacrifices still went on.

More than anything it was the pain. That she had run from. To. The city was light flooded with air. It looked a lot like hope. But pain studded every corner and no one seemed able to do anything about it. Not the white spirit teachers. Not the people in the next world, the one nearby that she had seen. They all went about their lives as though the anguish had nothing to do with them.

Like Stephen, lost behind the mountains, who in such fear refused, would not give himself away in word or deed. Who would not betray the pain. He had tried to heal them, the rest. He did not succeed.

He was like a monk. Like a priest. Through my fault, through my fault, through my most grievous fault. They had learned that in school, and he had never understood how alone he stood, how shadowed, because he would not say what he meant. He wanted to mean everything, be nothing. To live quietly with the anger, the lying, the blood. He did not ever want to acknowledge the brutal terror that was the certain measure of their lives. At home and here.

A whisper in the wind. A gesture, sure and demanding. But not to be understood. Maybe he feared that she, he, were nothing after all. Feared disappearance as she feared it, with every whisper of her blood, every aching of her bones. But the futility of what he tried to do—the unanswerable incontinence of it, he who like a wiseman, a cacique, demanded everything and required nothing. Maintaining in that way some tenuous hold. Sometimes she thought that maybe he didn't know. Maybe he couldn't see how many were dying, were murdered, how many used guns or knives against themselves, against somebody else. But he had to know. He lived there, every day.

58

The stories he told her. Jeering, softly, eyes bland against the light, voice soft and unhesitating on the telephone. The tribal council. The tribal cops. The bleeding people, heads, ribs, caved in, guts ripped open, eyes put out. The women beaten beyond recognition, who went home after being treated at the clinic where he worked. They had no place else to go. She would be enraged by this, sickened. He would keep on talking, joking about it, relentless.

The one story he told her that she couldn't get out of her mind for a long time was about a boy they had thrown in the tribal jail because he was a faggot. Stephen had bailed him out and talked to his folks. His dad wouldn't relent. He should be whipped senseless, the man had said. He should be killed. He had brought shame to them.

The boy's father beat the mother regularly, savagely, methodically. He made all the children watch. If they cried or tried to intervene, he would beat her worse. That story. Those people. Who were enraged with shame because their son was queer. The rage. Pouring. Pounding. The fury. The cursing in the shadows. In the dark. The twisting of tongue, bitter in her mouth when she spoke against white people, what in her mind she saw. The mother, beaten, bloody. The boy frightened almost out of his mind.

She had run from all of that. Uncomprehending the cruelty, she had gone as those before her had gone. She wondered if they had moved away for the same reasons she moved away now. She remembered the words of her Navajo friend who, gazing in shock at the bloody leavings of a fight between some of the men, grieved, raging, "Sometimes my peoples make me sick." Yes. That was a fact for sure.

The White Forests Are Sweeping

She joined a therapy group. Everyone in it was white, some men, some women. Almost all were pretty young, going to school, starting out in their careers. She didn't understand all that went on. Sometimes she thought she understood nothing.

But it was warm there, filled with hope. The people she met with had something to believe in. They believed that they could change themselves, that they could be mad at someone, that they could make something right. That kind of thinking comforted her, strangely. She didn't exactly believe it. She didn't disbelieve it either. She attended the group doggedly, learning how to act in that place, learning to say out loud her imaginings. She was careful in what she said. They might think she was crazy for real if she told them all of it. She knew no one would believe the tales she could tell, about the cursings, about the dyings, about the grief. She stuck to the ordinary things they all talked about, bosses, children, dreams, forbidden feelings, fantasies. She was often surprised at what frightened them, at what caused them pain. But over the months she grew to believe that the world was like they described it to be. That it was mostly safe, mostly within her control. How she longed that it be that way, and the rest just her interpretation, her bad dream.

One of the people in the group was a woman named Teresa. She was somewhat older than Ephanie, and had a couple of kids who were almost grown. She had long curly black hair and white white skin. She was a large woman and usually wore long skirts and colorful shirts. She always wore hiking boots.

One night after group she had invited Ephanie to her house, and Ephanie had gone. The kids were staying over at the Soucies' house, so she didn't have to worry about getting home on time. Teresa had a small, crowded flat in the Mission, a distance from where the group met. It was littered with books and dusty objects—knicknacks, pyramids, water pipes, crystals, ashtrays that were overflowing with cigarette butts, and plates with leftover food on them that looked like they had been there a long time.

Teresa scooped some clothes and papers off of one of the chairs and told Ephanie to sit down. She went into another room and returned with a bottle of gin and two gritty glasses. She went back out and came back with a bottle of orange juice and some ice. Shoving some books aside, she sat heavily on the couch, poured the drinks, talking all the while. Teresa barraged Ephanie with questions, hardly stopping long enough to listen to one response before rushing on to the next query. Now and then she would look openly at Ephanie, her dark blue eyes probing, questioning. Then she would drop her gaze and ask another question. Where had Ephanie been raised? Had she read this or that book? Did she attend traditional Indian events? Did she go to the sweats? How old were her kids? What did she do in the evenings, on the weekends? Did she like having kids?

Ephanie was beginning to tire of the seemingly unending stream of innocuous questions being aimed at her, but she sat quietly in her chair, smoking and sipping her drink, trying to look composed, self-assured, polite. At last Teresa leaned forward slightly, and looking speculatively at Ephanie for a second, said, "Actually, the reason I asked you to come over is because I wanted to read for you. Have you ever had a psychic reading?"

Ephanie shifted in her chair slightly. Slightly she moved her head downward, slightly dropped her gaze. She felt herself shake, a spasm pass through her muscles involuntarily. She struggled to smile so that Teresa wouldn't notice her face as the spasm passed over it. She thought of the red hand she had seen posted on windows here and there, and of her wish to go into one of those places to find out what went on. One time a small, elderly woman had stopped her in the street, grasping her arm. The woman had whispered urgently, "Come inside. I have something important to tell you." But startled, Ephanie had pulled away. She had smiled apologetically, shaking her head, mumbling something about having no time right then. "Come back soon. As soon as you can," the old woman had said. She had looked squarely at Ephanie before turning away and going back inside her shop. Ephanie hadn't gone back, had told herself that the woman only needed to make a few bucks just then and had spotted Ephanie as a likely prospect. But the event had stayed in her mind.

Now here was someone else making a similar offer, someone it wouldn't be quite so easy to shrug off without sounding rude or foolish. Ephanie took a careful swallow of her drink, careful it went down the right way. She was very tense, maybe frightened. "No," she said. "I don't think I've ever had one. I got some Tarot cards, but I haven't had time to mess with them yet." She inhaled carefully, let the breath out carefully, then continued. "Maybe sometime I'd let you do one, but right now I'm sort of spacey. It probably wouldn't be good to try it this evening."

"Well," Teresa said, "I really think you should get one. I won't charge you. But I keep having this very strong feeling that they have something important they want to tell you. The spirits, I mean." She didn't smile as she said it. Her broad, square face was friendly and serious. "I don't want to make you do something you'd rather not, but I really think you should listen. If I don't say something that makes any sense to you, that's okay. Maybe we could just fool around with it a little so you can see how it goes."

Ephanie felt her resistance collapse with a suddenness that startled her. "Sure, why not," she said. "Might as well try it out." She looked back at Teresa almost defiantly. Thinking, this white lady can't scare me. Feeling scared all the same.

Teresa leaned forward and took Ephanie's hands in hers, resting them on her own lap. She looked into Ephanie's eyes for a moment, then off somewhere into the space between their faces. "Now, listen carefully," she said, "because some of this is going to be hard for me to get right. A lot of it is about stuff that doesn't make much sense to me, but I just have to say whatever they tell me to. It's not supposed to make sense to me, just to you. Okay?"

Ephanie nodded. "Okay," Teresa continued. "The thing is that they want you to know that someone is watching out for you. She's an older woman with white hair. She wears a particular pin on her dress, it's a small turquoise and silver one, shaped like a spider. She wears thick glasses and she's smiling and nodding. Do you recognize her?"

Ephanie nodded. "They also want you to know that there's some trouble that has been going on for a long time. They say you should investigate it. Investigate? Yes, that's right. Investigate it." Teresa paused for a time, staring into Ephanie's eyes but not seeing her. Her eyes seemed to be focused somewhere else. "They say it was a long time ago, and that it's important that you find out about it. They say that it won't be easy, but you gotta try. They say you should get a gold ring and wear it all the time. It will protect you, like a talisman." Ephanie nodded. She felt confirmed, somehow. She had been looking at gold rings, for no reason she could figure out, for some time. Everytime she went by a jewelry store she looked at them. Thinking it was some sort of romantic fantasy half buried in her head that made her look so stubbornly. She had felt pretty silly about it, and somehow embarrassed.

"There is some danger here, so they say be cautious. Take your time. Did you get that?" Teresa looked at Ephanie suddenly, her eyes focused again. Ephanie realized that for a few minutes they had seemed almost black, but now they were the bland color of the mid-morning sky. "I hope that all makes some sort of sense to you," Teresa said, lighting a cigarette. "It seemed important." She took a long drag and leaned back against the couch. "There," she said, smiling. "That feels better. I get so uncomfortable when they want something. They nag and nag at me the whole time until I do what they insist I should do. Now. Want another drink?"

Ephanie shook her head. No. "I think I'd better get home now," she said, looking vaguely around for her shawl. "It must be late."

"You can stay here if you want to," Teresa offered. But Ephanie was suddenly in a panic to get out of there. "No, I'd better get home. The kids will be home early tomorrow. I'd better be there when they come home." She picked up her shawl and wrapped it tightly around herself, securing it over her shoulder with the strap of her fringed bag. "Thanks, Teresa," she said. Heading for the door.

"Sure." Teresa went behind her. "Let's get together again soon. I hope the reading didn't upset you."

"No," Ephanie said. "No. It was alright. It was about what I had thought." She closed the door behind her and went down the dirty grey stairs out into the fog filled night.

They Lived Out Their Imaginings, Dreaming

She knew she should do some very real thing. She should canvass the city and get some kind of job that meant something, that they could be proud of back home. They could say things about her and not be ashamed that she was gone.

And she should go more places, see more things. There was a lot to do in this place, almost everything. She should get up in fogfilled mornings to active rooms, filled with cool warm friends who were doing important things. Making the world happen. Politics, arts, learning, adventuring. She saw that there were many like that around her. She saw posters about everything. Poetry readings, therapy groups, encounters, demonstrations, marches, symphonies, concerts, films, plays, dance recitals. She was excited by each of them. Wanted to go to them all. But somehow she didn't. She went to work, came home, did housework, ran errands, took care of the kids. She tried to work at her art work, mostly beading and painting, but some pottery too.

She had a friend from around home who lived south of the city. Sometimes they'd get together and go out in her pickup to the pastures around Cupertino to get a load of cow manure. They'd fire some pots and sell them at a powwow. But she didn't do much of that. It took a lot of time and planning, and her life wasn't like that. Once they had gone out and gotten some willow branches and she had made a couple of baskets. They had come out alright. At least the coils were smooth and the designs were almost evenly spaced.

She had gone to an ashram a few times to see a visiting guru. She had been transfixed by the chanting and the incense, the sense of tribal coming together she had felt. The women had been seated on one side of the room, the men on the other, as was right, she thought. She heard the white women she had gone with make apologetic noises about it, and nodded as though she agreed with them, but she didn't. As far as she was concerned men and women should meditate or worship separately, as they did most things. She had been very moved by the activities there, and had felt herself somehow held within the mind of the guru. When he left to go east, she missed him.

On his last public day there she had taken Ben and Agnes to the blessing. She wanted them to see this man, who uncannily changed color and shape before her eyes. They were bored by the experience, but she had felt it was important for them even so. The guru had blessed them and given them a special candy he kept for the children. Her friends apologized about that too. They didn't think sugar was good for children. But she thought about her uncles and her grandfather who had always given candy to the little ones. It was a way of making friends that she recognized. She thought sugar was less dangerous than no love at all. But she nodded and said that candy wasn't the best thing for them to be given. Still, she'd said, maybe it would help them remember the guru and the ceremony they had witnessed.

She thought a lot about being successful here in this strange place. She wished for a victorian flat with a real fireplace, for clothes that looked fashionable. Not like her country clothes from the trading post in Guadalupe or the Family Store in Albuquerque. She went to stores to try on outfits, but she usually left without buying anything. A friend at the Indian Center had given her a fine pair of boots. They were wine-colored and laced up with shiny black laces that you wound around hooks that were also black. They had high heels and were really good looking. She wore them when she went out to a movie or to a coffee house like she did sometimes in the evenings or on a day off.

But mostly she wore levis and mocassins and some shirt or blouse that as comfortable. She almost always wore her dance shawl, which was enough most of the time and made her feel held.

She made friends at the restaurant where she worked, and in the therapy group she went to faithfully, and after a time these new friends filled most of the time she had for socializing. She went to the Indian Center or the Inter-Tribal House less and less. She felt guilty about it, and ashamed, and she made resolutions over and over to spend more time there. She'd go on Friday night for the weekly dinner, she'd promise herself. She'd go to the next meeting, she'd promise.

Somehow the Friday went by, and the meeting was half over before she remembered she was supposed to go. Somehow time slipped away in the fog and the wind and the sunlight and the wishing and the promising. She went less often to pow-wows, sending the kids with someone else, or dropping them off there. Or she'd go in for awhile and leave after a couple of dances. She spent more and more time with the people she was getting to know, in the city that was the farthest west on the continent, the city where dreams, fantasies, imaginings, were supposed to come true.

She knew people who were doing alright. Down at the Indian Center or at the University. She thought of the people around her, the white people she spent time with who expected her to do things. Could not understand her lack of focus, her aimless wandering through her days. She imagined that they wanted her to see things from the outside, objectively, and she tried. She wanted to belong with them, to be a part of their world of hope and power and fine things. She admired them. Their easiness with words, their accustomed sense of understanding, in some way, whatever happened. As near as she could tell, they could explain anything, something she had never been able to do. And having explained something, whether poverty or fear, joy or distress, they would make plans about it. They would end poverty. They would transform fear. They would increase joy, extend it, spread it all around. They would banish distress, grief, pain. What a wonderful dream, she would think. And long to be part of it, to feel the hope that dream bespoke. They are so full of courage, she would think. They are so free.

She thought they disliked her silences. Her incomprehensible jokes. Her diffidence. Her way of not seeing what they saw. As they saw. Valuing what they valued. She did not try to explain, knowing that it was senseless to try. That she couldn't make it clear. Anything clear. Not to herself, or to them.

She was not the Indian maiden she was supposed to be. She knew that. Not the Indian they imagined and took her to be. Then felt angry when she wasn't what they wanted. She was not noble, not wise, not exotic. She was just an ordinary woman. She was well read, interested in a lot of things. She had gone to college and had studied literature and gotten involved in political struggles. She had passed out leaflets for Civil Rights, had stood in circles and sang "We Shall Overcome." She had dropped out in righteous rage at political injustice. She had sat at booths and harangued passers-by. She had returned to school and gotten a degree. She didn't have a single portrait of an Indian leader on her wall. She had smoked dope and worn miniskirts, had protested, however mildly when job interviewers asked her questions about childcare arrangements and her marital status. She had supported the Alianza and refused to drink Gallo wine. She had sent money and passed out petitions in support of the occupations of Alcatraz and Wounded Knee. She had sung the right songs and said the right things, but she hadn't occupied either place. She guessed that she didn't belong to any of them.

Once one of her friends had told her, "You don't seem Indian to me. You talk like a New York Jew, not like an Indian at all." He was disappointed in her lack of romantic appeal. She always forgot to keep her eyes cast down, to say nature loving things. She ground her chili in an electric blender and made jokes about her electric metate that made nobody laugh.

She supposed they got angry that she wasn't who she was supposed to be. She was always getting lost and they'd say, "How come you got lost? I thought you were supposed to be an Indian." They looked disgusted when she couldn't tell them where to get a good buy on blankets or jewelry. And she did not understand, really, what it was they wanted her to be. They wouldn't tell her, denied that they wanted her to be anything.

She Didn't Know God Made Wooden Headed Indians

Her mother came to visit her and they talked about the weird white people once again. It was a familiar conversation, full of unspoken understandings, like home, making Ephanie believe for the time it took that she understood what she otherwise could not comprehend.

"I don't know where they got the idea that Indians are dumb. Dumb and silent. Stoic. Noble. Have feathers. We don't molt, you know. There are Indians who aren't too swift, and there are those who are geniuses. How come they don't know that?" Her mother sat, gazing wide eyed at Ephanie as she thought about the strangeness of whites.

Looking at her mother, Ephanie thought again how round her mother's eyes were. Most Guadalupes had wide eyes, round and widely spaced in their heads. Or else they had almost square eyes, like Grandma's. Only those who had Navajo blood or something like that had slightly slanted eyes. "It's probably because we don't talk English the same way they do. I think Indians must sound slow witted in English," she said.

"Yes, that may be it," her mother said, staring off into space. She had a habit of looking outward into herself when she was talking. It had always fascinated Ephanie, who would sit as quietly as she could so as not to disturb that look. For it would become focused and sharp when her mother was talking directly to someone, talking about something directed to that someone in particular.

"Yes, I think that's it," her mother repeated. But the Indian languages are very complicated. Indians can think things that just can't be thought in English. Or Spanish either. That's why so many of us read all the time, I guess. And why we like opera and fine books and white art, if we get a chance at them. In them the whites seem almost like Indians. The bookmobile was through last week, and I was late getting there, and it went to the other villages first, so by then all the good books had been checked out. The woman who takes care of it, oh, she's a librarian, I guess, you know her, Mrs. Jansen, she always seems so surprised when we take out all the literary books she's got."

She looked disturbed for a moment, a line creasing the center of her forehead, running like an arrow shaft between her eyebrows. Then the lines cleared and she smiled. "Do you remember that time when you were, oh, around nine or ten and we went to Denver?" Ephanie nodded, remembering. "We went into the dining room there, for dinner," her mother continued, her eyes far off in some private distance. "I think your dad had some business to do there. It was just after the war."

"I remember," Ephanie said. "That dining room I especially remember. All that silverware. I was scared to death that I wouldn't know what to eat with. So I ordered what you ordered and then I just watched what you did so I could do it too."

Her mother leaned back, putting her head against the cushions of the couch. Her hands lay idle for the moment in her lap. She closed her eyes, smiling. "Well, do you remember the waiter? He was a stuffed shirt. Pompous. I had on some nice suit I had gotten, and my squash blossom necklace that your dad traded for at Feast that year. I had had my hair done in the beauty parlor at the hotel that afternoon after we got there. Anyway, this waiter came up and handed me the menu, of course he handed each one of us one, but then he just looked at me when he gave me mine. He just stared. I could see amazement all over his face. His mouth almost dropped open. I knew he was thinking, 'I don't believe it. A real Injun.' I just looked straight at him until he noticed me staring back, and then he sort of stammered something and backed away." She laughed quietly, remembering. "I think now that he never thought an Indian would even be able to read the menu!"

"Yeah," Ephanie said. "He must have thought you only ate dog stew." Then they both laughed, remembering Grandma Campbell's story about how she and her brothers would talk to the white people who sometimes came to Guadalupe. They would ask the children, "What do you people eat?" And the children, impish and sophisticated even in that faraway place would answer, "You see that dog over there?" And there was, inevitably, a dog nearby. "Well, that dog's for our supper. We're on our way to catch it right now." And they would run off, chasing the dog, leaving the tourists looking sorely distressed behind.

How amazing that was. That the children knew so much. The children who lived on a ranch way off in the hills on the edge of the reservation in the outposts of New Mexico. Knew that some Indians did eat dog stew. That whites thought all Indians ate it. Knew that the idea of eating dog meat horrified the whites who thought all Indians were the same. The children knew there were many kinds of Indians, and only one kind of white. They knew that the Guadalupes were as horrified at the thought of eating dog as the whites were, so their joke was doubly, triply funny. It was convoluted and complicated. It moved in and out like their languages and their minds, in and out like the belts and kilts they wove, in and out like the clans and families in their relationships, in and out like the dances, the pottery designs, the rugs, in and out like their stories and their lives.

Ephanie did not talk Guadalupe. Her mother seldom spoke it at home. Her father spoke it at the store, but not at home. She did not know the tongue, but she knew the thought, it's complication that piled one thing atop another, folded this within that, went from within to without and made what was without within. She knew that everything moved and everything balanced, always, in her language, her alien crippled tongue, the English that was ever unbalanced, ever in pieces, she groped with her words and her thought to make whole what she could not say. She was obsessed by language, by words. She used the words she had lavishly, oblivious to their given meanings. She did not give to them what was theirs, but took from them what was hers. Ever she moved her tongue, searching for a way to mean in words what she meant in thought. For her thought was the Grandmothers', was the people's, even though her language was a stranger's tongue.

"Grandma always said that whites are stupid." Ephanie started from her reverie at her mother's words. She had forgotten her mother was there, sitting across from her in that room where the light filtered through the shadows all over the room. "She said they couldn't think as completely as an Indian. That we must be patient with them because they were like children. They made things simple so that they could understand. She used to say, 'Poor things, they're so simple, they're just like children.'" And she giggled, putting her hand over her mouth, shrugging her head down into her shoulders. She looked just like Grandma Campbell then, laughing like the old Indian ladies everywhere laughed. Ephanie looked blankly at her for a time, then began to titter with her. Like two girls they giggled and hummed in mutual recognition of Grandma's penetrating thought, her wit.

There'll Be No Dark Alleys, When Jesus Comes

Her white friends seemed to want very much what she had rejected. They were preoccupied with nature, with what they saw as wilderness, with living what they called a simple, natural life. They seemed to believe that things had been better at some earlier time, that Indians cared deeply for the earth and for their own welfare. They were betrayed when she suggested that it wasn't that way. They didn't want to hear it. And she didn't anyway want to tell. They all seemed to think they could be Indians, if only they were recognized as sincere, nature-loving souls. She often wished it were that way. That she could be so easily accepted, too.

But she liked them, because they didn't ever beat each other up, because they wanted everyone to have enough and to be happy, because they talked of strange and wonderful things, because they did not believe that living in poverty was bad. Because they chose to live that way. And she scorned them for all those things.

Oh, they'd get drunk and rowdy sometimes. Sometimes someone would have bruises and a black eye. Usually they had gotten in a fight with some drunk. It blew over. They seemed above all to be such earnest people. They told stories about the world they'd seen. On the road. In the bars. On the streets. They fed one another. They acted like they cared. Even some who were old and tired, used up, who knew like she knew that courage had long since gone the way of vision, off into the blue distances with the old warriors, the buffalo, the grass. That the world they dreamed about, that they had never known, had given ideals up to concrete sophistication and steel unconcern. The world had become an endless highway, bounded by a chainlink fence that read KEEP OUT. Their world. The one they wanted. That they could not ever have. She thought that, and so did they, some of them. Some of them were not yet convinced. They thought you could still change something that wasn't yourself. They tried.

Listening to them she would remember one of the stories Stephen used to tell about when he was working in Gallup at the Navajo hospitality center, a place where folks could come and get together that wasn't a bar. There had been a piano there, and Stephen had played in the evenings. A Navajo coffeehouse, he'd called it. Some of the folks would ask him to play hymns, and he would. One of them was called "There'll Be No Dark Valleys, When Jesus Comes," but the way he told it, they used to sing it another way. "There'll be no dark alleys when Jesus comes," they'd sing, laughing. She would sing it that way too, especially when down in the Tenderloin she would see some brother sleeping on the filthy sidewalk. Leaned up against a cold, dark wall, a broken bottle nearby.

71

And she'd remember the people she would see in Guadalupe, by the highway, at a bar that was there. They would be out back of the bar huddled around a fire in the trash barrel. Even in the cold they'd stand around, laughing, drinking, having a good time. She knew the city wasn't remarkable for its dark alleys. They were everywhere.

And all around her she sensed what was growing, south, north, west and east joined together, fused together in fear and rage, the mute twin angels binding them above and below. And sleep became a tightening band around the eyes of all the people who could not see, who loved the pain, their eyes open forever, unseeing.

And all around her in that city of pain and grief and foolish, futile, destitute hope, everything was moving, always, always moving. The pall crept eastward across the bay toward the mountains, the deserts, the plains; south through obliterated pastures, hills, forests, crept into the once fertile valleys; slunk across the coastal range and into the sea; and north into the rivers, and southeast. Alongside and over. Beneath. The pall of despair that like a curse shrouded everything of brightness, of clarity. All over the land it grew and hovered. And over and within the sea.

And had she understood what they wanted her to be, she supposed, she couldn't have been it anyway. Tonto. Sitting Bull. Red Cloud. La Malinche. Well, maybe she could manage La Malinche, she who had led Cortez to Mexico City, to conquering the whole of the Aztec Empire. La Chingada, some angry Chicanos called her, The Female Fucker. But Ephanie supposed she didn't have enough sheer orneriness even for that title. La Malinche was a traitor, they said. Ephanie also thought she was guilty of betrayal, but she understood exactly what had been betrayed. The Aztecs were the enemy, from Marina's, La Malinche's, point of view. They had made her a slave. Ephanie wondered if selling out your enemy made you a traitor.

And Ephanie's people weren't exactly her enemy. They had not enslaved her in any noticeable way. They just took care of business, and if that business included her exclusion, well, that was only right. They had to draw some lines somewhere, she supposed. And she wasn't sure she wanted to be part of that

72

rage and destruction that was the full measure of their lives. I have enough of my own, she would think, pondering. She remembered an odd thing. About how she had longed as a child to belong to the village her mother had been born in. How she had imagined that she would grow up to be bronze and slim, with long raven hair and lithe limbs. How she and Elena would stalk cattle over the land, pretending to be Indian maidens who were brave and strong and beautiful. Indian princesses. Safe and sure in the arms of the tribe. She felt ashamed when she remembered that longago fantasy. But she understood the lure of the powwow circuit then, of the dyed skin and fake black hair she had seen some of them using. You could do that sort of thing here where everything was for strangers. At home everyone knew who you were, and exactly what you looked like. She had wanted to be a squaw. She was ashamed that she had ever wanted that.

She was determined to make another kind of life. To avoid the pain, banishing. The nightmares, the anger, the fighting, the blood, the silences that shaped her days. She would find life and live it. She wanted that. And death hung like dirty air over the land where once had walked the peaceful ones in the land of California, the golden land rumoured to have been the last dwelling of the Mother, the Grandmother, Earth Woman. Star Woman. The Woman Who Fell From the Sky. Where the ancient ones had set their eyes westward and the white ones, the strangers, had followed, destroying everything in their path. For two hundred miles in front of them they had spewed death. Of the animals. Of the birds. Of the reptiles. Of the insects. Of the plants and the herbs and the grasses and the trees. Of the people who died, who still danced and sang and fished. Who gathered wild grass seed. Who lived there still, though in another space. Not this one where the pall crystallized into asphalt and concrete, blood on the sidewalk, blood pouring from hands and faces, from arms and eyes.

One night she had gone with Teresa to a coffeehouse. When they came out and got into the car the glass in the door had shattered with a noise like a shot. "It's starting!" Teresa yelled. They looked around them and saw a dark shape running in the opposite direction. They saw a man holding his hand, blood coming from it. Or something dark that poured. Shivering, they got out of the car. "Get an ambulance," Teresa said as she moved toward the injured man. "Hurry." Ephanie ran down the street the way they had just come. She had cut her mocassined foot when she ran around the car. Limping, she ran toward the lights of the place they had just left. Ran inside and to the phone. "Ambulance," she said to the startled eyes of the woman behind the counter. "Somebody's hurt." And followed the woman's eyes to the floor where she had stepped. It was red and slimey. "Oh, shit," she said. "I've ruined my mocassins."

They Live Where The Wild Grass Still Grows

She saw them one night. In her room. She had been meditating, chanting, burning sage, remembering. Casting her mind like a line into the night. The spaceless shape of night. She heard singing, high and sweet, and saw around her their faces, the people. In boats made of tulles that were filled with long stalks of some kind of seeded grass. They were gathering the grass into their boats, pulling great sheaves of it down low then beating it with a heavy wandlike instrument. They saw her watching and smiled and beckoned to her. She did not move.

She knew that they were the people who had lived around here. That they still did, she hadn't known until she saw them. But she was certain that those she saw were not ghosts. Unconcerned, they knew who they were, and that she was watching them. They welcomed her. Like she had read, they did not know fear. Left to themselves for ages, they had no way of understanding what was happening when the strangers rushed in to find gold, to get rich, to make their own alien dreams come true.

The beatings then, the massacres. The grass people had not known how to fight. They didn't even have weapons. The strangers went into their villages and bludgeoned them to death, or shot them in the head, and so uncomprehending were they they did not move to defend themselves. The strangers could beat the people to death with rifle butts and clubs because the people didn't fight back. They didn't know how. They didn't

74

understand killing. All of them dead. The bloodsoaked grass of the villages had become the bloody concrete and asphalt of the cities. All that dying. Hundreds of thousands of them. Gone.

The descendants of the strangers now said when Ephanie would tell them the history of this place, "But we didn't do it. Don't blame us." And she knew that they believed what they were saying, that they did not see the connections, did not know that every time they turned on the water or the lights, an Indian died. Not long time ago, but now. And in some way they were right. They were no more guilty of those deaths than she, than those who had died there, who did not die, who still lived where the wild grasses grew. But still, her friends' incomprehension of the enormity of it made her seethe with rage.

One day Agnes came home from school angry. "They're making us read 'Old Yeller.' Out loud. I had to read it today. And Billy, a boy who sits next to me had to listen too. And I asked him how he could stand it. What they were saying. Mother, he passes for Chinese. He was surprised when I said I knew he was an Indian. He's Navajo, but he tells the others that he's Chinese." Her dark face was tight with anger. She was fighting tears by clenching her fists, so small and slender, so strong. She felt so weak, Ephanie knew, as she knew the feeling from every day of her own life.

"What does the book say?" Ephanie asked. "I've never read it."

"It's about a little boy, he's white, gets a dog to protect their livestock against the Indians. They call them savages. They're living in Arizona somewhere. It's Indian land and they stole it. But they don't admit that. They call the Indians savages, robbers, and they have dogs to kill them. A little white boy. And he's proud of that. The book makes him sound like a hero. Our teacher wouldn't have us reading it if it was about blacks. He knows you can't say things like that about black people anymore. But what about Billy? What about me? Why doesn't anybody care about us?"

Ephanie put her arms around the girl and held her. "I'll call the teacher and talk to him if you want me to. Did you say anything to him?"

"Yes, I told him the book was wrong. I was so mad!" The girl began to sob, with rage and fear. "How can they do that," she wailed. "Why do they tell such awful lies?"

She Gathers Some Seeds

She wrote Stephen long letters. Talked for hours on the phone. Never mind the bill. She was hungry for the voices of home. The laughter, the cynicism, the gentle jokes. Stephen's arrogant gentleness, his every story and pose. The gossip he passed on to her, keeping her in touch with what went on around Guadalupe. Who had gotten married. Who had split up. Who had been out all night. Who was being talked about and ostracized. Who was backing who in the next tribal election. Who got fired, who had made a bundle. Who snubbed who. Who had gotten their names on the rolls illegally. Who had been removed. Who had been hurt, maimed, murdered. Who was starving. Who had died. He kept her up to date on everything she had left behind, that she wanted to forget and could not leave, could not change, or fix, or help. That she could not wipe from the corners of her mind.

In their conversations she demanded, mute, unspeaking, that he understand her, reassure her, admit he was wrong, admit she was real. Say he would come to San Francisco and be with her. And all around her was the city's pain, beating at the windows, rumbling and shaking the floor. All the loss and aching pain of home that she understood and wanted to make go away. To leave her and her children alone.

Her cousin wrote her. Had Ephanie heard what Sammy had done to her cousin's sister Lucy? He'd driven out to her place one morning after her husband had left the house. He had a friend with him in the car, his lover, John. He had gone to Lucy's house with this boy and a gun, gone inside and forced her to undress. He ordered his lover to rape her. At gunpoint. He forced them. "He's crazy," her cousin said. "He's crazy. He was drinking. I don't know why he wanted to do that. He's out of his mind. Everybody's in an uproar over it. They say they're going to kill him when they find him. If they do. He's run away, nobody knows where. He left John at Lucy's and ran because Lucy got away somehow and called her husband. He came right away, because he was just over at the post office. Not far. And Sammy ran out of the house. He dropped the gun when he got in the car. They haven't seen him since. He hasn't showed up anywhere.

Ephanie hadn't heard. She called her mother, who cried. Who was sad because Sammy was her favorite, because she loved him a lot. But he had always been strange, always in trouble. She didn't know what to do. There was nothing to be done.

In that same call her mother told her that Juanita had died. Poor thing. She had died of cirrhosis, finally. It had taken such a longlong time. Years. "At the end there was nothing left of her. She looked like a corpse for years. Well," she said, her voice matter-of-fact, "she's gone, poor soul." She didn't say "Good riddance." But Ephanie thought that was how she probably felt.

And then she told Ephanie about the Sais boy. The little one who had hung himself the week before. Or was it the week before that. "He was only ten," she said. "Why'd he do that. His poor mother, she's half out of her mind. And his dad's gone. Hasn't been home since they found Emmett dead. There by the river, hanging in the trees. Some older boys had seen him earlier, playing down there. They said he had a rope, was tying it to the tree. They didn't know what he was going to do, so they went on about their business. When they came back by they looked to see if he was still there and he was dead. Hung himself. Such a terrible thing. We went to the funeral. It was so sad."

Ephanie didn't know what to do with all the stories she heard. Or the ones she lived, or was afraid to live. So she tried to bury herself. In occupation, in preoccupation. New ones, ones she hadn't tried. Old ones, comforting and familiar though tinged as always with the dread, the fear.

She spent more and more time with Teresa, who called herself a witch and said that she would teach Ephanie the craft. Ephanie, who knew witches personally wasn't convinced that Teresa had it in her, but she was interested in learning whatever Teresa knew. She hadn't forgotten what she had been told that first night at Teresa's house.

She got out her Tarot cards and learned to use them. In the Guadalupe way, she got a crystal ball and practiced with it, staring into it for long periods. She saw a lot in it—faces that she didn't recognize, that were occupied with whatever they were occupied with. Some of them were contemporary, from everywhere on earth. Some were dressed in costumes she recognized from other periods. They didn't do much, and she thought and heard nothing when she looked at them. They were just there, in the ball as though on a screen.

"Try just holding it and closing your eyes," Teresa counseled her. "See if you get anything that way."

So Ephanie tried that, and it worked. Something worked, anyway. She held the ball in her hand, resting it in her lap. She closed her eyes and focused her attention on the center of her forehead, as Teresa had instructed her. As the cold crystal grew warm in her hand, she began to see a series of images. She told Teresa about them as they came.

"First everything was just dark. Then I was walking down a tunnel and I saw a door at the end of it. It was painted blue, like they paint them at home. I looked down at my feet and I was wearing some sort of dark sandals. I could see the edge of my dress and it was purple, sort of like those red grapes, not red or purple really. I can't remember what the color's named."

"Say it in the present, Ephanie." Teresa advised.

Ephanie looked at her blankly for a moment then closed her eyes again. "Okay. I've got this dress on that's a sort of purple red and it's made of some sort of rough weave. I'm going toward the door that's blue, now I'm opening it. I can see blue light pouring through it. Now it's open and there's this grassy place. It seems like it's on a hill. There's someone coming toward me. The light is very bright, so I can't make out who it is. Now he's right next to me, and he's saying something. I can't understand what he's saying, but I feel very happy." She felt herself smiling, felt warmth spreading through her chest and belly. "Oh. He's saying that he's glad to see me. I wonder who he is. He seems really familiar. He says he has someone who wants to talk to me. We're walking toward trees. They're big and they have lots of leaves. Now I see that there's a lot of people there. It's like a picnic or something. We go up to them and now I'm looking at a woman. It's Grandma Campbell. Oh, boy." Ephanie brushed away the tears that were coursing down her cheeks. She could hardly control her voice, its trembling. She felt so safe, so good, so warm. "Now," she said quietly, struggling to make her voice loud enough for Teresa to hear, "she's holding me."

She Is Learning To Tell Time

When she was small, she and Elena used to go down into the big arroyo near her house and dig out clay. They would make balls of the damp clay and resting them on the cement of her front porch would roll them out into long slender ropes. These they would coil like the women did, to make pots. They would shape them and smooth them when they were shaped. They would leave them in the sun to dry.

The pots always crumbled. Always fell apart. When she would ask her grandma why that happened, the old woman would say, "That clay's no good. You have to have the right kind of clay." They would continue to try to make a good pot, one that wouldn't fall apart, but they never could. "The clay's no good," they would solemnly assure one another. "You have to have the right kind of clay."

Her grandma used to tell her stories. That was when she was almost blind. She would sit next to Ephanie and talk to her, as old ladies will. Half in and half out, she would talk. She would be silent. Her eyes, hugely magnified by the glasses she wore, would peer at the granddaughter. Birdlike, she would peer. She would say things that didn't make much sense. Because she would not remember whether she had said those things yet, to this certain child, or not. She often thought she had already said them, so she would not finish them or would say only a piece of them. Leaving Ephanie, the child, to make those pieces whole. It seemed to the child that her grandmother talked from far away. Leaning into her mind, back, back into her mind, the old woman would talk to the child, and the child saw how it was with her. She talked from someplace far away from the place where the others lived.

79

One story she told Ephanie was about the giantess who chased a little girl. The little girl had gone hunting for rabbits to take home for dinner. While she was hunting she came across this huge, huge woman. A giantess. The giantess chased the little girl, who was small but could run very fast. The child ran into a small cave and huddled there, far from the giantess' reaching arm. The giantess went off and got a stick. She used it to reach around in the cave opening, trying to sweep the child out with it.

But the little girl stayed out of the way of the giantess' reach, and didn't say anything. Then she heard a small voice, saying her name. "Little girl," the voice said. "I will help you if you want." The little girl looked all around and she saw a spider on the wall. "Do you want my help?" said the spider. "Oh, yes, thank you," said the child.

"Well," said the spider, "just take your hunting stick and blow this on it." She gave the girl some powdery stuff. The little girl did what the spider said. "Now," said the spider, "reach the stick out when I tell you to. Push it out very fast and whirl it around in a big circle as hard as you can."

When the spider told her to, the little girl did as she said. She heard the giantess let out a yell. Then it was very quiet. Soon the spider told the little girl she could go out now. "It's safe. But when you go out, make a special call that I'll show you. Two boys will come. They are my grandsons. Tell them what has happened, and they will go after the giantess."

So the little girl did as she was instructed. When the war twins came, she told them about the giantess. "Don't worry," they said. "We'll get her." And they went off and found the giantess. They killed her and flung her head in one direction, her body in another.

"You know that big rock by the road on the way to Montecilla?" the old woman would say then. "Well, that's the giantess' head." And Ephanie, the child, would nod, her eyes huge, wondering. For some reason, that story stayed in Ephanie's mind.

The Bearer of the Sun Arises

Thomas

There was a man who had come into her life, into her, feeding her, feeding on her. She told him about magic, and the mystery she knew about. But Thomas didn't believe. Said that was why she was there on the tatami raised a foot above his apartment floor, in the center of the Nisei man's room.

He talked pleasantly, not looking at her mostly, just talked hypnotically. He cooked supper as the long sun set over San Francisco, talked as they ate seated on the tatami. They talked and drank, she talked about magic and he talked about his work. They ate food he cooked on a brazier, Japanese style. "I'm Nisei," he said. "There are these: Issei, Nisei, Sensei, Yonsei. They are generations in America. The Issei are the old ones. I am Nisei. We are the only people who count the generations," he said.

She remembered her own clan, descended of Iyatiku, Earth Woman, Corn Woman. There were four corn clans, then her clan. "I am Oak," she said. "The fifth. My uncle, Oak Man, helped Iyatiku in the beginning. He assisted her in laying down the orders, the rules. The way the people would live. How they would be. He was the first War Captain, the first outside chief. We begin to count from the time the people came here from the last world, just like you."

When it was late, when the sun had long set and the fog was thick against the glass he undressed her like a doll and took her to bed on the tatami altar where they had eaten. He transformed the table into a bed, and laid her down upon it. He entered her, slowly, mastering his time, fucked her, his face gone from her, intent on his own straining to appease something unspoken within him, something far away and deep inside that he did not acknowledge with even a flicker of his eyes, not even a flicker of a look in her direction, he fucked her like a doll, and lay beside her, and went to sleep.

She looked at him then. His small body. His brown skin rippling still as the muscles went slack. As slack as such muscles could. The sheen of his skin she gazed at, for a long long time.

She wondered as she watched him sleep safe in his own place far from her why she thought only of hurt. When she was near him, why did she cry. His lovemaking was good. Solid and

81

certain. Unfumbling. Free, somehow clean. Like his neat apartment. Like his clean food. It was good. But though her body responded to him, he was very far from her, from any place she usually lived. His eyes, open or closed in sleep did not touch her, and while he fucked he said so little, nothing at all really addressed to her, just the formula utterances he'd learned by rote to say as he was getting off. And when he was through he turned and slept, and waking took her home. Politely. Smoothly. And she cried. She didn't know what to make of this. Of his confidence. His desire. His isolate sureness. Like Stephen he refused to make her real.

Maybe he was a spirit man. Maybe both he and Stephen were spirit men. Maybe they were in her life like others were in her dreams. Significant. Laden. Pointing to or away. From sleep to sleep, from shadow to shade, from need to need. Down in the arroyo she had learned to dig useless yellow clay and shape it into bowls for the sun to eat. Coiling the ropes, smelling the sweet smell of earth, she had made clay forms with Elena beside her in the tall shadows that the high arroyo walls cast. Digging, she had gathered the earth. Smoothing, she had made it. Alone in a place that had few shadows, she was alone and she was afraid. Riding the high wind on a sunspun morning she went out and came in, wondering. And in the darkness of late night, when the children were long asleep she lay, eyes huge in the shadows, feeling his pain. "Thomas," she would say, testing it on her tongue. Yoshuri. Nisei man. And rubbing her palms against the satinedge of the blanket she would lay in the shadows of that northern night, coiling her mind into sleep.

And dream. Of walking down corridors in a museum. Where no one recognized her, no one acknowledged her. Walking down endless corridors, marble shining and gold leaf trimmed, halls where people walked, shadowed faces turning away if her eyes met theirs, turning toward the wall rather than face her, look at her, see her. In these halls she wandered, unable to find the way out. Not the way she had come, not the way she was going, a silent scream rising up in her always rising but never uttered in those silent, marble halls. No one ever spoke to her there.

In the dreams she would sometimes enter a room full of people, would sit with them and await the speaker, the film, whatever was being offered for enjoyment or instruction there. And would find herself unable to stay, needing to orient herself, to still the panic that had a voice saying over and over, you are not here, you are not. And she would leave to once again walk the corridors where walls appeared in the place that a doorway had been, where stairs that had once led down now only rose, obstructing her from getting by in her search for someone she could not find. And she would awaken, aware only of the cold coiling terror in her belly, the trembling of her veins as the blood tried to make its way through their branches. Branches branching like the tree that had stood outside her windows in that other place, the one she had left.

In one of those dreams she saw her mother, walking along the corridor near the wall. Agnes and Ben were with her. They were talking and laughing as they walked swiftly along. Ephanie tried to cross the corridor to them, but there were too many people and they were all walking toward her. She called to her mother, but she didn't look in Ephanie's direction. She called Agnes, she called Ben, but they kept walking toward her and never looked her way. Then they were past her. She turned, looked after them, tried to go after them but they had vanished as though they had not been there at all. She woke then, tears pouring from her eyes. Nobody knows my name she thought. And arose in the fog-chilled early light to enter a kitchen she did not recognize, to wander through a flat she did not recognize, to stare at bowls and cups, pottery and photographs she did not recognize, to gaze long into the bathroom mirror under the hard, brittle light at a face she did not know.

83

Therapist's Notes. July 26, 1976

DREAM: "I am in a huge building somewhere. It's made of marble. I think it's a museum. There are a lot of rooms and all sorts of people. I can't find my way out. I'm looking for someone, I don't know who, but I get more and more lost and I never find them. As I walk the people coming toward me turn away as I pass. They turn all the way toward the wall sometimes so they won't have to look at me. They are all strangers. Now I see my mother coming toward me. She's with the kids and they're walking on the other side of this big corridor we're in. It seems like everyone is going one direction but me. I call to my mom and Ben and Agnes, but they don't act like they can hear me or see me. They just keep going, in the direction opposite mine, talking and looking around. They're looking around but they don't see me even though I wave at them to get their attention. They walk on past me and I try to turn and go after them but as I turn around I can't see them anywhere. It's like they vanish into thin air."

THERAPIST: "Be the people."

EPHANIE: "Okay. I'm the people. We're walking down the hall at the museum. We're on our way somewhere, and it's almost time. There's an important lecture and tour going on, and we don't want to miss it. There's this woman going the wrong way, but we don't pay any attention to her. She's not going the same way. Some of us have to go out of our way to avoid her, and that slows us down. We don't like that, but we're not going to let her interfere with our purpose. We have something important to do and she's not going with us. We don't know who she is, only that she's going the wrong way."

THERAPIST: "Be Ben."

EPHANIE: "Okay. I'm Ben Atencio. I'm nine years old. My grandma is taking me and my sister to see a show at the museum. This is a special show that she wants us to see. We're hurrying so that we won't be late, and Grandma is telling us about what we're going to see. She keeps telling us to keep up so we won't miss anything. I'm feeling excited about the show because she's been talking to us about it for a long time. It was hard to get in here, and we have a long way to walk before we get to the place where the show's going on. I wish there weren't so many people. They scare me. They all walk so fast and they're tall and I can't see much except Agnes's face. She's acting like a girl right now so she's not laughing and fooling around like she usually does. I'm scared and excited and kinda mad because I don't want to walk so fast. I want to stop and look at some neat things that are in cases along the walls. And I want to look out the windows we go by. Grandma says we have to get a good seat, so we have to hurry. She's holding my hand so I don't get lost in this crowd."

THERAPIST: "Be Agnes."

EPHANIE: "I'm Agnes Atencio. I'm walking with Grandma and Ben down a long hall. It's a very wide and beautiful hall with big windows and cases with beautiful things in them. It's the museum where they put special things for everyone to look at and admire. I admire the things. There's dishes and bowls, there's things made of gold and jade from China and Egypt, things from Africa and South America and Mexico and Europe. Paintings and statues, carpets and hangings. I'm all dressed up. I have on new boots with almost high heels and a nice plaid wool coat. I have a hat that's made of fur and it's soft and it looks really good on me. It makes me look like women in the magazines. Grandma and Ben and I are walking in a hurry with all the people who are going to the show. It's a display of ancient things, with a film. They've made everything just like it used to be, Grandma says, and we're really lucky to be going to see it. I'm glad she treats me like a grown-up. She helped me fix my hair and she bought me this fur hat. I wish my mother would treat me like Grandma does. Take me places and talk about hairdos and makeup and clothes. Sometimes she does, but she's not very interested in them. I wish she was going to the show with us. She'll be sorry to miss it. She has to work all the time, and she's always so busy and so tired."

THERAPIST: "Be the mother."

EPHANIE: "I'm Saichu Kawiemie. I'm taking my grandchildren to see a special show that's here at the museum. They're like my own children. I keep them for my daughter a lot of the time. I wish she could make more money, and that she could be here with us today. They're good kids, though. She does the best she can, and I'm glad to help her with them. I miss the kids when they're gone, and having little ones around keeps me young. They have so much energy and they're so curious about things. They help out a lot around the place too, so my husband and I like to have them. I don't like this crowd, though. The people are all pushing and hurrying. I want to see the show, and I want Ben and Agnes to see it too. Agnes is growing up. She's so smart. She'll go a long ways, that one. Her grandfather always says that. We have to make sure that Agnes gets a good education, he says. She'll make something of herself. That's what he says. I hope we get there pretty soon. We've been walking down hallways for a while. I feel lost in this crowd of white people. Everyone is dressed so nice. I wonder why nobody smiles or talks. I guess that's how they are in the big city. I wonder if my daughter remembers the time we took her to that play from New York when she was a little one. Maybe she does, and that's why she moved here. It's not as far as New York, but a lot goes on here. I hope she comes home sometime, though. I miss her when she's gone."

THERAPIST: "Be the museum."

EPHANIE: "I'm the museum. I'm huge and imposing. I'm square and shining and clean. All these people walk around in me and admire me. They see how tall and big I am, how full of special things. I have almost everything anyone would care to see. From everywhere in the world. Lots of the things here aren't on display. There is much more hidden away in me, in vaults and storage rooms than is ever put out for people to see. I have a huge staff of people who work here and keep things running smoothly. I am a bulwark. A strength. Half of what is stored in me is unrecognized by the people who work here. They can't begin to understand the knowledge and the treasures that I hold in me. But I keep these things safe. For sometime when there will be those who can understand, who can recognize what the artifacts and treasures I keep are worth. They think the things are about money or history. They think they will put them away because of their beauty. They are afraid that the beauty will be lost. But I know the truth of the matter, a truth that is carefully kept in the records that are filed carefully away. Someday they will be read and understood."

THERAPIST: "Be Ephanie."

EPHANIE: "I am Ephanie Atencio. Ephanie Kawiemie Atencio. I'm wandering in the great museum and I am hopelessly lost. I recognize nothing. I can't find my way. I can't see anything because I don't have time. I have to meet someone here, but I can't find them. They aren't here. There's a lot of people here, but they are shadows. They won't look at me. I don't recognize anyone here. I am walking against the traffic. I am lost and frightened. They look so threatening, so alien. They won't look at me. They're all in a hurry and they just walk by me, moving aside to get out of my way. They won't touch me or look at me and I'm afraid to stop anyone to ask where they're going or how to find the way out. The walls are so high, so smooth. I don't belong in a place like this. It scares me. I'm scared of it because it's so big and so alien, so strange. I don't understand anything I see here. Why do they put those things in a big building? Doesn't anyone use them? What are they for? I feel so stupid, so helpless. I see my mother and my kids. They're walking along the corridor. They don't see me. I call them, I wave at them, but they just keep walking on by like I'm not even here. I am so frightened here, and nobody even cares."

THERAPIST: "Tell them that, Ephanie."

EPHANIE: "You don't care! I'm so frightened here. I'm lost and frightened and you don't even care." (Voice barely audible)

THERAPIST: "Louder, say it like you mean it."

EPHANIE, shouting: "You don't even care! I'm lost and you won't even look at me! I am so scared and you don't even care. You dumb stupid idiots, quit looking away from me. Look at me, goddammitt. Look at me." (Starts strong, ends almost whispering)

THERAPIST: "Louder!"

EPHANIE: "Look at me! Look at me! Look at me!" (Said in a stronger voice)

Below On The Lower Hills He Strides

One late night after Ephanie had gone to bed, after the children were long asleep, somebody knocked at the door. It was Thomas. He came in. She did not turn on the lights. They sat in the streetlight lit front room of her flat and talked in quiet tones. She wondered why he was there. He said he needed to see her. He began to kiss her, almost desperately. He fumbled in his clothes, unzipped his pants. He dropped them slightly and pushed her down on the couch. She protested. "No, Thomas. Not now. I can't right now." She couldn't say she was having her period. Shyness, inarticulate fear rose in her at the thought. "Please," he was muttering so low she could barely hear. "Please." There was the sound almost of a sob in his voice.

She let him push her down. She let him lie on her. He pushed her gown up, reached for her panties, thin, nylon briefs. With one pull he had torn them, pushed them aside. He was moaning, saying her name. "Ephanie, oh Ephanie, I love you," he was saying, "oh, please let me, Ephanie." And with his strong brown fingers between her legs he touched her, slid a finger inside her, found the tampax and took it out, spread her legs farther, saying more and more strongly, like a chant, like a drum, "Let me, Ephanie, let me. Let me Ephanie, let me."

And with his hand he pushed his half flaccid penis into her, almost sobbing, "Damn thing," he cursed, moaning, "Damn thing."

And cursing, breathing with sobbing breaths, he held her shoulder pinned against the couch. He buried his face in her breasts and he wept.

And in the dim light from the blinded windows he arose and straightened his clothes. He pulled his pants over his slim, firm hips and zipped them with his strong brown hands. He buckled his belt and then looked down at her torn face. That had gone silent and remote in the dim half light. He reached down and touched her hair. He pulled her gown over her legs. He went out into the night, the darkness of the city night that was never complete. He closed the door.

And left her there to ponder the pain of him, of her. "I don't want to live," she whispered to the shadows that waited quietly

in the room. "I don't want this to go on. I can't make it stop."
She said that, whispering so the children wouldn't hear her, so
she wouldn't hear. "I don't want to live this anymore." And after
awhile she arose and slowly, whispering the words that came,
she returned to her room and got into her bed.

You Be My Snag, I'll Be Your Snagaroo

Two nights later she went to the Indian bar. She went early
and it was almost empty. There were a couple of men she didn't
recognize at the bar, talking together in low tones. They wore
work shirts and heavy silver and turquoise jewelry. The bartender looked up as she sat on a tall stool. "Hi, Ephanie," he
said. "Gimme a Bud," she replied, speaking quietly so no one
would notice her. She didn't want to see anyone right now. She
just wanted to sit in whatever comfort was available here. Sit and
not think about anything at all.

The man brought her the beer. He was a Miwok man, tall
and heavy framed. His black hair fell in a line over his forehead.
His huge hands sported several large, heavy Navajo rings. He
went back to his place at the other end of the bar after he served
her, and picked up the girlie magazine he had been looking at,
his impassive face eerily lit by the dim bar lights.

She looked around at the scarred bar, the simple kitchen
tables by the window. She didn't want to look into the mirror
that faced her. Restless, she got up, went over to the pool table
that took up most of the room and began to shoot. She didn't
bother to set up, just shot the balls that were left from the last
players.

A man and a woman came in. He was very large, and so was
she. They got a couple of drinks and went over to the other pool
table. They were pretty drunk, Ephanie could see, so warily, she
laid down the cue stick and went to sit at a table crammed against
the plate glass window.

It was getting toward late evening. The fog was settling
down over the city. She sipped her beer and smoked her
cigarettes, staring out at the sidewalk, at the street.

The man and woman began to talk in loud voices, and suddenly the woman exploded into a rage. Ephanie turned to look their way. The woman was yelling in earnest now. She was screaming. "You bastard," she yelled. "You rotten son of a bitch! I'll show you, you lousy lying bastard!" And she began to hurl the balls at him. He ducked and she kept pelting him. The mirror over the bar shattered. No one moved. The bartender and the two men had turned to watch. They were silent. She threw the balls with enormous force. Ephanie froze for a few moments, then ducked under the table as the wildly pounding billiard balls began to come toward her. The plate glass of the window she had been staring out of broke, glass flying everywhere. She crouched under the table, holding her head in her arms. The only sound was of the breaking glass, the thuds as the billiard balls hit the wall, hit the tables, the woman's cursing voice, shouting her pain and her rage.

She threw all of the balls, then hurled the cue sticks. Storming and raging, she threw everything within reach, then ran out the door, shattering its heavy glass as she slammed it behind her.

Slowly the people in the bar began to move. Slowly Ephanie came out from under the table, looking at her hands, her arms, to see if she was bleeding. Slowly the men began to talk, laughing, they began to pick up the billiard balls and the cue sticks. The bartender began to sweep up the glass. "Bar's closed tonight, folks," he said. "Sam, you son of a gun, don't you bring that woman in here drunk again."

Sam, his brown face ashen, nodded drunkenly. "No, Jake," he said. "I'm not gonna bring that woman anywhere, drunk or sober." And he began drunkenly to laugh as the other two men slapped him on the shoulder. "It's okay, Jake," they said. "Want another beer?"

Ephanie went into the ladies' room, splashed some water on her face. She looked into the mirror at eyes that were squinted into glittering slits: "Right On, sister," she said. "I know just what you mean."

She Had Stopped Dreaming

"Ephanie, you can't marry Thomas!" Teresa's usually placid face was pinched and mottled with red spots. She was angry. "It's the same thing all over. Just like your ex. He'll be rotten for you. Why do you want to do this to yourself!" She lunged out of the deep chair she had been sitting in and paced angry around the room, gesturing sharply with her hands, her arms, jabbing at the air as though at Ephanie's eyes. "Open your eyes, for chrissakes, Ephanie. Don't do it!"

Ephanie sat huddled on the couch, miserable. She understood Teresa's rage, agreed with it. Felt it herself. And she could see her friend's real fear for her. Teresa lived in a world completely different from Ephanie's. She didn't have to work. She didn't have small children to worry over. She didn't need anyone, self sufficient with her parent's money, her strong mind, her white mind. Ephanie longed to say this to her, but did not, knowing it would only deepen the rift, increase the pain.

Instead she sat, hands clenched tightly on her lap, head down, face hidden in the shadows of the corner of the room she crouched into. "I know what you're saying, Teresa," she said, "I know. But he's so lonely. He's had such a rotten life. He can't help how he is. Anymore than I can help how I am. How you can help how you are."

"Okay. So he's had a rotten life. So he was brutalized, hurt, made to suffer for other people's crap. But you can't save him, Ephanie, you can't make his past different. You're just gonna be his victim like he was their victim. Only he didn't have any choice in it and you do." She sat down then, crossed her long legs, leaned forward looking intently into Ephanie's face. "He as much as raped you, for godsakes. Aren't you even mad about that? Aren't you scared?"

Mad? Scared? Ephanie thought. All my life I've been mad. Scared. So what?

She wondered herself why she would think of marrying him, knowing that it was because she was too tired to fight. That resisting was not her way, antagonism was not possible. "After all the years of death," she finally said, almost whispering so Teresa had to lean close to hear, "you finally quit doing things out of anger or out of fear. You learn that mad, scared or not, some things just have to be." Bleak of face she looked at her friend. Reached out to touch Teresa's hand. Smiled carefully at her. "It'll be all right, Teresa," she said. "You'll see. The kids and I, we need someplace. We need something. We're alone too, and we're tired of it. The other day Ben asked me when he was gonna have a daddy—when I was going to get him one. He said he wanted three things. A daddy, a television and a car." She looked for a second at Teresa, felt the familiar spasm begin around her eyes, felt the tears rising in her throat, closed them off, looked away. Act relaxed, she said to herself. Act like you know what you're saying. Surreptitiously she pinched her leg, hard. She sniffed. Smiled. "Now he will have all three things."

Ephanie knew she could react to Thomas by hating men. He was like the other one, she supposed. Teresa was probably right. Or like Stephen. She could hate men, turn to her work, her friends, her children. Bury herself that way. Cut herself off from her rage that way. Like before she had cut herself off through Stephen. She could learn another way, the one the other women, secure in their politics and parties did. Pour her energy, hurt, into rage, defiance, rebellion. But rage took hope: a sense of meaning beyond herself, and she was bereft of meaning, of hope. She possessed only night dreams and unshared understanding and memory and history that made her alone. At least Thomas knew about it, that history, that death; at least he shared it. At least he knew what she knew, as she knew it. Bone and muscle, he knew.

He knew about confusion. Identity. Needing to be where he was. Not being there, wherever it might be. Not this or that. Not Indian or chief. Not Japanese. Not a cowboy. A dude. And he did not have even the comfort of knowing the earth, the land. Of being able in his heart and flesh to claim it, to name it, to watch it bloom and wither, knowing the rock, the dirt, the hills, the sky, knowing their voices in the mind of thousands of years within it, upon it. Nisei. Halfbreed. A tongueless way. A thorn bush. Frozen? By not being within secure. Closed? A door that had no inside beyond, no outside. Caught between, like her thoughts were always caught between. Between knowing and fury. Between despair and history.

She talked to his sister. Who came often to see them. Who one day brought a flag, saved as a token. A sign. It was the rising sun, reminding Ephanie of her home flag that also was a flaming sun on a clear field.

"We have this." Sally said. "I've kept it because I like the sense it gives me of being an American." She smiled, waiting.

Ephanie smiled, said nothing.

Sally smoothed the flag with her fingers. Its silk. "Because Americans all come from somewhere else. That's America. I keep it with the Gideon Bible I took from the first motel I stayed in. And some letters my dad's family wrote after he came over here. It's history, and I want to pass it on to the children. Mine or Thomas's. Probably Thomas's. At my age it's likely I won't be having any of my own."

Ephanie said, hesitating, timid. "Do you get confused? About who you are, I mean?" Then thinking the woman seated so tiny and contained across from her was a stranger after all, even though she looked so much like Ephanie's mother, aunts. "I mean, because your folks came over from Japan and you were raised to be Japanese in America. I mean..." Her voice trailed off. Embarrassed. She must think I'm an idiot, Ephanie thought. She began to twist the ring on her hand. Her hands fluttered, helpless. Fell to writhing, to twisting again.

Sally smiled. "Yes, I get confused. Sometimes I forget which language I'm supposed to be talking in. Or even listening in. Sometimes I forget the right way to walk. Or how to sit. Or how to eat. Or where to look with my eyes. So many things are different between the way my parents do things and the way Americans do. Sometimes I just want to cry I get so mad because I can't remember who's who." She shrugged. "But I get over it. In a way it's exciting, interesting. Because who in this country really knows how to be an American?"

"Thomas gets mixed up, I think. At least I think he does."

"Yes. It's worse for him because he's older. I don't remember much about the camps. I don't remember our house or anything before them either. The first house I remember was the barracks, but I was so tiny it was just where my mother was. But he

93

remembers it all. He remembers more than is good for him. More than he should." She shook her head, frowning. Sighed. Looked hard at Ephanie. "But you know. About being confused."

Yes, Ephanie thought. I know.

She married Thomas. The decision, seemingly sudden, was made a few nights after he had come to her flat. He needed her, he said. He wanted her.

And she, musing on what that need might mean, knew that she was also in need of someone to lend shape and focus to her days. And Thomas, who lived so quietly in such pain could do that, could give her some sense that pain and disaster were what you lived. Down or through. Perhaps around. That made your meaning sane.

But how could she protect him from the years? The pain of knowing that his face, his manner, his blood, had kept him from eating food his hands had planted, had picked? His family had spent time in one of the relocation camps the government had sent Japanese-Americans to. They had moved inland from there, finding work as migrant food pickers. He told her, his voice deep in his throat, his chest, how he had gone into stores there to buy food, and how they had turned him away, his parents away, his brothers and sisters away. There was no food for sale to them. How did a child grow, seeing his presence causing scorn and hate on those stranger's faces? She did not know. His pain was her own, and still she did not know. He told her about it quietly, detached, like a scientist talks about a project, an experiment on his past, that failed. And knowing the horror of it as he spoke, she wondered that he spoke so calmly. But he was years, a lifetime of that wounding: it was almost his friend; certainly it shaped his being. It was the shape and the container of his life. And she knew what he felt, hiding it from his face with the correctness of his language, the nonchalance of his description. What words were there to describe people who would damage a child beyond repair and at the same time eat the food the scorned scarred one had picked? No way to talk about them, the unspeakable ones. Probably better, she thought, to speak of it dispassionately, to use intellectual words to avoid it, to get away from the fact of it, to live with it and at the same time to make the memory of it pale into the distance. In the remoteness the pain could be disarmed, dismissed, banished, made unknowable, like dying in the snow. It could be put to sleep, laid carefully away like a corpse whose juices extracted would postpone rot, absorption into something larger and vital, for a longlong time.

What Is To Sweep Away

In that time they were murdered, starved, massacred into submission. The White Government wanted them rounded up, put away. The United States Army had nothing to do in New Mexico because they weren't fighting the Civil War anymore. But the territorial government was under military rule, and the governor, appointed by the U.S. for the duration of the military engagement in New Mexico Territory, wanted to keep his position. They needed a war, so they picked one. They went among the Navajo. Among the people, they went. They burned and pillaged. They stole and enslaved. They slaughtered the people and their livestock and their corn. They plowed them under. They salted the wounds. They ordered the People, Diné, to come in, as they called it. "Come in" to the stockade, where they would die of disease and starvation. And when many did come in, thousands upon thousands of Navajo, brown and starved, diseased and heartbroken, when they came in, those people, they were forced to walk to another stockade called Fort Sumner. They walked from Fort Defiance to Fort Sumner. They starved. They lost whatever pitiful goods they were taking on that walk. Their children were stolen from them, sold into slavery. They walked a long time. The children of Diné, starved, stolen by Mexicans and Pueblos, by Ephanie's people, by people not her own. Alien were Diné in all of that land, so they starved and walked, and like cattle were corralled, rounded up, slaughtered so that the Territory could indulge in war for just a while longer.

She remembered the stories from her childhood of the wild Navajos, the gypsies, her grandmother had called them. The old woman had warned Ephanie the child often. "Be a good girl," she would admonish, looking as stern as she could behind the thick glass covering over her eyes, "or the gypsies will steal you, they'll take you away." She remembered how often she had heard how the Navajo had stolen Pueblo children, Pueblo women, Guadalupes, and made them slaves. How often she had been threatened with that fate if she strayed from the confines of her village, of her home ground. Until later she learned how the Pueblo had stolen Navajo children, and sold them away.

It had been a long, long war. She knew that for certain, for sure. From 1590 until now, and they were still marching people, thousands and thousands of people, putting them in stockades to starve.

Ephanie knew the hurt that was in Thomas, knew it within her brown flesh, within her body's ache. Though he did not feel that hurt for himself. He felt nothing at all.

And pain was everywhere in those streets, the streets of the dead and the dying, the longing-to-be-born, the mercilessly hating, the loathing-the-self, everywhere surrounded by the fog and the pouring liquid sun, the blessing, blowing breeze. Like an obscure infection, pain dwelt among them, and it became flesh, deadly in its obscure power over their lives. And futile in her weakness, she raged and wept, longing to put her own self between Thomas and those who wanted him destroyed along with her, between all those who were wounded and maimed and their tormentors, between her living beauty and his moving death.

"In school," Thomas told her, "they taunted me because of my eyes, because of my teeth, because of the War."

"In high school we stayed apart, those of us who were Japanese-Americans. But we were so few in that state."

"In college," he said, "I was the only one. People used to look at me in that way they have, because of how I look—my teeth, my stature, my skin, my eyes. I was angry about it then. And I was ashamed. Not because of how I looked, but because of how they looked at me, scorn in their eyes, scorn on their faces."

At night he would usually drink himself insensible. Sometimes he would tell her gruffly to come to bed right then. Then he would take her in his arms. He would kiss her and stroke her as he should, as she longed for him to do. He would enter her. He would come. He would repeat his rote refrain all the while. He would turn away. He would sink into oblivion, sleep.

She would weep silently, quietly get up and walk around the flat, look out the tall windows to the fog-filled street. She would look into the children's room, stand at the door and watch them long and silent in their stupor, gaze at their faces, their hair, their limp arms and legs, their sleep.

She couldn't believe in much. Certain knowledge of how it is, like a bloody band tightened around head, made an ache in her chest just at the lower edge of her breastbone. She would wake in the middle of the night, calm for awhile before remembering, wondering how she had found her way into a world so cruel, so wrong. And would mock herself for running in her mind from the world they all had made, aping in her sorrow and confusion the tactic taught her by those who used torment as a way of life, a method she had learned all too well, that sucked her courage and denied her its sustenance. That made her forget the ancient secret knowledge of balance between opposing things.

"And the real horror of it," Thomas said, "is that they teach it to our children. How to hate themselves. How to hate everyone else. How to be dead within and act as if they were alive." He didn't say how well it had been taught to him. "Teach them to deny their heritage, their genes, their own special minds, their brothers, their reality," he said. "Lock them in the same prison that they themselves have been locked in for so long."

And Ephanie saw Thomas, like those he accused, deny all power that wasn't status and money, denying the source of vision, denying vision itself in his unending quest for vengeance, for righteousness, for forgiveness, for salvation. The ways of the ancient ones were not the ways he could walk, nor did he know the enormity of the distance between himself and the old ones, between him and her, between his mind and her dreaming. He listened to her talk about the spirit people, the old ones, the bear-powers, the snake-powers, and he would smile. He would listen like a stranger listens. Like a traveller who visits a land in quest of exotic lore. Listened, waiting behind his silence for understanding that would allow him to dismiss what it was she said.

"That's the usual superstition those people have" he would say, smiling slightly.

Denying all she knew and based her life upon. In the same way she denied her deepest knowing, her one true heart.

Once, The People Wandered

Her grandmother had told her about it. When the people were cast out of their pueblos. When they wandered, for many years, forty or fifty, maybe more. They were hiding. From the war, from the disease, from the warriors and the conquistadores. "Some of them came from Keresan towns. Some from other pueblos. Maybe some were even Navajos," she had said. "They hid over by Acu." She indicated the direction of that pueblo with her pursed lips, chin lifted and tilted, head turned to the southeast. "Over by the Enchanted Mesa, they camped out. My grandfather and his wives. They had more than one wife then. They were there, like refugees, I guess you call it, like gypsies." The old woman had laughed then. Delighted by the humor of a Pueblo being like a gypsy. "That was after the Pueblos rose up in rebellion against the Spaniards and threw them out of our country. They ran them out, all the way below the pass there at El Paso. That was a long way, hundreds of miles. But so many people had left their homes by that time, and they didn't come in after the revolt. They stayed out there, without even a village. They stayed out there for a long time."

Ephanie remembered that. She thought about the old woman's words. Her meaning. Her nods and winks. Her hands that stayed quiet in her lap unless she got very excited about what she was saying. Then she would gesture, hands like birds, soaring and circling, gesticulating with sharp, pecking gestures. She remembered the pin her grandmother had worn, the one that looked like a spider with a pale blue body.

The people had stayed out for a long time. When the Spaniards returned, they rounded up the people who were staying "out there" around Acoma. They promised to build them a mission, to deed lands to the people in perpetuity, to offer them help in defense against the mounted warriors of the Navajo, Ute, Commanche and Apache who threatened village dwellers, raided their fields, abducted their children and young women. And the truce agreed on, the people came in. They began the long trek back to their old homes. But part way back, they stopped near a large lake. There was a cluster of hills around it and a plain that offered shelter, water and earth rich enough for fields of corn and squash, chili and beans. They halted and told the small contingent of Spaniards and Mestizo Indians who accompanied them that they would remain there. Thus was Guadalupe settled. That was when the scattered remnants came in. They had been without homes or fields, without kivas or ceremonies for two or more generations. They were glad to found a new village, a home.

The Bearer of The Moon Abides With Her

Fragments. Sudden surfaces rising and melting into the fog and the sea, deranging. Smells. Sounds in confusion so strong, so pervasive that mind could not become tangible. Body a shredded surface, plane and curve unacknowledged and obscene. One evening, going home, threading her way through the voiceless noise, she passed a building and through the plate glass window saw old women and old men gathering in a garish victorian-restored lounge. The old men were sitting and standing in clusters, not speaking, not looking around. The women were sitting, silent, coming down the curved staircase, carefully dressed and stockinged, powdered, combed and rouged, carefully smiling into empty unwatched space, carefully holding spines erect, chins lifted, carefully blank, carefully unsurprised, even to see a brown young woman on the street outside staring in at them. She turned away abruptly, pulling her shawl tightly around her shoulders and breasts, ashamed in an obscure way, aware of their eyes, of hers, wondering if her shame was at being caught staring or at having seen.

Some weeks after that she left the city, left Thomas. She had to get away. From the confusion. From the pain. It was summer and the children were staying with their grandparents in Guadalupe. She was pregnant. She had to go away. She would go to Oregon. Agnes and Ben would join her when summer ended.

And in that time she spent where it was she spent it, in that place that was not home, that place that was strange, a stranger-place, the story she told herself was devoid of clocks. It was framed by afternoons and nights. Stoned-out and muddled streets, and rain. Those were the years of her dying she later thought, and wondered at her courage and her strength, the long time it took her to give up, to give in, to get out. Wondered at her blind groping away from sanity, from bright.

She sat at tall windows in the half light and still. She watched the seasons circling and sang her quiet songs about far away lovers and times that had never been. She tended children. She kept house. She sat and thought nothing at all, watched nothing grow within her mind and silent bear the blossoms of notime. She dreamed about being alive.

Once she watched blackberries turning ripe on the bush and understood the pain of deepening. The river ran still and silent at the bottom of the yard behind the house she stayed in, and strange flowering plants whispered their profusion around her ears.

She lived then in forests and tangled underbrush, watching the endless rain become an endless blossoming. She saw mountains a few miles away as towering on the edge of vastness. During that time she grew, silent, unaware of the growing, drunk or stoned much of the time, fat, mothering, uncomprehending, stupid and stupefied in her need not to know what it was she was knowing all the same, all along.

The tall trees comforted her slightly, and the enshrouding fog that curled around the forests and the hills making distance a surreal memory not to be believed. Regularly, there was the moon, lost early to the clouded and fog-shrouded sky. There was summer, rain, and little more. There was death. Everywhere. There was longing, carefully kept in the still private place she knew about but never touched.

Teresa came to see her. They played their special rituals through, the blue-eyed woman and the brown-eyed one. They practiced exploring other spaces not known to the streets and the walls. They traveled beyond clocks and any necessity for them. They journeyed in ancient ways, and along new edges of mind and being, hesitant and sure, open and closed to the fog and rain, to the befuddled stars.

And Sally came to see her. To see Ben and Agnes, who grew predictably enough, alive and vibrant, silent and shadowy, spindly and sturdy, growing into distance, into own self's being, away from her understanding, away from her complicity. Each child grew, learning to knit the stories of their lives into something that might be whole, might not shatter with the first touch of monstrous isolation that passed in her time for life. Sally brought Ephanie the flag. "For my nephew or niece," she said.

Shortly before the babies were born, Thomas came. To be with her during the birth and afterward. And at last far from home, the twin boys were born. They named them Tommy and Tsali. An American name and an Indian name. And there, a few weeks later, so far from home, among the blackberry thickets and rainshrouds, Tommy died. She had known he would not stay. She didn't know he would leave so soon. The doctor hadn't believed that she carried twins when she told him. He was surprised then when two rather than one baby was born. Tommy was blue with cold when he finally emerged from her body into the strong delivery room light. They did not let her hold him or Tsali. They kept her wrists tied.

22

Naiya Iyatiku Is Calling

The baby had died inexplicably. The twins had kept them up, sleepless much of the time. She and Thomas, trading baby-watch and sleep. In those few weeks there were two to tend, one was always awake. They were very different, those two. One so spindly, so bright. Who would gaze wisely out of wide blue eyes. Staring at the lamplight. Staring at the sunlight. Crying suddenly, inexplicably. "Wanting to be gone, outside to ride his bike," Thomas would say, grinning. "He doesn't want to be a baby," he would say. And it seemed to be true. There was something in the child that would not accept infancy. She could see it. Her mother could see it as well. She would say, "He's so bright, so aware. He is somebody the spirit people brought." And she would smile. And she would look sad.

Ephanie held him close. Because she knew he would not stay with her for long. She loved them both—Tsali, dark and active, sure and strong, and Tommy, frail and gentle, who loved to be held and talked to. But the hours taking care of twins who slept alternately, who cried separately and together, who were different in all ways from the start except in their need for each other, were exhausting her. She had not been strong during the long months she had waited for their birth. She had been sick and frightened. She had spent long weeks in bed, bleeding, frightened, almost paralyzed, dreaming sometimes. Waking at night screaming. Waking at night in the livingroom, in the hall, running. Away from some nameless thing. Seeing a face in the window, through the pane, in her sleep. Seeing something aimed at her. Seeing that something did not want her to live.

And always at such times she would say she had been dreaming, even though she knew that dreaming was not the true word. For often she had not been asleep but only lightly dozing, wrapped in reverie that precedes sleep, when the apparition would occur and she would leap, shouting, from her bed.

Nor did the hauntings, as she privately called them, stop with the babies' birth. They continued, and she shrugged them, the terror they evoked, away. "I am over-tired," she would say. "I must get some sleep."

"I am in a trance," she would say. "I must wake up." And would try, urgently, to awaken fully. Drinking coffee endlessly in her struggle to get awake, fully, completely awake. Or would fall senseless into bed, unable to believe that such exhaustion was possible. "I can't go on," she would say. "This is not possible."

But she would go on, after a few hours nap. She would again arise, feed a child, talk to a child, talk to a friend, feed a husband, do the laundry, do the shopping, sweep the floor.

Until that night. At four in the morning. After being up all day. Too exhausted. Two babies, crying. Or one then the other. Crying. Wet. Hungry. Colicky. Lonely. Cold. Restless. Bored. Not sleeping. She and Thomas stayed up with them. Ben and Agnes long asleep. Ben next door at a friend's. Agnes in her room, fast. At four o'clock, going to their bed. Closing the bedroom door where the babies, one in bassinet, one in carriage lay. They were still crying, the twins. But annoyed, desperate for sleep, Ephanie went to her bed, lay down. Telling Thomas, "Close the door to their room. Come to bed. We have to sleep. Let them cry." ⟶ blame

And Thomas, doing as she told him. His brown face lined with fatigue. Lying down next to her. Both of them plummetting into sleep, into dark heaviness, deeply deeply asleep.

And waking to screaming, to Agnes, sturdy body stumbling into the livingroom where Ephanie and Thomas lay, heavy and silent, deep. Screaming, the screams going into Ephanie's mind, arousing her, she raising up, her daughter coming toward her, mouth a howling hole, "My brother," sobbing, shrieking, "My brother!"

And getting up, not knowing, not remembering that action, ever. Thomas rising, on his feet just as hers hit the floor and running to the room, the open door, hearing Agnes sobbing, "My brother" and looking into the carriage, hearing the wails of the other baby, Tsali, in the bassinet, looking into the still, silent carriage. So still. So silent. The spindly bundle blue. Mottled blue. Still.

The Butterfly and the Rising Sun

The sun was shining, crystal and sweet the day they buried the baby. She had called his doctor when they found Tommy dead. He told them to bring the body to the hospital, and they did. Before that, as she wrapped the tiny, still form in a cotton quilt, she spoke to him. "I wish you hadn't done this," she wept. Trying to control the tears. "I wanted to raise you, to see you grow. I understand that you didn't want to stay here, and that it is best you go. But, baby, I wanted to raise you. How could you go? Why, why did you have to go?"

They never saw the baby after the attendants at the hospital had taken the body from her weeping arms. She and Thomas had taken something to the mortuary for him to be buried in. They had wanted him buried in something real, something white, something that mattered, that acknowledged his birth. They had wrapped him in the Japanese flag that Sally had given them. The one that had belonged to Thomas's father. The white flag, on whose center blazed the redred circle of the rising sun.

The funeral had gone quietly. Small casket wrapped thickly in white cloth, closed, heaped with flowers. As they stood at the gravesite listening to someone's soft words, a bright yellow butterfly came. It sat on the flowers for a time, then soared into the air. It circled and circled the tiny gathering. Seeing that, they smiled. They knew Tommy had come to say goodbye.

Naiya Iyatiku Was Singing

When Tommy died, Stephen came to see them. He entered the room and crossed to where she sat. He put his arms around her. "Hermano," she said. "Are you here?" And he looked silent and long into her eyes. "I'm here," he said. "I'm sorry about the baby," he said. "I wish I could bring him back to you." He held her for a long time. He said little more, except that he had notified the priests, the cheani, at Guadalupe. The small one's death had been noted. He said he would stay for as long as he was needed. To do what was to be done.

And her mother came, and Teresa, and Sally. They came and held Ephanie, held Tsali. Took Ben and Agnes in hand. Talked to them in the kitchen. The women came and went into the kitchen. They scrubbed and cleaned. They scrubbed the floor and the stove. They scrubbed the oven. They scrubbed the refrigerator. They washed all of the dishes. They scrubbed all of the pots and pans. They talked to Ben and Agnes in low tones. They talked to one another. They cleaned the flat. They washed the clothes and the linens. They waited.

104

Her father came too. He sat with Ephanie and Thomas. He said very little. He went out and came back with sacks of groceries. He arranged the burying. He talked to who came. Thomas's father came. He stayed, sitting quietly in a corner of the front room. He left at night and returned, staying quiet in the corner. He spoke little, but he and her father were there. That was why they came. And that was what she understood.

She understood little else. But there was some comfort from what was offered. The scrubbing women. The food they cooked. The silent men. Sitting there with her. Not like the others who came and said stupid things. Who explained that she shouldn't grieve. That the baby was somewhere, in what particular heaven only they knew. Who told her how much better it was. That she was sad, but that she would forget.

Or the nun at the hospital where they had taken the body. The sweet spindly boy who was not. Who was a corpse. Wrapped in his blanket they carried him. And entering the hospital met by the pediatrician who took the bundle. Somewhere. That she never saw again. The body bundle. That she held and wept over. That she talked to all the way to the hospital. That she scolded for dying, for leaving her there. That Thomas held. Weeping. Tears coursing down his brown, lined cheeks. Unheeded. "Now you can ride your bike," was what he said to the still, mottled baby. Holding him he said it and wept.

Then when the bundle was gone. The room they were put into. To wait. The nun who came, with a hypodermic in her hand. Aimed at Ephanie. "Your doctor said to give you this." "No," Ephanie tried to speak. "I can't take that. I can't take dope." The woman didn't stop. She took Ephanie's arm. In a trance Ephanie watched. She shot something into Ephanie's blood. "There," she said, wiping the spot where the needle had been. "At least you're not like some," she said, eyes bland and distant. Apart. "Not like the women who have abortions. At least he just died, through no fault of yours." She said. She said that.

Nobody did anything for Thomas. Who sat near her. Hands slack on his knees. Who blamed himself. Who didn't understand why he had to sleep. Who would not sleep right again. Not for a very long time.

She didn't understand what the nun was saying. She understood what had been done. To her. Later, much later, she would understand the rest. But she did understand the woman who came. Teresa's friend. Who was visiting one day, a few weeks after Tommy died. Who said, "Did you breastfeed?" Ephanie said no. "Well, that's why he died," the woman said. White doughy face serene. Mouth tight. A pale, bloodless prune. "That's what my doctor said."

And Ephanie understood that there was no way to understand. Anything. Ever. That what had occurred, had occurred. That there was no one to blame. Unless it was herself, who did not have an abortion. Who did not breastfeed. Who went to sleep. Who told Thomas to close the door. Or Tommy, who refused to live.

The Child Of The Water Now Is She

One day after Tommy died, Teresa, Thomas and Ephanie took the infant Tsali, the two other children, sturdy Agnes and silent Ben, and went to the ocean that was far away from where they lived, some hours drive. They went and she nearly gave herself to that ocean. Ephanie nearly went away into the water and did not return. She had been knocked over by a large wave in rough surf. The undertow kept her from touching the sandy oceanbed. She was not tall enough to get her feet, not strong enough to swim against the tug of the retreating water that pulled her out to sea each time she had almost fought her way back toward shore. Fighting silently for awhile, she looked around for Thomas who had been beside her when the wave dumped them. He was not there.

She began to realize her peril. Her lack of strength. Her lack of power. Angry she began to curse, almost under her breath. The sea that would drown her. The man who was not there. The weakness that imperiled her. "Damn. Damn. Goddamn." She chanted. Swimming, being pulled, helplessly, swimming too weakly, too slow, chanting. "Damn. Goddamn." And heard her mother's voice saying "Relax. Let it take you. Go with it. You must not resist what is too strong. Let it take you out. It will bring you back."

She had thought for so long that she would be happy to go out. To sea. To see what was beyond the sky. To go home.

Damn.

Damn.

Goddamn. She could see Thomas running along the water's edge, toward Teresa who sat on the sand. He was running away from Ephanie, who fought the pull of the water, of her soul.

She struggled with the water then, struggled relentlessly. No longer silent, no longer willing to give in. "I didn't come all this way just to die," she said to the water out loud. And repeated it, over and over, furious that it should come to this, that an ocean would try to drown her just when she had come to silence, to resignation.

Finally she began to call to bathers near her for help. She shouted loud, trying to be heard above the roaring surf. Men just a few feet away from her ignored her calls. She could see them splashing, knew their feet were firmly planted on the sand below the waves. They didn't turn her way. They acted as though they did not hear.

She struggled with rising fear. She couldn't get close enough to shore to put her feet on the ground. Was being pulled against her will out to sea and she was afraid.

Then as she was about to give in to the pull a hand reached out to her and she grabbed it, barely aware that it was attached to a human being.

Teresa, not much taller than Ephanie, had swum out into the pounding surf and pulled her out of the deeper water to where she could stand again on her own brown feet, walk out, lie on the sand, shivering, spent, mute. "I saw that you couldn't get your feet on the ground," she had said.

"But why did Thomas run away like that? Why didn't he give me a hand?" Ephanie was bewildered, frightened. "Where was he going?" She saw Thomas coming toward them, face creased with worried frown. "Where were you going?" She asked him then. "Why were you running away?"

He looked puzzled, hurt. That she was accusing. But she was angry, frightened. She didn't care, for once, whether he was puzzled, unjustly accused. "When the wave dumped me and I got back above water, I looked and couldn't see you. I got out as fast as I could, to get my glasses. I couldn't see your yellow swimming cap. I didn't know where you were." His face was closed. He stared at her, mouth tight.

"I was right there," Ephanie said, shocked that he had run from her, had wanted his glasses. So he could watch her drown? "If you had waited, you would have heard me calling you. But when I got above the wave, you were gone." She turned away from him, lying with her back to his helpless figure. She stared at Teresa's leg that lay along her line of sight.

That night, lying still in the dark, breathing, in her mind back home and in childhood safe Ephanie remembered something, about Elena. A hand out to help her across a long jump on the mesas. She knew something then. Something she did not say aloud. Something true.

And talking with Teresa through long days after Thomas went back to the city she could see how it might be. That whatever she thought he had done to her, he had done. Not out of hatred for her, but out of forbidden rage, hypnotized, tormented into isolation. Detachment his primary understanding, what he knew best, was locked into his breath in the potato fields of his childhood like Sally had said. Thomas was that child who was not allowed to eat what his hands had pulled from the earth. He was in that way bewitched, for all his contempt of the idea of witchery. In that way he was kin to the alien spirit that had grown over the land as the fog grew over the forests. When he was cold he was somehow seeing them, those who had tormented him, who had reviled him, mocked him for his teeth and skin and eyes. He jabbed her then, thinking she was them, and his own death smothered and terrified him, and he knew them as she knew and nearly drowned of it, neither of them ever inside themselves able to understand what had been done to them, what they had done.

As she, in recurring dreams saw an old woman's face, set against those who would betray, who would wound, who would kill. She would see that face, one she did not recognize when awake but that in the dream she always knew, and would remember the words coming from the ancient mouth, chanting

108

something, a chant or something. She could never remember, waking, the words or their meaning, but in the dream she knew.

"I have always seemed calm and quiet," she told Teresa during those days and nights they spent talking. "My grandmother insisted on that. My mother did, too."

And in that space of grief and realization, she understood the significance of her fear, her weakness, of Thomas's rage, his anguish, his disappearance behind closed eyes and why she had not said anything about it then, could not even now. For it was a dangerous comprehension, leading as it must back into her childhood and beyond to an old woman waiting, insistent that she, Ephanie, not let anyone ever know just what had gone wrong.

Therapist's Notes, March 21, 1979

DREAM: "I am at a house. Mother's there. Elena's there too, only she's my sister. I go into a large kitchen. 'Well, Ephanie, are you going to help me with this?' my mother says. And she looks like she's gone crazy or something. Like she's wild with grief or anger. I think, I'd better not let her know I'm scared of her. 'Yes, I'll help you,' I say. Elena comes in with a baby, it's Tommy, the one that died. But he has black curly hair. His pants are dirty. I'm glad to see Elena. I feel safer with her there. She talks gently, quietly to me. Reassuring. The baby looks at me as I change his diaper and I say, 'You know I'm your mother, don't you?' He says, 'Yes, I know it. And I want to go home with you.' I say, 'Yes, I'll take you home.' As I'm wiping his butt I see that he has shit in his eye, it's all over the place, all over him, his head, his face, in his eyes, all over his hands. I'm scared that I won't be able to get it out of his eye. I get a wet cloth and clean it, wipe his eyeball as he lies there quietly. I get him cleaned up and take him into the bathroom and put him in the tub. I wake up. I'm very frightened."

THERAPIST: "Be the kitchen."

EPHANIE: "I'm a very large room, I don't have much furniture. I'm in an old house. I have a lot of doors. They all can close. One goes to the outside and…I'm empty. I'm clean. No one uses me. I want my counters to shrink. I want to hold my breath. I want to pull back. I don't want to be seen, I'm thinking that I'm kind of shabby, that I don't shine very good and I can't look like she wants me to. I'm an Indian kitchen. I'm in a house on the reservation. An old kitchen, not very good. Not strong or pretty. Not like those houses they have in town. I'm like that, kind of battered and hopeless. I'm very clean but I'm too old and tired to really shine."

THERAPIST: "Be the mother."

EPHANIE: "I'm filled with fear, terribly afraid. I want to cry but I won't cry when there's someone here. I'm so mad. This knife, I want to use it on someone, anyone, because everything is so awful. I'm always alone. I work so hard and nothing is ever right. Nothing helps. Sometimes I want to break the windows, throw everything through them. Instead, I wax the floors. I'd like to use the knife on myself, but I'll use it on someone else instead. I'll use it on one of my children. Oh, I'm afraid that I might really do that. I might kill her because she just stands there, frozen, like she's afraid of me. When she looks at me like that, like I looked at my mother, so afraid of what I/she might do, I want to scream at her, make her quit smiling. I want to hurt her so she'll show some feeling, something real. I don't have to let her just stare at me like that. I have my knife.

"It's funny, you know, it's just a vegetable knife, and a good one. My grandma gave it to me when we got married, and it's the best vegetable knife I've ever had in all these years. They don't make things as well anymore, not even knives. The handle used to be red enamel, but it's all peeled off.

"That daughter of mine, she's so smug, so silent. She just stands there, she thinks I'm awful, that I'm stupid. She just smirks at me when I need her help. She knows something, I can tell. She thinks I'm crazy, that I'm not any good. That's what she thinks, I sure know that. She doesn't have to stare at me like that. I'm so scared because it's waiting—something I can't talk about is waiting. It's always been there, in the corners of the room. Everyone knows it's there, and they all just wait for me to do something crazy. Everybody. All my relatives, everybody, just waiting. They're so smug, waiting for me to do something shameful, I know what they say, what they're thinking, my mother, my father, my husband, my brothers, my aunts, my children, everyone. They say that I'm crazy. That I'm no good."

THERAPIST: "Be Ephanie."

EPHANIE: "I came to visit my mother. I'm afraid of her. I'd rather not be afraid of her. I want to feel safe with her but she looks so mad, so strange, and there's nothing I can do. I am afraid. I want to go away before she hits me and yells at me, I think she wants to kill me, to hurt me in some way."

THERAPIST: "Mother, would you give the knife to your daughter?"

EPHANIE, as mother: "I have this good knife and I can run away to the hills and take care of myself. I don't have to stay in this strange place they have taken me to away from everyone. I can run away and go back home to my real mother, my Indian mother, and I can take care of myself and her with my knife. I don't have to kill anybody. I don't want to hurt anybody."

THERAPIST: "So you will give your daughter the knife?"

EPHANIE, as mother: "No, I don't want to do that. I just want to cut vegetables with it. To know it's there. It makes me feel safe and powerful. It makes my whole family safe."

THERAPIST: "So your daughter can feel safe around you?"

EPHANIE/MOTHER: "Yes. Because since I have this knife she'll know that she has people who can take care of her and defend her. She doesn't have to be afraid of me because I can protect her if she needs me to. Meantimes I can use this knife to defend myself if I need to, and to cut things with for meals.

THERAPIST: "Ephanie, do you want her to give you the knife?"

EPHANIE: "No, I don't want it. I don't need a knife to feel safe and secure."

THERAPIST: "What makes you feel safe?"

EPHANIE: "Knowing something. As long as I know what's going on, I feel alright. Then I don't have to be scared or think that she's crazy or that she's going to kill me. When I understand what makes her look like that, or what makes me feel so scared, I can see that she's only scared or mad, not crazy or murderous. I can look at her and see that she cares about me and that she doesn't want any one to hurt me, ever, and I can see that she's only mad about something, or thinking about something. And if I knew what waited in the corners so secret, I could protect her, comfort her, make it go away. I don't think a knife will help me do that, do you?"

THERAPIST: "Why don't you say something to your mother to let her know that she's safe with you, and that you're safe too."

EPHANIE: "Okay. Mother, you're all right. Whatever is scaring you happened a long time ago. It doesn't have anything to do with you, and it won't hurt you or us. You don't have to worry about us anymore, because we're going to be just fine. You've got a good house here and lots of grandkids to keep you busy. You can do whatever you want to now, mother. No one thinks you're awful or crazy. I don't think so. I think you're discouraged and tired and sad. I think you're a good, strong woman and I love you."

EPHANIE, TO THE THERAPIST: "Then I would put my arms around her and we could cry. Then we could put the baby in the highchair, and Mom and Elena and I could sit around the table there in the kitchen and get stuff ready for supper and talk and laugh and feel good. But you know, even if I did all of that it wouldn't change anything. Even if I dreamed that Tommy was alive, he still is dead."

She Cursed Them, That's What She Did

Long long ago the people suffered from a terrible sickness. It was a sickness that made them break out all over with sores, and many died. The headclan's eldest daughter, Yellow Woman, got the sickness, and the people were very frightened. For if she died, something terrible would happen to them. But their medicine didn't work to heal Yellow Woman any better than it worked to heal the rest of those who were ill.

112

They had heard about a great healer woman who lived to the southwest of them. Her name was Gayo Kepe, and she lived far to the south of them in a house that had leaves for a roof. The people sent a runner to bring her to their village so she could cure Yellow Woman. The runner was dispatched. And after some time he found her home and persuaded her to return to the village with him.

At the edge of the first river they came to, one that flowed swift and deep, Gayo Kepe took off one of her moccasins to shake the sand out of it, and thus she caused herds of deer, antelope, buffalo and all the other animals of the forests and plains to spring into life. This frightened the messenger, and he hurried the old woman along. They rushed across the river and traveled as fast as he could urge her until they came to another river. Again she removed her moccasin and shook it, and birds flew forth from the wind her shaking made, singing. The messenger became even more frightened.

Again, when they came to a third river, she took off her moccasin, and as she shook it reptiles of all kinds came forth, springing into life from the specks of sand that she shook from her shoe. At this sight the messenger was ever more terrified. And more than that, he was enraged.

At the fourth river, Gayo Kepe again shook out her moccasin, and this time insects of every kind buzzed forth. In a mindless panic the messenger hurried with the terrifying woman to the village where Yellow Woman was waiting for death.

Gayo Kepe set to work immediately, bathing the sores on Yellow Woman's body with pure water from the nearby spring. That was all she used, but she used a lot of it, continuously bathing the young woman, and in four days Yellow Woman was well. Gayo Kepe then turned her attention to the others. She told the women what to do, and because of her knowledge, all who were alive when she arrived in the village were healed.

Meantime the village men had been talking. They were angry that this woman could heal with water when all their medicine and incantations had failed. The medicine men's society was especially angry. So they told the messenger to take her home, then to pretend he had returned to the village. But he was to go to the river nearest her home and bring back a party of men who would be waiting there. They would return to the old woman's house and kill her, because they believed that only in this way could their power and the people's confidence in them be restored.

So they did as planned, but when the party returned to Gayo Kepe's house, she met them at the door and asked them to come in. They refused, but said they would come back in four days to kill her and all of her family.

Hearing this, Gayo Kepe took up the broom that was leaning against the doorjamb and began to sweep. As she swept, she sang a chant that went: "Gayo Kepe is not like you. Gayo Kepe is one who knows. Generations will come and generations will go, before your disease's scars no longer show, before you will return to faith, because you have murdered Gayo Kepe."

When the fourth day had passed, the men returned to Gayo Kepe's home. They murdered the old woman and her brother and all of their families.

And when Gayo Kepe was dead, all the animals began to mourn: the birds dropped their wings and were silent, the herds slunk away into the brush and the forests and remained unseen, the bees and the other insects rasped their mourning, and all the reptiles crawled away and hid themselves.

She Makes a Clean Sweep

It was the most amazing thing. The whole place, the marble and the gold plate, the huge spaces uncluttered by so much as a bench, the marble staircases rising and falling out of sight, leading godknowswhere, footsteps unheard in the long marble corridors, the shadowy rotunda. People walked purposefully, carefully somber, eyes down, showing no amazement at all.

But it was truly an amazing place, this monument to established authority, one where only purposefulness was a suitable pose, where nothing of the street or the great grimy reaches of the city, the homes and the ordinary cares of the everyday, the informal, the familiar could enter. In one great room, marbled, spacious, where the walls soared almost out of sight overhead to the gold-leafed, fleur-de-lysed corners, the gold letters proclaimed: HALL OF RECORDS. Ephanie thought for a moment of the christian legends of a secret brotherhood, saw her name in a secret file containing the most private records of her inmost heart, where she would find the secret of her purpose here in this time and space, and she wished that the lost could be so stored and retrieved, even in this awesome institutional costume ball.

Up the spiraling stairs: surely Alice fresh out of Wonderland would have been awed, intimidated by this show of massive authority. The serene presence of the state, the faceless shadow of authority, of power, of those who controlled because they had seen fit to entomb themselves and their sacred honor in the vast caverns of city hall. No swaggering politicians, slightly rumpled from their labors stood around these halls gossiping like they did at home. None such stood or sat along creaking benches trading favors, gossiping, guffawing. No young or funky hung out among the tasteful echoes. Only file clerks and secretaries scurried silent here and there, and men with briefcases swinging manfully at their sides, properly dwarfed in the echoing vastness, insignificant.

Ephanie finally found her lawyer. He was waiting for her where the gold-leafed dome arched overhead. She had lost much of her sense of herself in her wanderings through the marbled halls, but she could see that the whole thing was a carefully constructed set, designed to create an illusion of unbreakable, everlasting power. In its own way it was a masked dance. Its priests and shamans wore different costumes, made different motions, but its intended effect was the same. She felt profoundly disoriented, an appropriate enough state considering the occasion.

Her lawyer raised a hand, signalling her. Modishly suited and mustached, hair fashionably frizzy, he was trying to create an impression of ease and elegance, to cast some glow of personal dignity against the cold white walls and floors of this unhuman place. But his thin figure and his bare maturity made his effort, like hers, futile. "Hello," he said, smiling.

"This place is amazing," Ephanie said, grinning at him.

He peered at her, eyes coming almost unglazed for a second, then shaded again with businesslike glinting. "You haven't been here before?" he asked, appearing nonchalant, pretending she was saying a tourist thing instead of another sort of thing entirely. Which was a difficult pretense to maintain, she thought, considering the way she was dressed. She wore the flower-emblazoned, silk fringed shawl she had worn habitually since she had made it years before. It covered a purple shirt and ranch-style levis. She wore moccasins. Not expensive, cool ones, but the simple ones she had gotten from the trading post near her home. "No, I haven't been here until now," she said, resisting the urge to pull her shawl over her head and face. "I think it's one of the strangest places I've seen yet!"

They went to the elevator and entered it. The small, dingy-carpeted box was framed by gold-tinged metal doors.

"The judge will be here soon," the lawyer said. He straightened his tie carefully. Something about judges set him off, Ephanie thought. "He'll ask you some questions," the young man continued, "but it shouldn't take long."

"Here's the piece of paper with the property disposition and signatures you wanted," Ephanie said, handing him a single sheet of cheap, unlined paper. I sound very matter-of-fact, she thought, considering the barely controlled anger and my terror at getting this written and getting Thomas to sign it. Considering Thomas's real or imagined pain at the whole thing. He hadn't wanted the divorce, she knew that, though he'd left her to run around with other women. He also wanted to keep the pot boiling at home. Well, she thought, the fire went out. I don't really want to pay his bills while he has a bang-up time, so to speak. And grinned wryly at her own unconscious punning.

"The property is divided more or less evenly, isn't it?" The lawyer gazed at her, expressionless.

She bit her lip. "Not really"

"Oh?" He looked surprised.

"Considering I pay the bills and he gets the goodies," she shrugged and tightened her shawl across her shoulders and breasts.

"Oh." The mustached young man gazed down the round hole in the floor. They leaned against the polished brass rail that encircled the shaft of the rotunda. "But, aside from that," he said, looking stubbornly determined to get through this.

"Sure," she said. "It's okay."

"And you understand that by waiving support payments now you're waiving them forever. You can't ever come and ask for them."

She nodded. Thomas should support us when we're divorced when he didn't while we were married, she thought. Out loud she said, "Yeah. I understand that." Her voice was deep and scratchy.

no Support

"It's okay," the lawyer said, "since you're..."

"...more than able to support myself," she finished his thought for him in a flat tone of voice. And him and the kids and whoever else comes along, she thought. I pay for my loving and I refuse to pay when they refuse to love. Shit.

She smiled coolly at the lawyer.

They went into the courtroom. Waited for the judge. The lawyer was nervous. She was nervous. She held her jaws tightly clenched. She wanted to smoke, but smoking wasn't allowed in the courtroom. You can't be overawed and terrorized when relaxed with a cigarette in your hand, she thought.

A fiftyish woman with too much makeup over her pasty-white skin came into the room. She looked fatter and older than she needed to because of the makeup and the neat, fashionless secretary's dress and toepointed shoes she wore. The lawyer went up to her and said something Ephanie couldn't hear. "Nine o'clock," the woman said, folding papers busily.

The bailiff, also old, also sickly white, yawned.

A man in a suit came in and sat down in front of the steno machine. He was toothless, his lips caved in against his gums. His washed-out grey suit matched his dingy skin.

Ephanie waited, hands folded in her lap, her moccasined feet dangling from the bench. Damn they always make the benches for Texans, she thought. Indians are short. At least my kind are.

"You'll go up there," her lawyer said. "All the way next to the judge." He pointed to the witness chair that sat forlorn and tiny beside the judge's massive desk at the other end of the long room from where they sat waiting. The chair looked isolate and humble. There was a microphone in front of it.

"All the way up there," she said, voice mechanical.

"Yeah." The lawyer smiled at her fleetingly. Bared his teeth at her, actually. He kept worrying about the judge. "I don't know what he's likely to ask, today. Judge Mather is one of the few intelligent ones," he continued, striving to reassure her with his knowing tone of voice. "But he gets picky. If he's gotten up feeling grouchy."

Ephanie's stomach felt twisted up. She kept wanting to laugh. Or tell the young man beside her that this whole thing was ridiculous and walk out. She picked up a newspaper lying on the long bench they sat on and began to read the front page.

"The court will rise. Case Number 651079." The lawyer read the number stamped on the documents in his hand. "Yoshuri versus Yoshuri." He motioned her to walk through the gates, past the tables where the stenographer and the secretary sat, past the empty jury box, up the steps to sit beside the judge's high desk.

Ducking her head and pulling her shawl tighter, she obeyed. She was conscious of the soft shooshing sound her moccasins made on the floor as she walked the long way to the steps, climbed them and sat down. Her fringes swayed as she moved, like at the Squaw Dance. Her lawyer followed her and stood in front of her at a safe distance. He droned the questions they'd rehearsed.

She answered each one in a strong, clear voice, surprising herself with her control. The judge, a large grey man, didn't look up from the papers in front of him. Ephanie's disorientation was almost total. She was so dizzy. The edges of her vision were blurred and dark. She fixed her eyes on the judge, who like the bailiff, stenographer and secretary, was well into his prime, very nearly beyond it. He didn't look up the whole time. She noticed that she, her lawyer, another client—a pretty Chicana—and her lawyer were the only people there under sixty. She wondered if that was significant. She and the Chicana were the only non-whites in the huge echoing room.

"The court grants the interlocutory. File the papers in Room 317," the older man told the younger. The stenographer pushed buttons silently, unseeing.

"You can go," the judge said to her.

She walked down the steps, past the over-aged secretary, past the long, empty tables, past the gates, looking at the blond mod lawyer who was signalling his client toward the witness chair at the other end of the long long room as her case was called. "Pacheco versus Pacheco" the bailiff announced. The tiny, dark woman walked the long way up to the tiny, isolate witness chair, through the huge, almost empty hall, as Ephanie closed the courtroom door behind her.

DIVORCE SETTLEMENT: Property

Cash, Checking Account Balance, Savings: $1,200.00 Divided evenly

Furniture: value around $575.00

Mrs. Yoshuri:		Mr. Yoshuri:	
	Couch		Tatami and table
	Three single beds		Futon and bedding
	End tables (3)		Stack tables
	Coffee table		Floor lamps (2)
	Table lamps (3)		High-intensity
	Curtains		reading lamp
			Rugs

Household Goods: value est. $750.00

	Dishes	Divided according
	Linens	to prior ownership/
	Bedding	need.
	Cookware and Implements	
	Glassware	
	Eating utensils	

Other Items: Car: Mr. Yoshuri. $4,600 balance due
Motorcycle: Mrs. Yoshuri. $2.560 balance due
Stereo, records, blender: Mr. Yoshuri
Typewriter, cassette tape player: Mrs. Yoshuri.

Personal Property: divided by original ownership. Gifts also divided according to ownership.

I find these disposals of our property satisfactory:

Thomas A. Yoshuri
Signature _____ Date

Ephraim Teruao Yoshuri
Signature _____ Date

PART III

PROLOGUE

A long time after their awakening from the bundles, the goddesses began to be unhappy with their lives and with each other. Uretsete, who was now called Iyatiku, Corn Woman, saw that Naotsete was always trying to get the better of her. She noticed that Naotsete would go off and spend long times alone, avoiding her company. She saw that they were not as happy as they had been. Iyatiku would go to Naotsete and would try to comfort her. She would ask Naotsete why she had changed.

Iyatiku and Naotsete had awakened at the same time, but Iyatiku liked to believe that she was the elder. Once, Naotsete complained that Iyatiku had gotten to bring more of the things in her bundle to life than she, Naotsete had. She wanted a chance to use her bundle more often. But Iyatiku argued. She said, "No, I am oldest. That's why I use the things in my basket more."

"That's not true," Naotsete had said. "We were sung to life at the same time, long ago, when they called you by another name. Don't you remember that?"

But Iyatiku was adamant. She enjoyed singing the things in her bundle into life, and instructing them in their proper ways. She didn't enjoy it as much when Naotsete did the instructing. Because of this, she would not admit that they were the same age.

Naotsete said, "Let us have a test to see which one of us is right. Tomorrow, when the sun rises, let's see who it shines upon first. I say it will strike us both at the same time, for we were created equally."

Iyatiku agreed to this. But she worried that Naotsete was going to trick her somehow, and make the sun strike her first. To outwit her sister, she went to the magpie and instructed it to fly far to the east, not stopping for any reason, and to spread its wings over the rising sun in such a fashion that it would shadow Naotsete from the sun's rays. The magpie agreed. But on its flight it stopped for food at a place where a puma had killed a deer. And in its haste to eat, it got the deer's blood on its back, wings and tail, but did not notice. It flew on as instructed, arriving at the sun's house in plenty of time. Placing its wing over the door of the sun's house, it made a shadow that would shield Naotsete from the sun's rays. So the sun shone on Iyatiku first, and triumphant, she claimed to be the elder. When the magpie returned, Iyatiku punished it for stopping to eat, contrary to her instructions. "From now on," she scolded, "you will not know how to kill your own meat. You will have to eat only what others have killed, and much of the time that meat will be rotted. And you will carry forever the blood stains that are splattered all over you now."

So the unhappiness between them grew. Naotsete spent more and more time alone, roaming the hills and the plains, even staying away for weeks. Once in her wanderings when she felt very lonely, she lay on a rock to watch the sun as it rose over the desert floor. It moved toward her, streams of light. In rose bright joy and power it grew toward the mesa she lay on. Slowly, the sun, Utset, sometimes called Uretsete, came. Filled with longing, Naotsete lay, legs opened to the light. She raised her hips so that her vulva was open, exposed to the rosebright rays as they came toward her. She held the lips of her vulva wide as the sun fell upon her thighs. She let it enter her womb. She lay there, open to the bright, warm splendor of the sun until it was gone, passing over her head on its way. After it was gone she lay for a long time, waiting.

In the proper time, Naotsete gave birth to twin sons. Iyatiku was with her and helped her in her labor. She helped Naotsete with rearing them. But the Spider came to them, angry that the twins had been born. They had been instructed to avoid pregnancy. Indeed, they had no need of children at that time, for they had much work to do. The Spider, She Who Dreams, told them that since they had chosen to follow their own inclinations instead of her instructions, they would be on their own from that time. "I will not help you in your work anymore since you have seen fit to take things into your own hands," she said. This did not distress Iyatiku and Naotsete, who indeed were glad to be left to their own decisions. So the women lived happily enough while the boys grew up. Naotsete gave one of them to Iyatiku as her own son, and for some time the tasks of rearing and instructing them took the women's attention and they were content with their lives and with one another.

But the trouble between them had not been completely banished, and after some time they became unhappy with each other again. At last, after thinking long about their trouble, Naotsete, Sun Woman, said to Iyatiku, "We aren't happy together. I think we should share whatever we still have in our bundles and then separate. I have many things left in my bundle. Look," she said, "here are domestic animals. I will share them with you, but remember that they will take much caring for."

Iyatiku refused the animals saying, "No, I don't think I want them. It will be too much trouble to care for them, and my children won't need them," she said.

Naotsete looked again into her bundle and found some seeds that had not yet been planted. They were seeds of wheat and certain vegetables and fruit trees. She said, "Here are some seeds we have not yet planted. These too take much care, but I will share them with you."

Iyatiku again refused the offer. She did not want them, and she thought that those plants she had already planted would be fine for her children. "See," she said, "I will not need those plants. I have corn and squash, beans and pumpkins already. I have tobacco and other foods as well. It will be enough," she said.

In Naotsete's bundle were many metals, and these she offered to Iyatiku saying, "I will share these metals with you, but remember that the use of them will entail much work." Iyatiku, Mother of the Indians, again refused these, thinking that she and her children had all they needed from her own bundle, and that Naotsete's offers might be tricks.

When Naotsete had looked very deeply into her bundle, she found something with writing on it. She offered this to Iyatiku, but again Iyatiku refused. Naotsete said, "There are many things that are good for food in my bundle, but I know that all of them will require much caring for. Why is it, sister, that you are not thankful? Why do you refuse to take any of what I have offered? I am going to leave you. We both realize that we will give life to a great many of our own kind, and in a long time from now we shall meet again, and even though much will have changed with us we will still be sisters. If you take none of the things I have offered you, I will have the best of you in that later time, and again we will be troubled in our hearts with one another. I don't want it to be like that when that time comes."

But Iyatiku persisted in her refusal, saying that she did not want any of the trouble that Naotsete's gifts would entail.

So, taking the child she loved with her, Naotsete went away to the East. Iyatiku stayed on where they had always been and she was sorrowful and lonely for a long long time. But she comforted herself as best she might, saying often to her son, who Naotsete had left with her, "Let us live here with all that the Spider has given us." Thus they lived alone for a long time, until the boy grew up. When he was grown, he became Iyatiku's husband, and she named him Ti'a'muni. Then she bore many children and the first, a girl, she named for Naotsete's clan, Sun clan.

Now Iyatiku came fully into her power. She did all her work in the ways she had been instructed: she took the babies when they were four days old and held them up to the sun as she had been taught when she came into the light, and she put pollen and corn meal that she had empowered with her own breath into each infant's hand. She taught this to every child she bore. And the brothers and the sisters all lived together, marrying one another and having children of their own. Iyatiku was the Mother and ruled.

And whenever a girl was born to Iyatiku, she gave it the name of a clan, teaching each the ways of the people as the Spider had instructed her so long before.

After A Longtime, Naiya Iyatiku Went Away

She lived on an island in the center of the lake. Her house was closed to everyone. Only the outside cacique was allowed to see her. He took her instructions and gave them to the people and the katsina as she commanded.

The people lived around the lake, near her. But she was seldom seen by them from the time she had ordered the villages and the caciques, named the clans and instructed the people in all of the rituals. She put her power into the sacred ears of corn, so that they might use that power when they had need. Only the cheani and the outside cacique would use it in the power ways.

When she made the corn maiden, she told the outside cacique to guard her house. No one was to come near. The path to her door was made of white abalone shell. It lay, soft and pale, tinged with pink, open to the sun and rain, open to the moon. Only Iyatiku walked upon it. Only she watched it, and only she knew what it meant. When she made the corn maiden, she took the power that was in the pale, glistening shell and placed it within the hollowed ear. She placed honey in the hollow, to bathe the shell in, to keep its glisten, its light. She breathed her breath into the hollow. She made the opening secure. When she did this, she remembered Naotsete, who was gone to the East, to the place of the sun's brightness. Remembering her sister, she breathed and she sealed the corn maiden. She gave it to the outside cacique. She told him that its power was love. It was the bond of honey and of golden morning light.

She instructed the people, in the last days of her tenure in their world. She taught them dances and prayers. She taught them the proper use of the corn maiden. She gave them dances for their pleasure. She gave them toys for their entertainment, and taught them games to play with them. This was after the people had moved to the beautiful white village she had designed and helped them build. She had told them to move there where they could raise their growing numbers in peace. Where there was sufficient land and good pasture. Where there would be sufficient rain, as long as they remained peaceful and respected her and her creations.

127

But good living affected them. After they learned to dance for pleasure, after they mastered the games, the young men among them got the idea that they could make up a game of their own. They made up a game that they could play in the kiva. It was a gambling game. They became so interested in this gambling that they forgot to go to the ceremonies. They neglected to pray. They forgot to plant the prayer-sticks. They stayed in the kiva sometimes during the dances.

And while they gambled they began to make up songs about the women, songs ridiculing the aunties and the clan mothers. Iyatiku was angry. And some of the old men were angry too. But the young men continued to sing their songs of ridicule and dishonor. They kept playing the gambling game. They got worse and worse, finally making songs that ridiculed Iyatiku, and when the outside cacique heart about it, he scolded them. He told them they must stop. Stop the gambling. Stop the songs.

They did not gamble or sing the shameful songs while he was in the kiva, but when he would leave they would resume. They even said that playing the game was more likely to result in gain to the players than the ceremonies of Iyatiku ever could. And hearing this, Iyatiku was angry. She said, "Then, if this is the way you are thinking, I will leave you to yourselves. Then you may see if it is not due to my teachings and my rules that you have prospered and have all that you will ever need." She told them she would disappear from their lives and remain silent. They would not hear from her again. And when she had spoken, Naiya Iyatiku disappeared.

But she told the outside cacique to keep watch over the people, "For they are my children, and I am always their Naiya Iyatiku. I will wait for them at Shipap, there in the center place, and I will greet them when their life is over."

This was the first time death was mentioned among them.

When Tommy died, the cheani, priests, had remembered him, her baby. Stephen had seen to that. He told her about doing that as he sat with her in her grieving. But she could not even thank the men who had done whatever they had done. She did not know what that might be. Only that the child had been with her and then had gone. She no longer longed to be reborn.

Still it was true, even in that brief space, that she had loved him. Probably too well. That's what the Christians would say. He had been perfect, brightness, the light of her eyes. He had loved the light, had gone in search of it, could not agree to darkness. That was what she had said, what she had believed.

But some had whispered about the little people. Maybe it was they who had claimed him. And there were those who had wondered about other things. About the hauntings or whatever they were, the strange, half real, half unreal visitations that too often had shocked her from her drowse, or from full sleep. The beings who were taking aim for her. Firing. She had thought they existed only in some dream space, but Thomas had assured her that she had not been asleep on one particular occasion when they came. Only she could see those beings, whose green, green arrows were aimed at her head. And she was helpless to stop them. She did not know what to do.

And some thought that the baby had taken the blow meant for her, the blow, curse, hex, whatever it was, taken it to deflect it from her, from the rest. Tommy had loved the light, that was true. He had chosen, perhaps, to just go home. The men in the kiva were silent about it. She did not go to confession to ask the Catholic priest. There had been no sin she could confess. Bless me father, for I have sinned. They say I was born a witch. Didn't they say that witches' babies die?

The spirit guide had said that the tiny bright baby had never been. But how could that be? Who had she held, then. Fed and sung to? Who had come from her own womb, hidden there behind his brother? Who had been the one the doctor wouldn't believe, all the long months of her pregnancy, was there? Who was it then that she mourned?

There were those who would never accept her grief. Would know that the dead child was a boy, and so was not to be mourned. Some of those, she knew, who were secretly glad. And others, glad for other reasons, that she did not know. Perhaps one of their arrows, realization of their anger, envy, the arrows that were so glowingleering green, appeared from the time she had not yet lived. Perhaps one of them, thinking evil in her direction, had aimed for her, for what was bright, for what was male, and he had died. Didn't jealous witches kill someone's babies?

Or perhaps it was as the doctors said. He had died because he could not breathe.

The Place Where The Four Sides Meet

The katsina had appeared near the meadow where Ephanie had been standing. She saw him and walked to his side. He was very tall and wore a mask. It was carved out of soft wood and painted. It was snouted with a long snout, the lip edges painted black. Or was it a mask. Or was it just how he looked. There was one horn that curved upward from the right side of the mask's crown. The eyes were ringed black. He wore spruce branches in a ruff around his neck. His body was painted white, with black stripes at elbow, forearm and wrist. She could see that his skin hung loosely from his arms. He showed her the convergence of four rivers. He indicated that the rivers were associated, identified, with the convergence of four books, and that the rivers and the books each flowed from one of the four directions, coming together as a cross. But they became one river, one book in a place they all met. She watched this, the coming together place that seemed eternal, infinite, still, trying to understand. He said that when the four waters had merged she would marry.

Long after that dream she understood. In her small quiet alone room, hunched within her books and papers, she read something and understood something that made it clear. The katsina was showing her the origin. The place of the mother. Shipap. The place of memory, the place of dream. The place where all rain, all knowledge, all connection comes from. The place that first and finally is home.

Stephen had been nearby in the dream. He had stood to one side, near a rise. The others stood on the rise and beyond it. He wore wedding clothes. White pants, a red shirt belted with the green, red and white woven belt of the people. He wore turquoise and silver jewelry and tall, soft moccasins. Maybe he was her guide to that place. Maybe he was the witness. Maybe he was the cheani, the priest.

Years before the time of her alonebeing, before she met, married Thomas, she had that dream. She had looked in shops and books in the years since then, searching for that katsina, his representation, but she had only seen a picture of one mask that resembled the one he wore. She had never seen a kachina doll made up to look like he appeared in that dream. After a while she had given up thinking about it. Dreams don't mean much, she had thought then, even when they were about the messengers of the gods.

But the sound and smell of the water. The image of the old spirit man's arm, halfway between elbow and shoulder, stayed clear in her mind over the years. In heaven, the Christians said, there is no time. The sagging, crepey skin told her that the katsina was very old.

Later On, She Went Home

It had to happen sometime. She had seen it in the apple tree that lay on the ground, split, almost dead. And in the tiny spring that used to be fresh, clear, cold, now scummy. She supposed she'd known all along how deep it went, that knife, looking in Teresa's eyes. She and Teresa had stopped for coffee on their way back to California after a visit to Guadalupe. The visit had released a certain strangeness in Ephanie's mind, stirring memories, fusing understandings of things she had run so far to deny.

Ephanie's eyes registered Teresa's face with affection. Over the years of their friendship she had grown very fond of the planes and lines of it, the pale, freckled skin, the wide blue-green eyes that slanted slightly at the tips. It was a sturdy face, broad and flat, framed by lank, dark hair that curled slightly in a damper climate, but here in the dry air, hung heavy almost to Teresa's shoulders. Ephanie had felt very warm and safe with Teresa since they had wandered around the village together.

Ephanie had pointed to certain things—the apple tree, the spring, the deep, wide arroyo, telling stories about them, laughing, reflecting quietly, sitting or standing for long moments in silence. And her friend had listened with animation, or had stayed quiet when Ephanie fell silent, or laughed when Ephanie told a humorous tale. The apple tree had taken much of their attention as Ephanie told Teresa about the hours she and Elena had spent secure within its sturdy branches, dreaming away the hours as girls will, pretending to be warriors or stolen children, or just lying quietly along some thick branch's length, amiable in their long summers. The tree was almost dead now. Only some parts of it still leafed. Ephanie felt fury rising in her at the thought of it lying against the ground, split in two. She remembered the sweet blossoms it had borne, pale and rosy like shells once. Now the old tree could bear no blossoms, no fruit. The sight of it made her rage, want to weep. She became enraged at whatever Teresa said, irrationally, a breath taken, a swallow of coffee; a knowing what she was rose in her like lies, like filthy, like the once clean air now burdened everywhere with death.

She knew that she was little more than a complex of molecules, like Stephen had so long ago said, and that those dancing elements were subject to all the vagaries of what she ate, what she breathed. That she was at the mercy of the air, that her thoughts were no more than the after effects of molecules combining and breaking down. A tape, she thought, a program. A biocomputer. A charade. And felt her thoughts leering and jeering at her, a vicious clown within that would not accept her rage, the pain of her grief.

She felt rise within her words and pictures, understandings and interpretations that were not hers, not her, alien, monstrous, other than her, in her, that wanted her dead, wanted her to kill, to destroy whatever was of meaning or comfort to her, like Teresa sitting here, like home, left behind.

She wished she could tear out the monstrous other in her, reveal or find the one within that matched her, loving, passionate, wild and throbbing, but the stiffness in her chestbackarms, anger and contortion face, waves of imprints not so like a machine that they could be changed like a tape, like a record. They were too familiar and warm for mechanical transposition,

132

disorienting her somewhere in the lost space between eye and nerve, sympathetic gaining over parasympathetic, she supposed, but no remedy applied—mechanical, medicinal or otherwise.

Certainly there was no cure, no rewiring possible to change this lifelong duality, dichotomy, twinning of her own self with a monstrous other. They were so completely intertwined. She hid carefully behind her eyes, suddenly cunning, sly, wary of Teresa's worried regard. She lowered her lids like shutters are lowered during bright day, blinds drawn so she couldn't see herself looking openly through the alien eyes that sometimes took over hers, looked through them. What was wrong?

Within her, no new words, no soft feeling, no magic lens to change, nothing that would diffuse the spasm-intestine coiled in her belly and weighing on her tongue. She could feel her feelings, the ones that were calm, clear, sweet, only like far dim echoes that were rapidly drowning in the waves of unwanted, terrifying, alien rage that surged through her round, round body.

She sat, frozen. Told Teresa that this was happening. Saw herself lost, Ephanie, moving away, clear away from the table they sat at, but fighting panic reaching with her hand and body across it with her eyes, "I am angry, I am furious with you. But it's not with you, this isn't about you, it's what happened when you didn't understand what I said a minute ago, what happened to me at the apple tree, what happened at the spring, about how it's all dying, all filthy and rotting and dying. I'm furious with you. It seems like with you. But it's someone else who wants me to be mad at you—only it, whoever, feels like me. Someone, something, trying to turn my mind, my eyes away from what I saw, we saw, what I said, what I know, about the dying apple tree." Begging Teresa with her silence to understand, to explain what was happening to her now, as they sat, facing each other across the table, the familiar face of her friend so alien, so strange. Teresa, help me, Ephanie prayed silently. Say something I can understand. But did not say that, could not make those words out loud, silently begging, desperate to be understood. She could not speak, could not shape the terror building in her in this strange, strange place. Knowing what she was saying could mean she was losing her mind, was disassociating, projecting, denying, that it was true, but not the way it seemed, that she was losing her mind, her safe fitting within it, it being taken over by something else, something that didn't want her to know the truth that she couldn't fight, she didn't know how.

Thinking, I'm not even sitting here. Someone else is. Then who am I here. Who is she across the tablecloth from me. The panic rising in her lashing her in waves over the length of her body. Because they have taken my body. They have taken my mind. Just like Thomas said. Because I don't live here in me. Because I have nowhere to go. Because I can't get out of here. Because you can't hear me, can't understand the danger I'm in. Because it is so real to me here, and it was as real in the apple tree, and in the spring and in the doorway of the house that wasn't there anymore, because they have stolen my name.

And that's what I don't want to know, to see, to say. I am possessed by someone who sees through my eyes, enraged. Someone who wants me to die, to kill. Someone who wants you to leave me to them. She said that to Teresa who sat regarding her with troubled eyes. Ephanie struggled to make clear what all of this meant so that Teresa wouldn't confuse her words with what a psychiatrist would say about her, her fear, with what a psychiatrist had said to her about this same event when it had happened in other times. And as she talked, the room seemed to grow darker, the shadows along the wall moved in to surround her, suffocating. "Let's get out of here," she said. "I can't breathe."

And led the way out, paying for the coffee on the way to the street and open sun, carefully not looking directly through the darkened edges of her eyes, looking instead at windows, ways to buy something shiny, to anchor herself securely to the street she was walking. She and Teresa agreed that Ephanie should be as deeply in this whole experience as possible later, perhaps when they were safely private, because Ephanie did not want to say, there in the face of red and white checked tablecloth and moonfaced strangers, those terrible words of accusation that were clamoring at her tongue, twisting her mouth and throat in the frantic raging effort to escape her lips. She bit down hard, bringing blood, bringing tears.

134

Which were not hers but which would be in her mouth, powered by her breath, driving Teresa away, destroying and destroying and which she must never say except in a way that made clear to both of them why they had to be said. Those words that were not about Teresa, never about her, but that came toward her anyway and would find release one way or another. Better some other way found to say them. Like with the shrink. Who was so far away.

Chanting, She Knew Them

She began her calming chant in her mind, shouting within herself to be heard over the panic and raging din, the flood. I am Ephanie Atencio. Ephanie Kawiemie Atencio. I am myself. This is Teresa who walks beside me. The sun is shining and I am on my way back to California. I know who I am. I will not give in. This is my hand. These are my eyes. My mouth belongs to me. I am Ephanie Atencio. Ephanie Kawiemie Atencio. No one else can possess me. No one else can control me. No one else can speak for me. Through me. This is my hand. My sturdy, strong, brown hand. These are my eyes. I know what I see. I am no one else. I am myself. These are my eyes. Ephanie's huge dark eyes. This is my hair. Ephanie's thick hair. This is my body. My small square round stubby body. I am on my way to California. I don't live in the apple tree spring any more.

But she knew that others owned such bodies, such eyes, such hair, such hands. That her own had come to her from another time and from people who were not her, who invaded her so long ago, before she was born. She looked like many others and she knew that even her flesh was not hers to own.

If my own dear mind, the words, the memories, the beliefs, the understandings, if the mesas I see in memory, the water my skin recalls, the food my tongue thinks it tasted, the painful, tearing, ugly, beautiful, loving, tender words my ears think they heard, my mouth thinks it ever spoke are not true, not mine. If I cannot believe that one single thing in me, in my mind, in my

135

body, my brain, is of me, is mine, is me, then how will I know which is me and which is the other, the others, the not-me?

Which is I. Which them. And wondered how she had come to believe herself possessed, how she had known, decided the possession was final. I must be psychotic, she thought. I must be mad. They don't burn witches anymore. Possession does not, cannot exist. That's what the shrink says and I must believe her. Or I'm lost. I'll never be able to live.

Shaking She Speaks This Time

They had gone to visit some friends of Teresa's on their way to Guadalupe. That was in Colorado. The women were political types. Wilderness buffs. They believed in a lot of things. They raised food. They wore natural fiber clothes. They organized things. Ideas that they put people in. Within. They sneered a lot. At people who lived in suburbs. At people who watched television. At people who worked the land and raised livestock and talked with a drawl. At women who wore pantyhose and aprons. At universities and students and professors. At doctors, lawyers and Indian chiefs. No, they drew the line at Indian chiefs. Maybe out of deference to her. They winked at her conspiratorially. Like she knew what they knew. And agreed. They talked a lot about Indians. About massacres and victims and Sand Creek and Wounded Knee. They snorted and shrugged, railed and analyzed. They treated her like she was the wooden Indian outside the trader's store. When she spoke, they waited, hanging on her every word. They laughed hugely at her jokes. They twinkled at every grin in her eyes, on her mouth.

After three days there she had begun to lose any sense of who she was. Of what she thought about anything. She wanted to like them, these friends of her friend. Who viewed her as an artifact, quaint, curious, fragile, wronged. She began to feel wronged. Fragile. Innocent and helpless. She wanted to be understood. They winked and nodded as though they understood, and she believed them. She talked more than she should.

She said things they hadn't the remotest idea how to understand. She thought they understood. She didn't remember that they couldn't. Not from the point of view they occupied. Not from the snorting and sneering and analyzing space they inhabited with familiar grace and ease.

One night, late, they were sitting around the kitchen, talking, drinking herbal tea sweet with honey from their own precious bees. They were talking about old Indian ways. Medicine men. Power. Black Elk. The centuries-long war. That was never over. About the tribal ways. About peace. About the mining companies. The uranium tailings piled up on nearby hills, that seeped radioactive water down into the creeks during runoff time. That radiated everything. About the people of Guadalupe who lived with the mines just beneath their feet. About the work that could be gotten because of it. About the money that had poured in. About the affluence and what it cost.

They spoke glowingly about the famous medicine man who had spoken so powerfully, so movingly at the survival gathering they had attended, spoken about the sacredness of mother earth, how the whiteman had desecrated it.

She told them about how this same medicine man had lashed out at some women she knew. He was angry and contemptuous because they were lesbians. How he had told them he ought to rape them. How they had put him out of their car. How hurt, puzzled they had been. How afraid.

They told her about the Navajo woman they had spoken to who had been so eloquent about being moved from her homelands to the other side of the reservation because the whiteman wanted her land to drill on. "We have to help these people," they said. "They are being moved off their own land. Again. Why doesn't the government leave them alone? Greed and profit is all it cares about. All America cares about," they said.

She told them that the disputed land was Hopi land, and that the relocation of the Navajos was a result of a decision made by the U.S. Government at the request of the Hopis who did not get along with Navajos since time immemorial.

They told her about the rising incidence of cancer among the Guadalupe Indians and some others that they had read about in some recently published book.

She told them that the stories weren't true, that there was no higher incidence of cancer among the Guadalupes since the mines than before them, and that the cancers they did get were more likely caused by excessive sugar and refined carbohydrate consumption than yellowcake from the mines.

Through it all she found herself getting angrier and angrier, her face burning and the muscles tight as she tried to speak quietly, simply, convincingly.

They told her about how Indians were dying of booze and lousy working conditions and ignorance and squalor.

She told them about the Vista worker who had come to Guadalupe and wanted to teach her mother how to keep house properly. About the government people who wanted to make sure everyone had indoor plumbing, so they got toilets installed for everyone. But some people had to put the toilets in the kitchen, and it disgusted them. "They refused to use them, of course," she said laughing. "One old man said he'd die before he'd do his business in his own house!"

They didn't crack a smile.

She finally gathered herself together enough to ask, "Where are you all from?" And grinned, gleaming, triumphant, sly and sick when they replied, "Back east."

"Of course you are," she said. "Of course."

Teresa had burst out laughing then. "You have to understand how westerners feel about easterners. They think you believe all westerners are primitive cowboys. That you see westerners as not very bright. Cowboys and rednecks. Indians and Mexicans. Who are exotic and bizarre. Who need to be educated in how to be proper, civilized Americans." She had sat there quietly through much of the discussion, so Ephanie was startled when Teresa spoke. But she knew Teresa was trying to convey something. Maybe she wanted them to change the subject. Find things in common to talk about.

She couldn't drop it. Some contrary sprite had hold of her tongue. She found herself getting mad. Madder. Because she had wanted to like them. To be understood. To understand. And all they knew was what they read. In some weird magazine. That told them how to think. What to say. In their red, white and blue handbook of western American culture. She thought. Anger pulling at her eyes. Making the room seem full of smoke. Making it hard for her to see.

Teresa looked at her, arching an eyebrow. "It's not that we aren't all those things," she said. "But we have a certain lifestyle, an ecology, a balance among ourselves, that makes our lives not the same as they sound when you describe them." Her look seemed to say to Ephanie, "Let me take care of this," but Ephanie ignored it. She knew that Teresa had some pretty strange ideas of her own. That she didn't understand, really, either. That somehow she, Ephanie, must tell them. Something. So they would know how it was for her. For all of them. Here. Filled with the same spirit, perhaps, they ignored Teresa too. Instead they began to talk about the traders who, they had read, stole jewelry from Indians, taking it in trade for merchandise that they sold at inflated prices, trading against the jewelry at far less than it was worth.

"Worth to who?" she asked.

"To somebody else. Like this belt," one of them said, pulling at the bright silver concho belt she wore around her slim waist so Ephanie could see it. "Do you know that I had to pay over seven hundred dollars for it? It's Indian pawn."

"Where'd you get it?" Ephanie asked.

"Oh, at a pawn shop that handles a lot of Indian stuff in Denver."

"Oh," Ephanie said. "It's very nice. You got it for a good price, too," she said.

"But I heard that a belt like this, some Indian might only get two hundred dollars for it from the trader—if that. Then he'll sell it to a broker and make a bundle off it."

"Sure," Ephanie said. "That's business." And didn't say that the trader and the broker made money because people like the concho-belt woman would pay seven hundred dollars to show off their awareness of Indians. Or that the two or three hundred dollars the Indian got was a lot of groceries. Or that the trader charged a lot for his goods because he had to pay a lot for them. That independent grocers and merchants didn't own the subsidiary companies that huge supermarket chains did. And that the local trader often carried people "on credit" for years, without repayment, without hope of repayment, and without

139

once asking for money on that account. Because they knew the people. Knew they would pay when, if, they could. Something that huge grocery chains, or pawn shops in big cities didn't do. Or that the traders she knew cared about the people they lived off of, putting up bail when someone was thrown in jail, paying for lawyers for them, giving them counsel. She knew that wasn't the official line about traders, and that there were plenty of traders who used the people badly. And that there were plenty of the other kind too. She didn't mention the losses that some of the traders took from theft of their stock over the year either. She knew she would just sound contentious, wrongheaded. That these fine people didn't want to hear that everything worked two ways, at least. That Indians were people too. Strong, capricious, willful, gentle, malicious, kind, vicious. People. Human beings. Not noble denizens of a longlost wilderness. Not romantic leftovers of some past age. Not downtrodden savages with boots on. But real live human beings, full of piss and vinegar, as the saying goes.

Instead, she cleared her throat and her brain. Began to talk of other, safer things. Of the white housewives who were dying of booze. And the college kids. And the squalor the radical fringe lived in. And the lousy working conditions at the restaurant where she sometimes worked. And realized she had fallen into some sort of trap. Knew she was run through on the tip of her own sharp tongue.

Knew it was pointless to argue with people who had read so much, who knew so much. Who were so sure.

"You sure seemed sure of yourself last night," Teresa said to her the next morning. "I'm surprised. You don't usually put up such a fight." She was smiling, but something on her face, in her eyes, made Ephanie think she was not pleased. I have angered her. I have made her mad. I should have kept quiet.

"I should have kept quiet," she said, eyeing sidelong her friend. Keeping her head down, watching the ground.

"No, you shouldn't have." Teresa spoke with quiet intensity. "I was fascinated by what you were saying. I wish you had said more."

"Really?" Ephanie felt better. But unsure. "What else could I say?"

140

"I think they, we, don't have much of an idea about how you live. All of you. We think in terms of the movement. Any movement. All the movements. We think in terms of black and white. Good and bad. Cowboys and Indians. We think about things in the west like things in the east are analyzed. Are thought about. We try to transfer what we know about cities and industry and government to this." She gestured around her. At the hills. The blue soaring peaks of the San Juan mountains. "Maybe we don't understand. How you see them."

"Maybe," Ephanie said. "But probably I don't know anything anyway. Probably it's just like they say it is, and I don't know any better. Probably I'm too dumb to know what's really going on."

"Well, I don't think you're dumb." Teresa stopped and faced her friend. She put a hand on either of Ephanie's shoulders. "You're different. You've lived all of it. We haven't. We live something else. Someplace else. Maybe it isn't a matter of who is right and who is wrong. Maybe it's a matter of how many ways there are that things go."

Ephanie averted her eyes. She didn't want to look into Teresa's blue ones. However fondly, sincerely, the woman looked at her. However she tried to understand. Ephanie felt a surge of anger. That she put carefully away. Somewhere in the place she had for such things. Safe and far from her eyes, her voice, her mouth.

"Ephanie," Teresa said. "Don't you think you're overreacting? Don't you think you're just tired, or upset? It's been a long trip. This is a strange place, filled with strangers. You haven't had much of a break from stress, from trouble, from pain. Maybe you should be kinder to yourself. To the rest of us." She dropped her hands, shoved them into her pockets. "You know I care about you," she continued in a low voice. "I hate it when you're down. I wish I could help, could take your pain and throw it away, far away where it wouldn't ever come to you again."

"I know." Ephanie felt embarrassed by her stubbornness. Her inability to take what her friend offered, freely. To hug it, her, to her. To respond to her plea, the look on her face, the tone of affection, trouble, puzzlement in her voice. "I guess I'm a little weird," she said finally. "I'm sorry. I didn't mean to upset you, or your friends. They're nice people. I'm sure they mean no harm."

"Dammit, that's not the point!" Teresa was flushing. Red. "Dammit, Ephanie, you know that's not what I mean! Why are you so bitter?" Then she stopped. "I'm sorry. I didn't mean that," she said. "It's just that it's so hard to understand. And you don't make it any easier, you know."

"I know," Ephanie began to walk faster. Trying to calm her agitation. She knew Teresa was reaching for something. To understand. To say. Wanting to make it easier for her. To protect herself. She bent to pick up a rock. Put it into her pocket. "Well," she said, conciliatory, "but maybe what they say is true. About the traders. About the cancer. About the medicine men. About everything. I don't know what's going on in Hopiland. Maybe we're talking about different things. We probably are."

"You probably are," Teresa agreed. "I read that they are relocating Navajos and Hopis from that area. Because of some deal with the mining outfit. And that the people there are really mad, but that they haven't been able to do anything about it. I know several people who have gone out there to help. Or are raising money, holding benefits...And I read just recently in a secret government report someone leaked that the cancer incidence among Indians in New Mexico, around the mining area, is a lot higher than it used to be. But they aren't letting anyone know about it."

"So maybe the tribal council is lying," Ephanie said without conviction. Thinking, they probably are. Everyone probably is. Why. Because they couldn't do anything about it. Because they needed the money. The jobs. Because the income from the uranium made everyone's life easier. Made them feel almost human in the whiteman's world where having enough money, white style houses, white style food and clothes and cars and schools made them feel like they might live. A few deaths of this one or that one from radiation, from working in the mines, drinking the water, eating food raised in polluted ground might seem a small price to pay against the alternative. The death of everything they cared about. Of everything they knew. Of the tribe itself. Maybe. Or maybe they were just bought. By the money. The power they wanted. That held them hostage in a world they could never enter, one they could never leave.

She felt exhaustion creeping over her. Felt the ache that filled her grow too strong to ignore. Felt the futility of trying to explain, to ever explain to anyone, to Teresa, to the people back in the house they were now walking toward, to herself. Felt the craziness building, building, rising in her like a summer flood when the dam up in the mountains would burst and the terrible water had come rushing down, carrying huge boulders, metal, trees, everything in its path downstream, raging and untamed.

"I guess what I mean is howcome everybody thinks it's the other guy who's responsible for what happens to Indians and never themselves? That's what makes me mad. They point a finger at everyone else, but never at themselves."

"Yes," Teresa said. "I know what you mean. I have to wonder about that too. But."

"But, nothing." Ephanie said, knowing what her companion was about to say. "But some are worse than others, right?"

"Ephanie," Teresa said, sounding exasperated, "you need to keep in mind that most people don't even care about Indians. Or ever give them a thought. I know that's terrible. A whole country full of people who never think about where they've gotten everything they have. But it's true. And these people at least have an awareness of that."

"Yes, of course," Ephanie said. "But what's the use of awareness if it only leads to more of the same thing? I mean, the words are different but the song's the same. You know?"

"No, I don't know! I don't think it's the same thing. Not at all!" Teresa looked pale. Her nostrils were pinched. Her mouth tight. She looked like one of the nuns when somebody stepped across some moral line and was about to get punished for the transgression.

But once again, the imp had hold of Ephanie's tongue. She wanted the conversation to go somewhere else. But she couldn't let go. "The people who use Indians to demonstrate their own personal nobleness are just as dangerous to us as the ones who rip us off in more direct ways. More dangerous, maybe."

"Ephanie, I don't know what's gotten into you! You know better than that." Teresa was walking faster, showing with her haste and agitation, her desire to leave the conversation and her arguing friend behind. "Do I?" Ephanie asked. "How do you know what I know? What I know is that no matter which side of this stupid discussion wins, it's Indians who suffer and it's Indians who die."

They walked the rest of the way back to the house in silence. Stony. Like the pink and pale gold rocks that studded the road they walked on, the yard.

She Left Again

Driving back to California. The long road there. Through Albuquerque, to Gallup. Where the red red rocks loomed, brooding and grand, edging the sky. Through Holbrook and Winslow, where so many Indians lived. Where the Harvey House had stood. Where the picture of a longlost aunt had hung. Her face young and fierce, a savage's face with thick hair cascading over blanketed shoulders, strong, bold jaw jutting. Rich, sensuous lips slicing straight across her jaw without a smile. Deep set eyes brooding. Savage. Like the redrocks, like the untamed sandstone cliffs. To Flagstaff where the godmountains stood, aloof, intent on other things, taking no notice of the puny works of the tamed people buying and selling, getting and spending on their slopes. To the Mohave. The grey and deep rocky spiney green stretching endless for miles, sliced by the straight black highway that stretched endless for miles between rocky, desolate mountains that stood aloft in the distances, growing smaller and less forbidding as they grew closer on the way.

And along that long journey, Ephanie talking. Thinking. Sitting quiet and huddled in the corner of the car. Driving with one hand on the steering wheel, puffing endlessly at her cigarettes. Talking, singing, talking. Sometimes squaring her jaw to keep the tears, the fear, from rising out of her control. In rage lashing back and forth with the power of her thoughts, her mind like the powerful tail of a wildcat, lashing. Back and forth. Back and forth.

"I can't understand what happened. The trip has been so pleasant. Everyone well at home. The kids looking good. Seeming so grown up. Except Tsali, of course. But he's doing great. He likes spending time with grandma and grandpa. He's happy living with Thomas. And Sally just dotes on him. Like he's her own son. I'd like to see more of him, of course, but I'm glad he's got this time with his grandparents. And Ben and Agnes too. I'm glad I get some time alone. But I can't understand why I freaked out like that. Like this."

"Maybe you're just still reacting. The baby's death and everything couldn't be so easy to get over. It will take time," Teresa said.

"Of course. Even though it's been three years I don't think the effects have gone away. But still."

"Well, maybe somebody did something that set you off."

"Maybe."

"What happened that made you mad? What have you been thinking about, chewing on?" Teresa, who was driving then, took her eyes off the road for a long moment to examine Ephanie's troubled face.

"Well, the main thing is what happened when we were in Colorado. That and then going on home and seeing everything so, so different." Ephanie looked out the window, ignoring Teresa's gaze. "I can't, it's hard to make sense out of things. Like being in Colorado at those people's place, the things we talked about. I know much of what they were saying is the truth. I don't know why it gets me so mad. They're good people, and they care a lot. I liked them, mostly."

"But." Teresa said.

"Well, being there, then going home, being there for Feast. Seeing the folks. Who never look like pathetic oppressed victims to me. They look like people. People I love a lot, or people I like a lot, or people I've always known. Like the Letos. Did you know their boy was killed in some freak accident? He was drinking. Probably on some dope of some kind. The car went over the bridge across the river. It exploded. Poor things."

145

"They seemed okay. Those were the people we ate with, the second time?"

Ephanie laughed. "Yeah. The third house we went to was the Costi's. They were the ones with the beautiful daughter, Agnes' friend."

"Oh, yes. I remember. That wonderful cake we ate there."

"Yep. That's what I mean. How many of the people you saw looked like down and outers, helpless, cowering victims of some vast conspiracy?"

"Well, no one. But you know that's not what it's about."

"I know." Ephanie sighed. She sat for a few miles silent. How to find the words. How to shape the thought. That was about the truth or that aimed at it at least.

"I know that so much that's awful, horrifying, has happened. I read the same books your friends read. I even listen to some of the same people—Indian activists, experts, anthros, media people, radical politicians. But somehow I can't shake the feeling that what I think, based on what I know, what I have lived in my own life, isn't much like what your friends think when we hear the same story."

"I'm sure you're right about that. But I don't think that's what upset you so much. You were really scared, panicky." Teresa reached across the seat and put her hand on Ephanie's. Ephanie began to tremble. A violent spasm passed through her. She let her breath out slowly, like the therapist had taught her.

"I know. Maybe it's because I agree with them. In my mind. But my body remembers wonderful cake and fry bread and warm, caring, good times. You know, a lot of my family are traders. Some good, some not. But I know them. They're my people."

"So maybe that's it."

"Yeah. Maybe so. Nothing's so simple, is it? I don't know who to be, how to judge anything. I can't come to easy solutions. There's always someone or something in my own life that contradicts any judgment I ever make." She began to weep, silent, the tears flowing silently down her face. She didn't raise her hand to wipe them. She just sat, head straight, looking at the road ahead, weeping. "What do you do when you love everybody on every side of the war?" she asked in a low, low voice.

146

"Oh, my dear." Teresa said, her voice low and husky too, her eyes filled with tears. "I don't know."

There's Four Sides To Every Question

It was inevitable, she supposed. That she did not know where she belonged or where to go. She had left, after all. She was always leaving. Fleeing terror and delusion over each next rise. Fleeing death. The infinite fool. She did not understand the nature of limitation. Could not understand that some things could not be understood. This lent to her character a certain obstinacy, and with it, a certain strength. She had dreamed one night of a grey-striped kitten that in the dream had been skinned by Teresa's Colorado friends. The pitiful little thing had bled, its bare flesh pink and oozing. But it had roused itself and walked to its dish. It had begun calmly to eat.

That described the nature of her peculiar dilemma, she supposed. To not understand that she had had enough. To not understand when it was time to lie down and quietly die. Not that she was obviously stubborn, or obviously strong: her muscles did not ripple, her gait did not command. But she stood, wavering, tirelessly. Almost, it seemed, forever. Weaving, bobbing, leaving, but never giving up. Like water. At some point she knew it all came together somewhere.

But this time the leaving had been hard. She could barely get out of the two rooms she had rented for the summer after her visit home. She had difficulty expanding her awareness even so far as the kitchen or the tiny hall. She seldom thought of the entryway or of the sunrainstreets beyond her tiny apartment. Her contact with the world beyond these two rooms—one a livingroom where she sat and read and worked and talked on the phone and slept, and the other a tiny bathroom just beyond. The only good Indian is a dead Indian they said. She wasn't very good, then. She wasn't yet dead. She asked no quarter, but sat, brooding.

Like her grandma and her mother she could not go back. Though she had tried. To go back to confession, to husbands, to

147

Stephen, to children, to dreams that stuck in her throat, unrelenting, to lovers' arms. She had gone back often to walk the mesas and the road that curved around the village. But there was nothing she could hold on to there. Maybe you could go back, but only if the places and the people from some remembered time did too, she thought.

One thing she could not go back to, though she had tried symbolically, in dreams, in books, was the old heathen tradition. She had never been to a masked dance. She had not been allowed. Even her mother had not been there since she was a small child, taken by Grandma Sylvia, Shimanna, across the spaces between one village and the next, around the lake that was no longer there, to the square to see the katsinas, the gods, enter and bowing, stepping, dance, the spruce collars dipping and swaying gravely with their steps.

"I never saw them," she said, quiet, wistful, "because they left, and left me out."

When Sylvia left, when Ephanie's mother grew up and married out as well, those doors had closed.

Her Name Was Nightshade. She Bloomed In The Dark

Her name had been Shimanna. Nightshade. Ephanie remembered her. How she, Old Woman, Grandma, had come to talk to Ephanie as she wandered once along the cliffs near Old Oraibi. How she had come there to show Ephanie the way of waiting. Of keeping time. Oraibi, the oldest inhabited village in North America, where Ephanie had gone with Stephen to see Snakedance but had instead seen her long dead grandmother. Grandma had waited all the years of her life through. Even on the other side of the world she waited. Still. She did not tell Ephanie what she waited for, only that waiting and watching was for her, Ephanie, to do.

Shimanna, called Sylvia by the others, had gone to the Presbyterian mission school in Albuquerque. Then she had gone to the Indian school in Pennsylvania called Carlisle, where she had studied literature and latin and arithmetic and classical history. Western history, not any other kind. And in the summers she had worked for nearby white people as a servant, as part of the education she was being given. The man who had founded the school had pitied Indians. He had loved them. He was loath to see them die. He wanted to save them. He founded his school to teach them how to live down being Indian. He thought they would be able to survive if they'd just forget their homes and their languages and their ancient ways. Anyway, that's what he said when he went to Congress and whoever to raise money for his famous school. Famous in Indian country, anyway. He got the money because he was not only kind and concerned, but because he was a Colonel who had distinguished himself in the Indian wars.

After a number of years away among the whites in the east, Shimanna had returned to Guadalupe. She brought pots and pans with her when she came home, they said. She walked in balance, they said, because even though she cooked on a whiteman's stove, she baked her bread in a beehive oven and she ground her chili and her corn on the old grinding stones. She wore her special shawl to the dances, even though she married a white and bore his children. She wept when the clanuncle would come to see her. Ephanie's mother told her about that, saying, "I hated that old man. He made my mamma cry." She was a Presbyterian, but she never entirely lost her heathen ways. Did she reconcile the differences, or was she cut in two?

Ephanie couldn't know. She didn't dare ask. But she knew that the clanuncle didn't think much of Shimanna's arrangement. She knew what they did to those who married out. She herself had received too many blows from those who hated the strangers, even if they carried within their bodies the people's seeds.

"Just like a bunch of danged dogs," her mother would say. "Come up and sniff you, and if you're smelling a little strange they try and murder you."

She had shown Ephanie how that was when once Ephanie had caught a bird, young, picked it up because it had fallen from its nest. "Poor thing," she had said, crooning over it. "Poor thing. Mother, what shall we do?" Her mother looked at the tiny creature in her daughter's hand. "Well," she had said, "probably we can't do much. If you put it back in the nest it'll smell of your hand. Its mother won't feed it. Might peck it to death."

Ephanie felt sick. She had only tried to help. To be kind. To save the poor shivering pathetic creature. But sadly she put it back in the nest, as her mother advised, saying, "Put it back right away. Maybe not too much harm's been done yet." She put it back in the nest, praying that her hands hadn't made it smell unbirdlike. She had peered into the nest the next day, climbing high up in the tree to see. It had died.

When Shimanna died they had buried her in Albuquerque next to her white husband. There had been no water jar broken and placed over her grave. Maybe that meant she didn't have to return to the village as the rain. Maybe the Shiwanna, the rain people, excluded her. But it didn't mean she didn't care. She still came back, if only to her granddaughter, to tell her how to wait. With no water jar, how could she bring the rain?

They Left Even When They Didn't Go Away

Ephanie's family had lived in the village, but they might as well have lived in Timbuktu, as her mother used to say. People didn't come to their house on Feast Day, not even the relatives who would have been expected, required by duty, to come and eat on that certain, central day. They were shunned. Not overtly denied, confrontation was not the people's way. But covertly.

Ephanie remembered with pain and shame the time she had been visiting Guadalupe with Thomas. Her father had mentioned at lunch that one of the nearby Guadalupe villages was having corndance that afternoon, and suggested she take Thomas to see it. They had driven up the road to the village, parked and walked to the danceground. It was around two in the afternoon, about time for lunch to be over and the dancers to come out again. The square was completely deserted. There was a slight wind, stirring the summer dust around them. It was very hot, and there was no shade to stand in. They could see that dancing had been going on. People had left chairs and belongings scattered here and there, but no one came out to greet them, to invite them inside for some food, as was their usual custom.

Nothing but the wind and dust moved. After waiting in the bright hot sun for some time, maybe thirty or forty minutes, she had shrugged. Looking down at her shoe, she had mumbled to Thomas that they had better go. Hurt and pain had stuck in her throat, making her voice harsh and whispery. Sad, angry, bereft, she had turned away then, leading the way back to their forlorn car. She had not tried to go to corndance ever again.

She knew that her mother had felt the rejection, the ostracism keenly. Lived in an isolation that was almost complete. She did not talk about it often, only sometimes alluding to it but not to how she felt about it. She just kept to herself, tending her family and her house, growing a few things in the garden that she, unlike the rest of the villagers, kept; growing plants that were sturdy and self reliant—hollyhocks, geraniums, wild roses, marigolds, zinnias, and a few stalks of corn.

The only family that welcomed them in their home, who came often to Ephanie's home, was Stephen's family. His father Ben and his mother, Margaret. His brothers, tall and warm, smiling, quiet, hardworking, shy. His sisters, much older than Stephen, but always ready to laugh and joke, filling the kitchen with strength and a certain joy that for Ephanie was the most exact sign of home. Those women she had called Aunties. They had taught her to cross stitch in the Guadalupe fashion on aprons they taught her to sew. She learned to make the perfect, tiny stitches that with patience became roses, deer, antelope and rainbirds.

But none of Stephen's family was her own age, and Ephanie, taking her mother's cue, stayed apart from the rest of the villagers too. Or maybe they avoided her, and she thought she was the one avoiding them. However it was, she had made friends with Elena, a Chicana girl her age, almost, who was also an outsider, a stranger. Together they had made up a world that filled and satisfied their needs, one that they were cowboys and Indians in, one that was composed of thunderheads and mesas, rambling and imagination. One that was private, but not lonely, not alone. Because of Elena, she supposed, she had not noticed how solitary her life, her family's life, really was. Until now when she found herself alone in the city, living in her summer rented apartment, cut off from everyone she knew.

She didn't like solitude. The shadows, the noises the building made, frightened her. She was most afraid to go to her closet, one that was too large for a closet, too small for a room. One with a highhigh ceiling. With a heavy pipe that ran across the narrow width, high above her head. She always thought she could hear voices there. Though there was no one, no place they could have come from in such a way that only the closet contained the sound.

In her childhood she had heard the talk of spirits and ghosts. The koko man, as she and her sisters called the katsina who initiated everyone into being one of the people. They had tortured her with his name. She had wakened at night crying in fright because she thought the koko man had gotten into their house and was coming for her.

She had listened to the older ones talking about those who had loved too much to ever leave, of lakes that dried up when the lake katsinas left for other places. Lost, beyond recall. Had seen that happen, the lake vanished in the dirty air of what at Guadalupe they called bad thoughts. They said the angry, jealous people did that. The disobedient ones. The ones who mocked the holy ones. Or who did not believe. And that because of them the lake spirits had to leave. She thought it was the suicides that had finally made them go away. The lake had dried up after the war, when so many soldiers came home, uncleansed, changed. Angry and twisted up inside. Wanting things they'd never had. Hating themselves and their futility they had begun to kill themselves and each other. Wanting to be done with the old ways, the holy things, they had lately begun to hate the Spider, to ask why their God was not a man. She thought it was also because of the land, which allowed too much mockery, abuse, and did not demur. She thought it was the heavy presence of the new fundamentalist churches there, the missions they called them, sent from the easterners to spread death.

And pondered these things in the night watching the shadows move along the walls, dark on dark, questing in her mind the course of these things, not comprehending what it was she understood, seeing in the light of remembered fires that flickered on midnight mysterious hills around the longago

152

village, some necessary counterpart of home and daylight, of comfort unseen but not less known.

And that was far different from what she had been taught all those years inside a dark box on her knees trying to find comfort in heavy velveteen curtains and knowing joy on mesa, on treetop perch, where she sang to the sun and the clouds, the very sky singing with her, a counterpart to her joyous pealing. Or from the confessional to run behind the convent where she lived as a little girl, to run behind it to the alfalfa field and throw herself down among the sweet blooming stems to hide and watch the sky, the clouds, wheeling. To weep. How foolish I have been, she whispered as she realized what had been done. To her. To all of them. They made me be like this. The sisters at the school. The priests in the box. And clenched her fingers tight against her palm. Helpless with grief. With rage.

As a child there in that alien place, she had learned to believe that the god of the boxes would sing, would bless her when she knelt down within their musty velvet to confess and to pray, crossing herself with the sign of disease: "Bless me father for I have sinned." Shrinking inward. Closing off her body like spoiled fruit, trying to feel the sinning, herself in the act of sinning, the accompanying thrill of hot intense shame, of guilt, of release, that she would ever after experience in the arms of her lovers. Hoping then that in that progression of emotion, of sensation, would come blessing. Which later she recognized to be what it was, the terrible infestation that had taken place in her own only beloved body's soul.

Kurena, sunrise. Fingers touching thumb. Spreading. Blessing another. Saying, "The sun." Shiwanna, the people who live in Shipap. The rain.

"Bless me, Naiya Iyatiku, for I have been wronged. Make me remember to understand. To send the evil away."

She would sit for hours, comparing memories. Making in clear and exact detail pictures of the places she had been, the people in them, the words. What she had thought. What she had understood.

She grew to understand that there was no meeting between the several sets of memories, experiences, she carried in her mind. The sheepcamp meals. Sandy, gritty beans. Flavored sweet with small chewy bits of salt pork or rendered pork rind. The bread hot from the beehive ovens of her grandmother's yard. The chili, hot and biting, laced with tender bits of fat and meat. The coffee, almost creamy it was so thick. The calm voices. The laughter. That was one set. The other was something quite different.

Long, empty, polished corridors. Silent white faces of women whose whole heads and bodies were encased in black heavy fabric. Whose rosaries hanging dark and heavy down their legs clinked with every quiet step they took. Of those white faces, almost always unsmiling. Of those white hands that never touched a child. Of those white faces smiling, tight and stiff, as though that simple expression caused great pain. Who said she must pray. Must ask to be forgiven. Must remember to walk quietly. Never to run. Never to climb a tree. Never to have messy hair. Or a dirty dress. Never, never wear jeans. Must sit quietly at the table. And never ask for more. Who must eat when told, sleep when told, wake when told, play when told, work when told, study when told, piss when told, shit when told, and must never never use too much paper to wipe her butt. Her tiny child's butt.

She thought about the first poor people she had ever seen. Poor scarecrow people. White people who came to live in an abandoned house on the far outskirts of Guadalupe. The children, a boy and a girl, were so pale. She thought they must be very sick. She thought they might not have enough to eat. They wore flowersacking. She wanted to get to know them. She must have been four or five at the time, but she wished for a way to make friends with those two who looked so slack, so vacant, so white. Her mother felt sorry for them. Sent a little food, as a welcoming present, she said. To let them know they were welcome there, she said. But really, Ephanie knew, so they would have something to eat. So they wouldn't feel ashamed.

The next white people she knew, the stranger kind, were the sisters who owned the convent school in Albuquerque. They did not go without food, though the mission sisters near Guadalupe often did. These sisters were rich. They had good sheets for the beds and plenty of meat at supper. The girls who attended

154

the convent school never went hungry, though the food they got was tasteless. Boiled for long hours. Never seasoned. In all her years there, she never tasted sweet pinto beans or hot chili stew or fresh from the oven good bread.

She remembered the two sisters who, for a brief time, did not look half dead. Sister Mary Grace and Sister Claire. Sister Mary Grace had been at that particular convent forever. For decades, at least. She wasn't a young woman, nor a pretty one. She was so myopic that she wore thick, thick glasses, like those Ephanie's Grandma wore. Her white face was pinched in around her thin nose, and her mouth showed strain and age.

Sister Claire was sent to the convent school when Ephanie was in high school. She was young and lovely. Big blue eyes and pink smiling lips. Tiny white teeth that she showed in laughter and smiling. Small delicate hands.

Sister Mary Grace and Sister Claire spent a lot of time together. They both taught math, and that was the reason. They said. The girls noticed that suddenly Sister Mary Grace was beautiful. That her usually pallid skin had a glow to it. That her dark eyes snapped and sparkled. They even heard her laugh.

One night during the usual after dinner recreation hour, the two sisters were clowning around with some of the older girls. Ephanie was sitting on the sidelines, watching. She was grinning a lot, too. She loved Sister Mary Grace. She liked it that the old woman was having fun. That she looked so happy. That Sister Claire wasn't a dry, dreary woman. That they finally had someone there who didn't sneer at them, or spend all her time scolding in sharp, bitter tones.

Sister Mary Grace and one of the other boarders were playing the piano. Sister Claire had rolled up the sleeves of her habit, pinned the long veil back, decorously, as they often did when they were going to scrub the floor, instead she began to dance. She grabbed one of the girls and began to whirl her around. Sister Mary Grace turned to watch. The tall, heavy girl and the tiny, delicate nun danced and laughed with delight. The girl playing the piano struck up another tune. A polka. The girl dancing with Sister Claire went spinning off to sprawl, laughing, on a chair next to Ephanie. They crowed with delight. Sister Claire danced up to Sister Mary Grace. She drew Sister Mary

Grace to her feet. She pulled her out onto the floor. They began to dance, laughing, giggling like girls. Their faces growing rosy and gleaming from sweat and exertion. They danced the polka and laughed.

About a week later, Sister Claire was gone. Sent to another school. Or back to the mother house, the place where they were trained and where they lived when they retired. The girls talked about it in whispers. They eyed Sister Mary Grace. Whose face was heavy and dull with grief. Or with something that was not joy. They knew, sort of, what had happened. They were subdued. All of them. No one laughed or danced much the rest of the year. Sister Claire had been sent away and Sister Mary Grace must have wept.

The girls said, they must have been in love. And nodded to each other. And whispered. No one said anything about it being wrong. Ephanie thought now, all these years later, how glad they had all been that someone there was able to love. To laugh and shine and work and play and dance. And how very bereft they all felt when that love was sent away.

"I had forgotten that, I suppose, or I never knew," she said when she was telling Teresa about what she had discovered. She was elated. She knew she had uncovered something very important, but she didn't know why it mattered so much. But somehow it gave back to her, whole and entire, the memory of racing with the sky, the clouds, a piece of ripe juicy fruit, full of moisture and joy. She danced then, in recognition. Alive at last for that moment within that blessing so long craved, sought, prayed for, searched for through penitence and plague, that had eluded her for all these years.

Misunderstanding the significance of these things when she was too young to understand much of anything, she had grown to walk heavy and bowed with the weight of sin and grief. Like Sister Mary Grace had walked after Sister Claire had gone away. "Because they told me that only in such a burdened down way could I ever find the gold of comfort and salvation, of sanctity that was the only joy, the only lasting peace," she raged to Teresa, and in the midst of raging, began to laugh. "What a dunce I am. I get an F." She went over to the unused corner of the room where the stereo sat, lonely and covered with dust. She picked out a record and as its strains and pounding beat began to warm the room she turned grinning delightedly to her friend, held out both of her hands and said, "Come on, Teresa, let's dance."

Life Is a Vale of Tears They Taught

So in that way she discovered what it was that had been done. To her. To Sister Mary Grace. By Sister Mary Grace. Life is a vale of tears, they had often said. Those cold white faces in those black black veils. She had thought they were saying that life was a veil of tears. She understood that. How the veil could be pinned back for scrubbing the floors. But not for dancing.

Dear Agnes,

I am writing to you to tell you some stories. I hope you will understand what they mean. They are concerned with some things I have been thinking about. And with some of what I have been reading.

You know the joke about how when the whiteman came he had the Bible and the Indian had the land, and now the Indian has the Bible and the whiteman has the land? Well, I've been thinking about that. About what it means. We always laugh when we tell it. And we always know it isn't exactly so. Certainly the Bible isn't ours. Or if it is, it's ours to prove that God likes whites more than Indians. We aren't even in it, like the old Duwamish chief Sealth, the one they call Seattle, said.

Anyway, I was thinking about the land. And the food we eat, we used to eat. Before you were born. In a lot of cases, before I was. The way I figure it, they took the land, then they paved it. Cut down the trees. Plowed the plains. You know the story.

They took away our food, and gave us their food instead. Sugar, white flour, macaroni, rice. They took our corn and squash and beans, our herbs and condiments and meat. They tied it all up one way or another. But the strange part is this: they took it and they didn't keep it for themselves. They just lost it.

They don't eat good corn or potatoes or meat or fish. They eat another kind of these things, a kind that can't feed anyone.

All the nourishment has been taken out of it, one way or another. And that's not all.

After they took our good land and food away and gave us their Bible and their idea of food—sugar, flour, macaroni, canned beans, they came back and scolded us. "Why are you eating that lousy food?" they said. "Don't you know it isn't good for you? And why do you drink so much booze? Don't you know that Indians can't handle booze? You better learn how to eat right and lay off the bottle!" they say. "We only want to help you so you won't get sick. So you won't keep dying young like you do."

I just want you to know this. So you will be able to understand what's going on. When one of them decides to save you. From themselves.

And, my sweet, that's the history lesson for this week. Are you having a splendid time? I hope so. When you guys come here we'll go to the museum. The natural history museum. That's where they put Indians.

Love to you my dear one,
Mom

So she understood them. The people like Teresa's friends. Who could never replace within what they had lost. When they were tiny. Infants. Toddlers. What she had always known, in spite of pain and terror. For she had been given food. It was not she who was starving. And she understood that they looked out of their starvation eyes and saw Indians. And not really did they see Indians. They saw only their own hopeless fear. Their own unowned rage. Their own unfelt grief. So they hated Indians. Or petted them. Her. Nodding and winking. Cursing and making fun. Scolding in cold, sharp tones. Talking of the victimization they would not own. Themselves who forever died on the bloody, torturous cross. Which in their minds they forever nailed someone else to. Her. Her people. All others who had known real food. Of body. Of heart. Of mind. Don't pity me, she thought. Pity, pity yourselves. Who have always tried to make us believe that only in pain and sorrow, only in rage and weakness, only in selfdestruction and selftorture would we be free.

"They're always telling me what victims we are," she said then to Teresa. "Don't they see that they are even more victims than we are? Do they call us victims over and over so we will believe it? So we will believe that there is no hope, that we are forever and forever helpless, maimed? They tell us over and over how we have been destroyed. Isn't that how hypnosis works? They always sound so sure. They write books and make movies about it. How can we escape the snares of pity? Of smiling, gentle eyes? Of sweet, giving, generous hands?"

"Yes. I see what you're getting at," Teresa said. Frowning slightly. "But Indians have been slaughtered, destroyed, forced into being like white people, Christians, slaves, workers. Their land has been stolen, with pitiful amounts left to them. That the government, in its largess, has reserved for the Indians' use. And taken all the rest."

"I know, I know." Ephanie drew a breath. Let it out abruptly. Lit a cigarette. "Of course we are victims. Who isn't? But we have a history too. We didn't just stand there and have all of this done to us. We helped the cause along. We are not victims. We are co-creators. They make it sound like we're poor noble idiots. Who couldn't do a damn thing. But we could have done a lot. Only we didn't understand that there were so many of them. That no matter what they said, they'd wind up with everything. And that's just what's still happening. Now they've got our land and our water and our air, they want all of our power, all of our dignity, all of our ideas, all of our rage, all of our grief. First they said we had to be Christians. Now they say we have to die, to save what's ours. Don't you see?" She looked pleadingly at her friend. Who looked stony at her. Who tried to look friendly. Who couldn't. Who smiled and said, "Of course. Sure. Yes, I see what you mean." But who didn't see, not really. And who shortly after that put on her coat. Saying, "Well, it's been a long evening. I guess I'd better go on home." And who left. Shutting the door behind.

Ephanie sat. Still. A long time. Staring at the closed door. Numbed. She tried to think, to read, to write something in her journal. But her thoughts were only colors, red and grey, roiling, tumbling, like clouds in the summer at home used to be. Just before a storm. Piling and piling. Up. And she couldn't see the pages of the book she picked up, held stony in her lap. And the pen was a dagger that she stabbed the notebook with, leaving gouges several pages deep.

All she could hear herself saying, somewhere off in the foggy blue distance of some corner of her mind was that it was hopeless. She could not make Teresa, could not make herself, could not make anyone. Understand. How it was. How it had been. What had been stolen. Taken away. Destroyed, abandoned, poisoned. So that, no matter what, the people would never return to the old ways. The earth, the water, the sky had been stolen away. The dreams had been colonized. Now even Teresa had gone away.

She began to pinch herself brutally on the thigh. Began chanting, almost out loud between clenched teeth, don't let them know, don't let it show. And the words grew and grew in her mind.

Promise Her Anything

Dumb Indian.
Stupid Indian.
Flesh slashing Indian.
Savagebrutaldrunken Indian.
Dirty Indian.
Dirty savage Indian.
Dirty vicious hostile heathen savage drunken stupid Indian. Injun.
That was what they said. Those were the words. Some of them. The others were nice words. Said with friendly, warm, sympathetic smiles. They worked as well. Perhaps better.
Noble Indian.
Earthloving Indian.
Wise old Indian.
Ugh. Indian.
Who guards the earth.
Who waters it with blood.
Good Indian. Dead Indian.

The First American.

The Vanishing American.

Our Indian.

Exotic quaint American.

Indian.

Thinking about it. About the picture postcard people. They were. They had become. Seeing herself, moccasined, shawled. What it meant to tourist friends. Who only cared for what they had created. Because that was all they would ever see.

Vicious.

Hostile.

Bloodthirsty.

Savage.

Yes. Her blood was thirsty. She was dying of thirst.

"Well," she said to the spider in the corner by the stereo, "one thing's for sure. When that old woman Gayo Kepe cursed, she didn't fool around."

The spider sat. Dreaming. Still.

She Dreams Another Dream

The words rose in her ears, loud and precise, in spite of her efforts at humor. She found herself cringing. Blushing. Skin hot and tight. Smile fixed against her teeth. Must not let them know. I must tighten every inch of flesh to avoid touching anyone, anything. So I won't get anything dirty. Like Sister said. Like all the sisters said. Their pursed lips. Bloodless faces averted from mine. So they won't have to see me. So they won't know.

She finally saw it. Finally heard, loud and clear. What had been done.

And mouth opened wide she began to howl. Wondered where the sound came from. Did not recognize it as her own. Thinking only, filthy, filthy, I will never be clean. I must die, I must kill myself, I must die. Thinking that only by her death could she be veryvery sure not to pollute anyone, anything. My poor babies, she wept. My poor babies. I must die so I won't get them all dirty. With my love. With me.

The wailing went on and on. She wondered who it was, making un ungodly noise like that. Did not notice her arms clutched over her belly. Her body bent almost double. Did not notice the water pouring from mouth nose eyes. Did not notice any longer the terrible crashing torrential anguish of muscle, chest, heart, bone. She had a focus, finally, for her grief. For her shame. She knew what she must do. Now.

Moving methodically through the apartment. Turning on every light. Heedless now of the curtained windows. The shades half-drawn. The rooms. Their emptiness.

Intently she went about her task. As though she was readying supper for friends. Who would soon arrive. She dug through the cupboards and chests until she found the rope she had stashed away one day, thinking maybe she would string up a small clothesline in the bathroom or out on the backporch. She rummaged through the kitchen drawers until she found her hunting knife. She carefully sharpened it until it was razor sharp. She wiped it carefully on her jeans to clear it of shavings. And all the time the intermittent wailing, the moaning, the water pouring out of her, unheeded.

Muttering. She could hear someone muttering in the closet. Where she seldom went, leaving her clothes and coat slung wherever they happened to land. Where she went now, rope in hand. Where she looked up at the ceiling's height. The strong pipe reaching across the center of the narrow enclosure nearly a yard below the ceiling, but still far enough above her head. She estimated the height shrewdly. Returned to the kitchen for the knife, a chair. Put the chair down in the livingroom when she remembered a light highstool she had seen on the backporch last time she had gone out there. Got the stool and took it to the bedroom. To the closet. Flung the few clothes hanging there onto the bedroom floor. Cut enough rope for the job with her knife. Put the knife in her backpocket. Absently. Weeping madly sometimes. Sometimes working in concentrated silence.

And as she worked, again and again the words. All of them. Would rise up in her ears, sometimes shrill and taunting, sometimes calm and sure. The only good Indian's a dead Indian. Die savage die. Lice. Indians are lice. Vermin. Gotta be exterminated. Terminated. They're all alike. Sly. Cunning. Vicious. Nits breed lice. Y'all come out of there with your hands up.

She stood on the stool and slung the rope over the pipe with a sure, easy motion. She knotted it carefully, made a loop at the loose end, tying a slipknot. Good thing Elena and I wanted to be cowboys when we grew up, she thought. Feeling smug, superior. Sure. She began to hum. A cowboy song. I'm an old cowhand. From the Rio Grande. I'm gonna get me an Indian, and I'll sing the blues. Got up on the stool. High enough off the floor. To hang herself. She was certain it would do. The work she'd just done, she thought, was good. She could kick the stool across the length of the closet, out of the way. Should die with my boots on, she thought. Sensing an urge to laugh building up in her. Uh-uh, Indian, she thought. No joking your way out of this one. Not this time. She lowered the loop over her head, drew it snugly around her neck. Kicked the stool out from under herself with her moccasined toe. Felt the jarring jolt, the knot cutting off her breath. Oh, god. What have I done.

Tried to hold onto the rope with her hands. Brain clearing, the red, the fog, moving suddenly away. Suddenly awake, aware of her peril. Oh god, oh god, help me someone. Tried to wedge herself between the narrow walls, but they were too wide for that. Reached up and held on to the rope, trying to raise herself up on it, like she had when she was a child. Tried to reach the pipe, but it was just out of her reach. Saw out of the corner of her eye a large spider lodged in the far corner of the closet. That seemed to be watching her. I'm hung, she thought. Wanting irrationally to laugh. I can't get down. I can't breathe. I'll die here, alone. Panic rising in her chest, toward her throat. Her almost windless throat. Unless I can hang on until someone comes.

Knowing no one would come. Or not for days. You stupid. Stupid. You dumb woman. Dumb Indian. Now what are you going to do? Die? In such a stupidstupid way. Well, at least they won't bury me a Catholic, she thought. They don't bury suicides in consecrated ground. Maybe they bury us in savage grounds. In the wilderness. In the ocean. In the sky.

She closed her eyes. Trying to be calm, now. Trying to think. How to get down. How to stop what she had started. And remembered the knife.

Reached into her backpocket, drawing it carefully out. Careful because the edge was so sharp. Because she was afraid she might drop it. Depending on how badly she wanted to live. Crying in short gasping cries. Whimpering. Clenching her teeth against the pain. In her mind swearing. Cursing. Those who wanted her dead. Herself for listening to them. For ever listening to them. I won't die, damn you. I won't die. I will live. I swear, I will live. Drew out the sharp, gleaming knife. Raised it high above her head, grip suddenly sure, swing smooth and wide. The second slice severed the rope. She fell several feet to the waiting floor. Knocking what was left of her breath out of her.

When she finally came to, got her breath again moving through her bruised, knotted throat. After she could feel again her legs, her hands. After she could see again in the harsh light of the bare bulb that hung far above her head like a malevolent spirit, leering. After she saw that she had not landed on the knife, that she had somehow flung it across the closet in her fall. After she had lay and recovered her wits. Contemplated her actions. Her crazy need to finally do something. Do something final. Something certain, absolute, clear. Realized how close she had come to finality. After she had begun to weep, quietly, with relief, with sorrow, with comprehension. Of what had driven her. The grief, the unbearable anguish, the loneliness. The rage. She realized how grateful she was. For air. For life. For pain. Even for the throbbing pain in her throat.

I did it, she thought. With luck and determination. With intelligence. I almost did it for good. Maybe in a way I did. She turned finally on her back, letting her arms and legs stretch out, and as she looked up she saw the spider, sitting unconcerned like spiders do. It seemed to be approving of her. To be nodding, maybe even smiling. She smiled up at it and said in her husky voice, her first words since she'd fallen from her near death, "Thanks, Grandmother. I think I'm going to be all right."

PART IV

PROLOGUE

It is said that one who is uninitiated, who walks a certain path might come upon the Spider. She will be sitting near Her shrine, which is a cavern or a small opening in the ground. Often the path is guarded by Her grandsons, the Little War Twins. But whether one is caught by the boys, or comes upon the Grandmother unprepared, one will be forfeit to Her.

For without the special protection that only knowledge can give, the song She sings will draw you, take you in. And in the supernal gleam of Her midnight eyes, you will sink, you will drown. You will forget that you have walked on earth, in the haunts of humankind. You will follow Her into Her cavern, into the deep, dark, shimmering hole of Her nest, and you will want to stay. You will never leave. For Her beauty is like that between the stars. It is heavy and sweet. It is crystal and night. It is a blinding light that will enable you to see.

She will call you when She sees you coming down the path. She will say, "Are you here? You have come at the proper time. Come, come, grandchild with me. Come into my home with me. For now that you have come, you belong to me."

And singing thus She will stand. She will take hold of your hand, as She has already taken hold of your heart. She will lead you within the cave. She will never set you free. Thus it is said.

And Her twin grandsons, the Little War Twin grandsons will enter behind you, barring the way. And they will take you by the hands and lead you forward into the dark that will seem as bright as day. They will take you to the heart of midnight, the heart of the sun. They will charm your heart away.

On the Other Hand, She Was War and Death

She made forays to the library and bookstores, amassing texts on the arcane. She wasn't sure what she sought exactly, but found hints and clues here and there. To take seriously. What is poked at you in fun. Thomas had said that. Had held her, dancing, murmuring in her ear in the dimness of a dance-floor, humming, whispering the sweet loving words of some romantic song. "They just say those things to get some broad to spread her legs," he snickered. She, frozen, smiled, objecting effusively. At such times she understood the rage.

Others she heard speak of it. How they would take gun in hand, knife, shoot, stab, carve their tormentors. She could see their thoughts shaped in stabbing hands, fingers, lips tight against sharpening teeth. But shrank into herself at such thoughts of her own. Denied the twisting knot in her belly. Could not eat for days after such conversations. Clenched her teeth cruelly for too many nights. Pictures of savage Indian women behind her eyes, denied, almost forgotten, wished to be forgotten. They with tangled hair, bare arms and breasts, sinewstrong legs crouching as they bent over helpless body, savage knife held poised over naked victim's chest. She could not imaging herself killing. She had been clearly shown what that meant, would mean, to herself, to everyone she loved.

In her trips to the library and bookstores she also sought the tales of enragement, searching for some protection she could not name. Hesitatingly. Denial screwed tight at her throat like a noose. About abuse. About rape. About things they said about that viciousness. And at home she would read and moan, weep. Not noticing the fist she made so tight her hand grew numb. Not noticing the pictures that slunk through her mind like unac-knowledged children. Pictures of mutilation. Heartgripping fury. Revenge. Vengeance is mine. Like he said.

He always said something true, longed for. She did not want to be vengeful, savage, to make their words, their images true. Though she had known all along what vengeance could do.

I must not think this, she would say, brushing the air with her upraised hand as though it were a screen on which the hated thoughts appeared. I must remember raspberries. Moving clouds.

Water. I must not think of pain. Her pain. This victim's pain. Mine.

"Promise her anything, but give her what you find cheap," they said. They did. He did, Thomas, though his promises had been small enough. Take whatever you can get and smile and kiss her if she objects. Or beat her. Up. Or take all her money, all her dignity, all her security, everything she worked and planned for, that you promised to share. Growl a bit. Sometimes that's all. It takes. Throw a tantrum. Slam a few doors. Or if she gets troublesome, try a little tenderness. Not too much. It will spoil her. Or, if all else fails, you can pull a gun. She thought, sneering. Raging.

She glimpsed the depths such thinking could lead to. But could not stop. Could stop no more. Had stopped such thoughts for too long. Thought them anyway. Trembling. Hesitant. Defiant. Hunched over her books. Coiled tight into her chair. Hands clenched or open in the light.

She wondered sometimes if what she remembered was memory or dream. Or if the memories were hers or someone else's. It doesn't really matter, she would think. I want to understand the chaining, whether mine or someone else's, it all links up somewhere, someway, it all adds up. And laughed. Snorted. Stamped her foot. If only I could be sure of any one thing, she thought. Anything at all that I knew for certain, for sure.

She spoke to Teresa often. Tracing the process of her repose. She denied her work, discounting, dissimulating. "I sleep all day," she would say. "That's what I need. Only some of the time do I read."

For if such things as she surmised, half glimpsed with the part of her brain that dwelt best in shadow were true, then nothing at all was alive. Not even the sun itself could shine except mercilessly. He had said that. Nothing is alive. How to keep reason in a reasonless world.

What am I doing here? She would rage, pacing, clutching her arms tight across her breasts. What kind of world is this anyway! And fearfully thought she knew.

It's not so bad, she would argue to herself other times. Stephen had been so convincing of that, showing her sunlight, calling it joy. She had thought she hadn't listened, but deep vein and bone had heard. And learned what passed for hope, so. Against her will. Forsaking in his golden eyes the sure knowledge of her own mind and sight.

Within which she no longer dwelt. Marble halls and adobe walls lost, crumbled away. Cold silence of stone. But not living network of flesh and nerve. Not incoming outgoing breath. Even these she understood were not her own. Someone forever else lived within them. But she said nothing about this, not to Teresa, not to herself.

The man had said as he hit her, "Why are you making me do this?" The weight of him. Pressed on her. Her screams making no sound. "Don't let them know," Grandma, Old Woman, had admonished, pinching her leg hard as she fought not to cry. "Don't ever let them know." Fiercely she had said it, and as fiercely Ephanie, the granddaughter, had obeyed. "Bless me father for I have sinned," she so long longed to pray. I don't know how or why, but he hit me and said I'd sinned. Suffocating her, his weight, her words, the ones she had never said. Forced between her legs. Hitting her he said, "You'd better smile. Smile now, baby."

Such things did not happen. She knew that. But her heart pounded each time she heard someone on the stairs. She thought instead about coronaries. Often held fingers to wrist, counting, seeing the seconds ticked off through out of focus eyes.

There Are Many Ways of Leaving

Kochinnenako, Yellow Woman, was grinding corn one day with her three sisters. They looked into the water jars and saw that they were empty. They said, "We need some water." Kochinnenako said she would go, and taking the jars made her way across the mesa and went down to the spring. She climbed the rockhewn stairs to the spring that lay in a deep pool of shade. As she knelt to dip the gourd dipper into the cool shadowed water, she heard someone coming down the steps. She looked up and saw Whirlwind Man. He said, "Guwatzi, Kochinnenako. Are you here?"

"Da'waa'e," she said, dipping water calmly into the four jars beside her. She didn't look at him.

"Put down the dipper," he said. "I want you to come with me."

"I am filling these jars with water as you can see," she said. "My sisters and I are grinding corn, and they are waiting for me."

"No," Whirlwind Man said. "You must come and go with me. If you won't come, well, I'll have to kill you." He showed her his knife.

Kochinnenako put the dipper down carefully. "All right," she said. "I guess I'll go with you." She got up. She went with Whirlwind Man to the other side of the world where he lived with his mother, who greeted her like his wife.

The jars stayed, tall and fat and cool in the deep shade by the shadowed spring.

That was one story. She knew they laughed about Kochinnenako. Brought her up when some woman was missing for awhile. Said she ran off with a Navajo, or maybe with a mountain spirit, "Like Kochinnenako." Maybe the name had become synonymous with "whore" at Guadalupe. Ephanie knew that Yellow was the color of woman, ritual color of faces painted in death, or for some of the dances. But there was a tone of dismissal, or derision there that she couldn't quite pin down, there anyway. No one told how Kochinnenako went with Whirlwind Man because she was forced. Said, "Then Whirlwind Man raped Kochinnenako." Rather, the story was that his mother had greeted Yellow Woman, and made her at home in their way. And that when Kochinnenako wanted to return home, had agreed, asking only that she wait while the old woman prepared gifts for Kochinnenako's sisters.

Ephanie wondered if Yellow Woman so long ago had known what was happening to her. If she could remember it or if she thought maybe she had dreamed it. If they laughed at her, or threw her out when she returned. She wondered if Kochinnenako cried.

The Way She Left Was Like This

Slyvia decided that it was time to go. She waited for her son James to come from California where he lived to see her on his annual visit. Then she put her good shawl on, the purple one with the dark fringe she wore to dances, wrapped it around her shoulders and breasts. She sat in the rocking chair. She rocked and rocked. Her children noticed something was wrong when they went to her house to see her.

"Come on, Mamma," they said. "You'd better come stay with me."

But Grandma refused. She knew what she was doing. Her sight was almost gone, and her hearing. She wasn't willing to go live with any of her children, helpless like that, unable to care for herself. "No," she said. "I'm all right."

But they could see that she was growing weaker. She even stayed in bed one day, didn't get up at all. Something very unlike her.

The chidren grew worried. "Come on, Mamma," they said. "We're going to take you to Albuquerque to the doctor." And they took her, and she was admitted to the hospital. There was nothing wrong with her. She wasn't sick. Maybe a sniffle, a small cold, but nothing fatal. Still, she was clearly dying. And in a few days, curled within herself in her bed, covered with her shawl, she did. She stepped over to some other world. She went back to Shipap, maybe. Or she went to heaven, where Grandpa waited.

When Shimanna was through living, being too worn to live her life for herself in her earthly form, she died. That's what she did.

She Looks For A Midnight Cave

Cool and clear that blue. The sky over. The voices calling Distant that bell and true. Sound of light in the day. She would heed it she said to herself. One fine spring morning.

It was the air. Wet and free. She raised up in hope. Rose each dawn to watch eastward, make an offering of golden corn meal to the dawn. She held it to the sun. She gave it to the wind. She wondered if birds found it later. That nourishment.

The spirit people came and went in the deep of the night, in the bright of dawn. Ephanie's true name, they said, was Yellow Corn Woman. To feed the birds. To make bright and nourishing the day. She was never sure that they had said that, later, when they were not there. Or was it Stephen. Or the body that groped, pressed on her. Or the dark.

At night, at dark, she counted the moons. Crescent to half to full to dark. She wanted to plant at the right times. She did not know how. Often she thought she saw water jars lying broken on the floor. Sometimes she imagined she lived near a spring, in deep, cool shade.

Sometimes other spirit beings would come. Once a huge serpent lay silent and dreaming on the floor at her feet. Once a bear came and stood by her bed. Once she awoke to see a huge round flame, steady, like a moon but almost red, close by her window, about fifteen feet above her bed. As she watched, the glowing ball went out.

Jump.

Fall.

Flying. You are. Do not walk down that path. The Spider Old Woman waits. Her twin grandsons will call you. You will never return if you follow them. Rest now. Close yourself gently to the noise, the moving. Enter safely the dark.

I can leave now, she thought dreamily one overcast day. No one will know I've gone. She longed for a rocking chair. She wished she had not lost her shawl.

Moonlight. On the floor. Shining. A voice in it saying words she did not quite hear. About two of them. Twin archers of the moon. Mumbled, the shadows, the silver light a bow, strung tight. Turning she moaned. Flung her hand toward the window.

Her head away. The moon warned her. About duplicity. About the shadows filling, growing around her, from the walls, from the floor. The curse of houses made like this. Things not wished for piling up, suffocating, in corners. No free entry for the wind.

The next month the moon was still. Desolate, Ephanie mourned the lost silver, her lost sound. She could speak of this to no one, though her eyes, her circling, fluttering hands tried.

I've been too long alone, inside. I need to open the windows. Let the air, the sunlight inside. I must clean up this place. The dust is piling high. She said. Wanting energy to surge through her arms, her back, her thighs. Felt her feet slap against the floor for reassurance. But they took her from bed to table and she began again to read, squinting to see in the dim, the half light.

She knew it had to come together. To knit in an invisible seam. To become whole, entire. In her thought. Her mind. Separation was against the Law. The one that the sun rose by. The one that let the water sing. Inside and outside must meet, she knew, desperately. Must cohere. Equilibrate. No one mentioned it. They said it was all within. They said it was all outside. But she was the place where the inside and the outside came together. An open doorway.

The tribe had two kinds of heads, chiefs. The Inside Chief and the Outside. They were the white chief and the red chief. They were the holy priest and the secular priest. They were the right side of Iyatiku and her left side. The life of the people, they held between. Iyatiku was their heart, they were her arms.

To all appearances, the scholars and experts, the occultists and the rationalists whose books she read, had never heard of such a thing.

Never of Uretsete and Naotsete.

Utset and Nausity.

Iyatiku and Naotsete.

Thought and Memory.

Sunlight and Shade.

Town and Country.

Home and Away.

Mind and Flesh.

Me and They.

174

And so she was locked in. Land locked. Stuck where the waters of the lake long since had been. Where the reed boats long since plied. Locked. Away from light. As she had been locked in musty boxes. Had locked her house against Stephen, fair, light, loved, abandoned, Stephen who did not go toward caves or shadows, who moved within his life like the spirits of the lost Indians she had seen moved within their boats. Gathering.

She had not known when she locked that door what she knew now. Or did it matter. Did anything ever matter. More than that, the spiders around her once again grew. Twins. Twins of twins. Drums, heartbeat, pounding. The cave near the path, forbidden. An open door, slanting into a darkened hall. Spiders silent and waiting. Spinning. Spinning. Only she would ever know what it was they spun. They spun it for her. She ached for the cave, for a Grandmother hand, voice, to guide her. For the low sweet singing that would call her into deep, into darkness, home.

And no one would break a waterjar on her grave, either. And there was no knowing where she would go.

When It Was Over He Left

Hame haa. They said that to start a story. Hame, long ago. Haa, so far. Long ago so far, Kochinnenako wanted to go gather piñons. It was that time, and all the people were going. The forest would feel so good in that late month, after so much heat. She begged her mother to take her. Now Kochinnenako and her mother were outcasts in the village. No one would play with the girl, and she was often lonely. Her mother felt sorry about this. She knew that they would not be able to join the rest in the gathering. But she agreed to go anyway. She gathered the provisions they would need, and some blankets for them to carry the pine cones on when they gathered them, and soon after the other villagers left, she and Kochinnenako followed. They gathered piñons, though they had to keep to themselves.

175

One afternoon, Kochinnenako was alone gathering the pine cones. She heard soft footsteps near her. Looking up she saw a handsome young man staring at her. She did not recognize him, but she smiled at him. She thought he might talk to her, and she was lonely.

The youth smiled back, and they began to talk. She told him a little about herself, and he told her that he came from the east, far away, from where the sun lived. He told her some fine tales about his journey to her land, and she was very entertained. After some time had passed, he took two piñons out of the pack he had been carrying. "I want you to taste these," he said. They were fine, fat piñons, so she took them and cracking their brittle shells by biting them carefully, she pulled them apart and removed the fat sweet nuts and ate them. They tasted very good. When she had finished them, the youth stood up. He said he had enjoyed talking to her, but that he had to be on his way. The long sun of late afternoon was slanting through the pinetrees, making a golden haze on the dark air in the forest.

Kochinnenako bid him goodbye, and watched as he disappeared into the golden haze. "My, what a fine boy he is," she said aloud. And stood dreaming for a time. Then she noticed that the air was beginning to chill, so she gathered up the pinecones she had picked and putting them into her blanket, she turned and went back to her camp.

Some time after she and her mother returned to the village, Kochinnenako gave birth to twin boys. They grew very rapidly, and in no time were frolicking about the yard and asking their mother and grandmother all sorts of questions. As they grew they learned how to hunt, how to plant and care for corn, and how to weave. All the things a boy should know.

One day they asked Kochinnenako who their father was, and she told them he was the sun. They begged to go and find him, and she agreed.

So they began their long journey, provisioned with food their grandmother had made them. Along the way they had many adventures, and met up with Old Spider Woman who vowed to help them. She told them some secrets they would need to know when they got to the sun's house, and explained the tests he would put them to so he would know they were truly his sons.

After they got there, they were greeted by the sun's wife, who was quite annoyed when they announced to her that they were the sun's children. "Humph," she said. "He says all he does while he's gone all day is go and check on his people."

But she treated the boys courteously enough, giving them some food and a place to rest from their long journey.

That evening when the sun came home she told him that these boys were waiting to see him, and that they said they were his sons. "Aren't all humans my children?" said he, knowing she was angry. "Haa," was all she replied.

Then the sun went in to see the boys who claimed to be his children, and told them that there were a number of tests they woud have to meet to prove themselves as his sons.

They agreed, and because of the knowledge and power they had gotten from Grandmother Spider, they passed all of the tests and were welcomed by the sun as his children.

He gave them many gifts, for themselves and for their mother and grandmother, and he sent them home. And with the powers they had learned from him and Old Spider Woman, they became the helpers of the people for a long, long time.

They even created some of the earth's features. They made canyons with their lightning bolt arrows, and they saved the people from the great serpent when he raged over the flooded lands of the first village.

In later times, they were turned to stone and stood on the side of one of the tall mountains where they guard the people even now.

And they live with Spider Grandmother, the Keeper of the Fire, the bringer of light, the mind and maker of the world.

She Tells The Time

Half mind half knowing. Halves, pieces. Halves, doubles. Halves, wholes. When doubled. Placed together in the right way. She wove her days in words. The pages turning. Her thoughts stricken into silence, watching. Hovering just behind her eyes. Waiting. "Watch and wait," that's what she said, Old

Woman, Beloved, Ck'o'yo. The words hovering just behind her eyes. Just beyond her ears. Long ago, so far. Watching for the few sentences that would finally form sure knowledge of what had been done. Hame Haa. To the lake. To the mountain. To the sky.

Sometimes impatience would overwhelm her. At such times she would grasp the books, piles of them, shout and fling them against the walls. She knew the exercise of painstaking hunching over undecipherable words, eyes coming unfocussed and following somehow the tangled texts, was senseless, foolish. She already knew, in the secret places in her mind, what was true. But she needed to see some confirmation in the books, from the printing machines, so like a factory had she become, so unlike a cornfield in the wind. In spite of herself she kept on, hunting, dogged, reading each sentence, each word, writing some of them in the slick spiral notebooks she stacked on the floor near her chair.

She seldom wandered far from them. Seldom wandered anywhere. Intent. A hawk readying herself for the kill. She was herself like that, felt the feathers covering her head, felt the piercing dartings of her eyes. Teresa would come sometimes, sit and talk to her, mostly of the doings of mutual friends, or of her own struggles with job, school, lovers. Sipping glass after glass of red wine or weak tea, offering comfort to Ephanie, strength, acknowledgment, making her who was fast becoming shadow feel almost tangible for the space of time when she was there.

Sometimes Ephanie grew too weak to keep on. Drew darkness into herself, around herself, in a small acknowledgment of cramped muscles, stiffened spine. Sometimes even her eyes refused to follow along the lines. At such times she would give up. Get up and taking her keys from the dusty armchair where she usually left them, pick up her coat, shrug into her shoes and go outside. Where she would walk, look in windows, stare at herself unrecognizing for long minutes, try to remember how to breathe.

Her once sturdy frame grew birdlike over the months. Her eyes, slightly uptilted at the outer corners grew ever more dark and huge. Her hair thinned, grew long and lank around her shoulders. She would look at her hands sometimes, shocked at the slender fragility they had become, or at her thighs, thin as birdlegs beneath her jeans.

Help me, I'm dying. It was nothing she could say, looking at her friend when they were together, pleading. She would at those times feel the fear rise in her. Would beat it down into the place she reserved for silence, knowledge of bone and anguish, a place just behind her heart. Sometimes she sang to the empty room, or scattered crumbs from her window for the birds. Much of the time she slept. And ever, reading, musing, singing mindlessly, praying, feeding the birds, knowledge grew within her like the sun, like the night, growing fat and glowing, growing steadily and serene.

Grandmother of the Sun, Grandmother of the Night

Before the world was made, in the vast shining midnight of the eternal void, the grandmothers slept. They meditated. They sang. Alone in the darkness they sang. And coming together, they thought. They dreamed of making the darkness shine so bright. They dreamed of making the stars. So they came together, so they thought. So they dreamed. The heart of midnight, they dreamed. And after long thought, after meditation and singing, they said, we will gather up morsels of darkness, the gleaming darkness that is the heart of heaven, the heart of the void, and we will breathe upon the darkness and it will begin to spin, it will begin to sing. And these morsels, our thought, our breath, will become the stars. So will the meaning of our midnight be complete.

And they gathered the darkness. Morsels of the midnight dark they gathered, calling it to them with their song, calling it to them with their thought, and when each had gathered sufficient morsels of midnight, they together made one thought, and together did they sing.

And the pieces of darkness they had gathered began to turn. Faster and faster turned they. Spinning were they, as the grandmothers sang, as they thought. And spinning, the morsels of midnight went back into the night, and spinning, they began to

179

glow, to gleam, to shine. And then the grandmothers were pleased, saying, we have made the stars of midnight that will forever shine. We have made the stars. We have made a universe of suns.

And then for long eons, they slept.

As She Gathered It Began To Dawn

Qué lejos. Á donde va. A fluttering beyond the blinds. Pulled that night. She had slept through much of the day. Had not remembered the drawn blinds. La golindrina. La paloma. She awoke with that image on her mind. Those haunting songs. "Que una paloma triste muy de mañana le va cantar. They say that on certain mornings, a grieving dove comes to sing. A la casita sola con sus puertitas de palimpar. To the lonely little house whose windows are shuttered. They swear that this dove is none other than her spirit. How I long for her, who is dead, so tragically." Or something similar, close, to her clumsy translation. The soul of the dearest. Beloved. Mi alma. No llores. My soul. Don't cry. "They say that I don't eat, that I don't do anything but drink, because my beloved is dead." That was what the song said, the song she had learned when she was very young, had loved for its plaintive power, for the picture it made in her mind of the sad lover, the lonely, grieving dove that came to comfort.

She imagined the tiny village in the song as a circle of adobe homes. Like the ones she knew so well. And in her image, endlessly around the village the white bird flew.

If there is a place you can ever go, it is also in your mind. Stephen had told her that once. She knew there were many such places. She had them by heart. He hadn't said they were in her heart. Maybe that was what he had meant. If only she hadn't been so damaged. Her throat. Her lungs. Her heart.

The truth she knew, she sought, was contained in a simile. Simple after all. A matter of snowfall. Of midnight. Of light. A matter of fact and mind. Of heart. Called seizure, called spasm, it flowed. Around her chair. Alongside the shadows that also

180

grew. Among the endless, minute, grains of dust. If only she had more time. A simile that was so simple, once made. But when examined became so complicated. So very complex. Made as it was of bits of everything.

She had never meant to be alone, never intended it. Though others had tried to convince her that alone was her place, she had resisted, fought, bitterly enough sometimes, and always failed. She had finally acquiesced, given in to what she had come to believe was inevitable, had learned to be alone, to love her isolation. She suspected that it would drive her mad, more mad, but she persisted because within the isolation she felt secure. Somehow comforted. Safe. No longer needing to fight anyone, to confront her strangeness, her estrangement, a world in which she did not ever make sense, that did not, to her, ever make sense, a world that was safely confined to memories, dreams, ghosts and pages of prints.

Of which she could make whatever she chose. They did not tell her she was wrong, those silent pages. They did not sneer. They did not smile or pat her head, making in their silence openings for her blooming, belladonna, tobacco, nightshade, her blossoming within the shadows of isolation, calm at last, safe utterly beyond tears.

But so long before, when she was a child, even while she was young, she had wanted to be together with them all, all the people around her, all she knew, all she saw only in the stores, on the streets, to love and to be loved, but it had never quite happened that way. Because of her perversity, she supposed, because of her shame. Sometimes the longing, the old need so painful that ache, a torrent, a forever rising crescendo would shake her to her bones, the thirst for company, for companionship. But she had given into that need many times, walked that darkling path may times. She knew that it led to disaster.

She thought her grandmother, Shimanna, whose name in English would have been Nightshade, had died of that disease. She knew that a man who married an Indian was ostracized from company, a squawman. She also knew what happened to an Indian who married a white. Or an Indian from another tribe, or a Mexican, or a Black. It was not good. But Shimanna had clung to her life beside the village, alongside of it, walking, they still said long after she died, in balance. She had walked precariously, Ephanie knew. Abandoned probably. Maybe stoned. Certainly ignored. Knowing the eyes and the bitter tongues were about her. Did she ignore them, Ephanie in the shadows of the results of her grandmother's longago choice wondered. Her mother had said, angry, sad, "Uncle Beatsie made my mamma cry."

Yet she also knew the passion with which her grandmother had clung to her Indianness. How she had gone to the dances, whether the Presbyterian minister liked it or not. How she had clung, stubbornly, to both ways, the way of the white Christians and the way of the bronze heathens. Maybe it had been her particular wisdom to make no judgments about either, but to take from each and give to each what might be of use. But how lonely, how terribly lonely, she must have lived. After Grandma died the lake the village depended on had dried up. Vanished.

Ephanie herself no longer had the strength or courage for faith. Courage, of the heart. She could only cling, in her time, precariously to breath on the edge of the city. Hame haa, longago so far, only her determination to see this last necessity through could carry her. Will. That was what she was growing. Or at least stubborn, unspeakable determination. The final passion was her consuming need to know. What had happened. When. To who. She knew it had happened to her, that it was that particular unknown event that she was dying of. And that all attempts to evade it were futile. She had tried evasions, every possible way. She had tried.

The small one, the baby who had died, the lost twin, had taken it on himself. As so often the weakest do. He had taken the arrow that had glowed green in the half light into his own chest. He who had loved her as an infant loves, blindly, out of desperation, out of need.

And how could she love anyone after that? Expose them to that certain destruction, that death of mind, of hope. How could she allow anyone at all to touch her. To risk what they could not know. And what could she say. "I'm cursed. Don't touch me or you'll die?" Who could accept a statement like that. Teresa tried to act as if she did. Thomas had tried. Stephen, hermano, had left it alone. He alone, of her blood and meaning, had known. Had said it himself one day when the March wind of New

Mexico blew hard and gritted itself against the windows, the doors, the sky. "I can think of no one I would rather marry," he had said. "If I were younger, that's what I'd do, marry you. But I can't, I know I would only destroy you."

And had risen stiffly. Gazed at her, eyes deep and bright with the pain that she did not, he only understood. But she had understood eventually. Had seen what it did, the mystery. Had learned exactly the true measure of despair. Had found out exactly, precisely why shadows and sleep grew monstrous around her on too many mornings. Had learned how much she could never tell anyone, could never say.

Until finally she had submitted to the terror, to the dread. Head bowed like a burro in a sandstorm, trudged through the hours of waking. Grim in her stubborn determination to discover exactly the measure of the shadow that lay like plague on her life, like plague on the land she was born, to, could not leave, had left too many times. She wondered if she would, could, ever see it again.

"Que lejos estoy del cielo donde he nacído. Al verme tan solo y triste qual oja al viento." How far I am from the skies of where I was born. I go alone and sad like a leaf in the wind. I want to weep, I want to die, from the strength of my lonely feelings. That song too was each day on her mind.

She knew it, whatever it was, would come for her eventually. As it had come for the rest. Or left them to live. Or not to live, really, as vital and joyful, but to walk through their days and wake and mumble through their nights.

But she wanted to find out what it was. She knew how it would go, as she poured over the books and the pages she had written about their lives—all of their lives. The stories were clear. The evidence lay everywhere. The dead spoke in her ears, whispering. Telling her exactly how it had been. But she had trouble hearing clearly. Or believing what it was that she heard.

They told her it was the arrow of jealous furtive superstition. Of believing that who had more in the basket was inevitably going to do you in. There were so many stories about that, its folly, its essential wrongness, and the terrible losses that such beliefs always entailed. They had so many stories. So many about the consequences of selfish, suspicious actions. Like the one about Iyatiku and her beloved sister. Who went away finally because Iyatiku could not get over the fact that Naotsete's bundle contained more seeds and other things from the start. Who was so angry at what she believed was a slight that she had punished and punished her sister. So angry that finally Naotsete had gone away. So angry that she would not take the gifts that Naotsete had tried to share with her. So angry that she had given life to a people who conspired to murder the old woman who saved them from plague because her medicine was simple and much more powerful than their own. Who had been forever cursed because of their jealous fear.

They had a way of getting significance into words, the children of Iyatiku. They piled details, confusing, twisting and turning them, around and around, in and out, over here, over there, as her own life twisted and turned, confusing itself, melding with herself, as her mind did. So that as the events piled up and turned over and into and upon themselves the meanings became clear, though the meaning was never said in so many words. The people of the corn were wiser than that.

Not that it made any difference in the long run: they died anyway.

Once, when she had first thought about what the stories said, the stories that made up her life, the lives of the ones she knew, the ones she had never met, those from time immemorial, those as yet unborn, she had tried to fight back. She had trained. Had learned to be a shaman. Had learned to order the rainclouds. To foretell the rain, the end of drought. To change her shape at will. To talk to the shifting vapors that often curled and spiraled around her. Stephen taught her. Then Teresa. Finally the spirits themselves.

She had battled every thought that moved her brain, smiling in the face of everything, conciliating, mediating, trying to think only good, only hope, only bright. Once she had so tried, but no more. She had lost anyway. She did not have the power to resist whatever it was that stalked them, held them hostage to bitterness and to pain. Some things were like that, and nothing could make them change.

She hadn't stopped laughing then, in fact had laughed even more. The laughter that only those who know the worst can laugh, that only those who have been to the grave far too many times can make. The laugh of pure defiance. The laugh of triumph. The laugh at anything. The pain.

They made jokes out of everything. The skinnings of live human beings. The pictures of whitemen performing the savage acts Indians had long been accused of. They saw as they were seen by others, and that made them laugh. And drink. And die. The bitterness alone, without laughter, was otherwise too much to bear.

"When you've seen for generations how everything, everyone you love dies so hard, you laugh. A lot. At everything," she said.

She despaired at never understanding or of being understood. Not agreed with. That wasn't necessary. But of being comprehended, what she was meaning, what the terms of her life were, what she, like a particular fleshly story, was about.

She talked, her thoughts ran in circles. Which couldn't be helped. Indians lived in circles, did not care for lines that broken went nowhere. For her the sun was a clock, a calendar, like her body, like her eyes that were the meeting place of light and flesh, were circular. Like the winds. Like the sky. Like the entire galaxy that wheeled, holding the earth in her outflung arm. She thought in accretions, concretions. Like pearls grow. Like crystals. Like the earth. She gave up talking.

The curse laid upon her flesh was her gift as well. She knew that with certainty. That she was always, unendingly, aware of the pain. Of the people. Of the air. Of the water. Of the beasts and the birds. She could not escape that knowledge. In every eye, in every mind, the pain lay, blossoming in bewilderment, in blood. They never knew why they suffered. Nor did she.

All she knew was that they were always dying. And that she was exhausted with the torrential urge, frantic, to make the dying, the senseless, brutal, meaningless, terrible unending pain stop. And they also understood the gift, the curse, some of them. They brought their stories to her like wounded beasts, gazing at her with longing eyes as they placed their gifts of agony in her lap, in her hand, left them shyly beside her door, on the steps, in her eyes. They thought she could make them well.

She couldn't. She could not understand. Its nature. Its source. She lived it. Carried it within herself like a seed. Raged and swore. Laughed and laughed. Touched and held. Retreated, endlessly retreated into the helpless bewildered comfort of the dark. And whispered to the dead the tales of the living. And wept together with them. She was certain that if she could understand, they would, she would, be healed.

The pain of the earth. Even the sky stood helpless. Dying.

She knew all the ways there were of fighting. Of caring. Of taking care of. She also knew how all those ways never fixed anything. Never solved anything. Never changed anything. Never, never, never healed but only made the wounds deeper, more agonizing. All the ways of fighting played into the destruction. The little war twins had caused more grief than they had ever assuaged.

Like the time they came to save the people from the drought, from the results of the young men's mockery of Iyatiku who had given them gambling as a way to pass the time until it would come, the rain. She had left because they gambled only and mocked her. She had left them to themselves, to learn the hard way the exact measure of that they had done.

And the little war twins had come to save the people. From the Mother's decision. They had gone to talk to the lake spirit people in the villagers' behalf. And had somehow angered them so that the lake spirits decided to bring rain. Lots and lots of rain. And the terrible flood that had come. And the people had drowned, except for a few. Who had somehow made it up the side of the mountain, following on the heels of the little war twins. Who from the lofty peaks watched the water rising, rising. And the great serpent that came with the rising flood. Who the little twins slew with their potency that the Spider had given them. That had come from the sun. So that it looked like they had saved the poor shattered remnants of the people. From the consequences of their acts.

All the ways of fighting played into the destruction. Killing more people, beasts, trees, rivers, clouds. They even knew how to kill the rain, those who were set to destroy. Even knew how to turn the light into a murderous pestilence. A huge, mushrooming blaze of vaporizing vicious light. She knew that. And she knew how small, how very small were her hands.

That was how they'd killed her son. How they'd murdered themselves. Fighting over nothing. Over their own graves.

Death is like the stories, she thought. Death turns on itself. On ourselves. Death has no ending. Everything furthers death. Bless me Naiya, that I might live.

Not that dying was the problem. There was a way to die that was blessed. That was clear water. Clear air. That was the mountains and the skies of home. But that kind of dying had gone away, as Iyatiku had gone away. It had gone with her. And that kind of death was one that healed. It was the source of all that was good. Of all that was alive.

They had stories about it. In time immemorial, they said. Long ago so far, they said. When the animals talked to the people. Before the Katsinas went away. But something had changed all of that. What.

The First Time They Died

The way it happened was like this. The boys who had mocked Naiya Iyatiku had also mocked the Katsina. But a certain Katsina had been in the kiva where the mocking jokes and the imitations were going on, and he was angered by what he saw. He left the kiva and went home to Wenimats where the Katsina lived. He told the others what was going on over at the village. They were also very angry. But some of them counseled peace. They said, "Never mind. Let it go. Let's ignore it. They're just foolish boys, and they will soon grow up a little. We can just wait."

But this particular Katsina didn't want to be tolerant. He was angered at the insults he had seen and heard, that were directed at the Katsina who, after all, were only interested in the welfare of the human beings, and who always did as Iyatiku had instructed them. "No," he said, "I don't think they should get away with this. Come on," he said, "let's go over to the village and settle some things with the people. They can't be allowed to treat us like that."

He told them what he had seen and heard, exaggerating everything in a way that finally enraged them. But the peaceful Katsina kept saying, "Leave it alone." He tried to remind them that their duty was to care for the people, not to punish them, but nobody was listening, they were so caught up in their righteous rage.

"Let us go to the village," they said. And in their rush to avenge the wrong done to them, they stampeded over the Katsina who counseled peace, injuring him.

In the village the people had grown very uneasy. They knew that something terrible was about to happen. They could tell by the shudderings of the earth, the surliness of the strangely darkening sky, that the Katsina were angry. They began to plant prayer-sticks, hurriedly, but it did no good. The Katsina were in no mood to be placated.

The little war twins were in the crowd of people that was gathering behind the country chief on the square. They hoped that the troubles would be settled without too much harm. But when they saw the furious Katsina descending on the village in a rage, striking the people and killing them, they became frightened. They ran to their house and put on the clothes of power they had brought back from the sun's house, and they gathered their weapons. They even took down the hunting sticks that their father had given them after cautioning them not to use the sticks unless serious trouble was occuring. The little war twins knew they would need those sticks now. Rushing out of their house they ran to the square, all the time giving the war cry that their father had also given them as a means of calling on the power of the sun. They rushed among the fallen bodies of the people. The country chief and the injured Katsina were also there, trying to stop the fighting, calling on the combatants to put down their weapons and make peace. But their words were scarcely heard.

Into the battle the little war twins rushed, and hurling their hunting sticks at the Katsina, they soon ended the battle. The magic weapons decapitated all of the warring Katsina, who fell headless to the ground and ceased to move. Then the twins realized the horror of what they had done. Then they began to weep, for this was the first time any of them had seen death.

And seeing the bodies all around them, the injured Katsina and the country chief began to tremble. "I think we have done something wrong, or else how could such a thing happen?" they said. And when the remaining Katsina asked by whose power had the Katsina been killed, the little war twins said, "We are responsible for this. It had to be done, for they were murdering the people. We know that the Katsina are sacred, but we also know that it is their sworn duty to protect the people and to take care of them."

And though the little war twins restored both the dead Katsina and the dead villagers to life, things were never the same in the village again. For the people quarreled with each other constantly. They were suspicious and untrusting of each other. They were no longer at peace in their lives.

And the Katsina went away then. They would never come directly among the people again, but would only come through certain dancers on their appointed days.

After this many of the people began to move away. Sometimes large groups, sometimes only a household of a woman and maybe one of her sisters and their children. But they began to move from the first village, hoping to find some other place to live in peace, where it would be like it had been.

And now death was everywhere.

What Is Divided In Two Brings War

It was just a matter of time. What Grandmother Spider had taught, had left them to study in the full measure of their lives. At Guadalupe, recognizing the nature of her silent instruction, they called her Thinking Woman. She who is thinking. She who is waiting. For them to understand, to come in their hearts and minds to peace. The only possible hope. The only possible help. Which was why they waited, that long line of women who had gone before Ephanie. Within the walls, on the cliffs, beneath the mesas, beneath the ground, among the stars. They were waiting for the time when the people would recognize the causes of death, would come to understanding through thinking on the meanings of the stories, of the lives. But the thinking had to be intertwined with open hearts. And not ever with any sort of death.

What made good thinking hard was the lies. That were bonedeep. Every story had been twisted. Even her own. Especially her own. If she could control her tongue. If she could re-occupy her own mind.

Spider thoughts. Small. One at a time. Quiet. Still. Building.

Spider thoughts. Building. Weaving. Hidden in the corners. In the shadows. So nobody would see. Until they were done.

But the words she had. The language wasn't built for truth. It was a lying tongue. The only one she had. It made separations. Divided against itself. It could not allow enwholement. Only fragmentation. And it was the only language they all knew together—the people in her world. The tongue that only knew how to lie. The only words she had. The only containers for the food, the water, the soil of recovery, uncovery, discovery. To re learn. To re member. To put back what had been shattered. To re mind. To re think. The beginning so as to grasp the end.

So that stories, similes, piles upon piles of slick, wet, shiny metaphors that would breathe on their own, within themselves, among themselves, had to be made. And all the fragments of all the shattered hearts gathered carefully into one place. Tenderly cared for. Would grow. That truth. The one where all the waters would come together. Shipap. The Mother's home. The place of the one good heart.

In The Shadows She Sang, Remembering

Empty spaces. A room of long shadows, climbing. Sun that is simply there.

She looked up from the notebook she had been writing in. Noticed the slanting sun that shone around the edges of the shade she kept down. Heard the wind rattling the pane. She caught a memory that had been struggling in her mind for the last few hours as she read and scribbled her endless notes. For hours it had tried to get her attention, and now, by some flicker of sun or sound of wind, was sprung free for her to examine. I must have dreamed, she thought. Eyes squinting with the effort to remember. No. Not a dream. A memory. And all this time I've thought it was a dream.

"Jump. No. Out here. Get in the open when you jump. Don't be so tense. Imagine you are falling with the wind. You are the wind. You can sail out, soaring."

He had said that. She remembered. And remembering began to weep. With fear. With relief.

"Because she fell." Ephanie said it out loud. Crying. Smiling. "She fell. I knew it. I made a name for her, the woman who fell. Because it was important. The story tied to what I wouldn't remember. All along. What I always knew."

She understood at last that everything was connected. Everything was related. Nothing came in that did not go out. Nothing was that did not live nestled within everything else. And this was how the stories went, what they had been for. To fit a life into. To make sense. Nothing left because there was no place else to go. Nothing left out because everything was remembered. Everything was told. What had happened in time immemorial, as the old ones called that time before time, happened now. Only the names were different.

And not so different at that, she thought. A tree of light. A blooming apple tree. A woman who was pushed into another life, one she did not choose, one she had chosen because it came necessarily from her choice. A woman who married a stranger. Who was stronger than he knew. A woman who was stranger, a stranger. Who knew what she should not know. Who aroused her husband's jealousy, her husband's fear. Who fell beneath the shining boughs of the tree into sky almost forever. Who entered a new world and upon it planted her seed. Who gave the sun and moon their light. Who from death made life. Who knew nothing was ever ended. Who just went on.

191

The Woman Who Fell From The Sky

Once upon a time, long ago so far, a young woman was told by her dead father to go and marry a stranger. Being a strange woman, she did as he said, not taking her mother's counsel in the matter as she should have done. She journeyed to the place where the dead father had directed her to go, and there found the man she was to marry.

Now this man was a renowned magician, a sorcerer. He heard her proposal that they marry skeptically. He said to himself, "This woman is but a girl. It would be more fitting for her to ask to be my servant rather than my wife." But he only listened silently to her, then he said, "It is well. If you can meet my tests, we will see if I will make you my wife."

He took her into his lodge and said, "Now you must grind corn." She took the corn and boiled it slightly, using wood he brought her for the fire. When the kernels were softened, she began to grind them on the grinding stone. And though there were mounds and mounds of stuff to be ground, still she was done with the task in a very short time. Seeing this, the sorcerer was amazed, but he kept silent. Instead he ordered her to remove all her clothing. When she was naked, he told her to cook the corn in the huge pot that hung over the fire. This she did, though the hot corn popped and spattered scalding clinging mush all over her. But she did not flinch, enduring the burns with calm.

When the mush was done, the woman told the sorcerer it was ready. "Good," he said. "Now you will feed my servants." He noted that her body was covered with cornmush. Opening the door, he called in several huge beasts who ran to the woman and began to lick the mush from her body with their razor sharp tongues, leaving deep gashes where their tongues sliced her flesh. Still she did not recoil but endured the torment, not letting her face lose its look of calm composure.

Seeing this, the sorcerer let the beasts back out, then said she and he would be married, and so they were. After four nights that they spent sleeping opposite each other with the soles of their feet touching, he sent her back to her village with gifts of meat for the people. He commanded her to divide the meat evenly among all the people, and further to see to it that every lodge had its roof removed that night, as he was going to send a white corn rain among them. She did as she was told, and after the village had received its gifts, the meat and the white corn rain, she returned to her husband's lodge.

Outside his lodge there grew a tree that was always filled with blossoms so bright they gave light to his whole land. The woman loved the tree, loved to sit under it and converse with the spirits and her dead father, who she held dear in her heart. She so loved the light tree that once, when everyone was sleeping, she lay down under it and opened her legs and her body to it. A blossom fell on her vagina then, touching her with sweetness and a certain joy. And soon after she knew she was pregnant.

About that time her husband became weak and ill. His medicine people could not heal him, but told him that his sickness was caused by his wife. He was certain they were right, for he had never met anyone so powerful as she. He feared that her power was greater than his own, for hadn't she been able to withstand his most difficult tests? "What should I do?" he asked his advisors. They did not advise him to divorce her, because that kind of separation was unknown to them. They did not advise him to kill her, because death was unknown among them. The only death that had occurred was of the woman's father, and they did not understand what had happened to him.

After deliberating on the matter for four days, the advisors told the sorcerer that he should uproot the tree of light. Then, lying beside it, he should call his wife to come and sit with him. He should by some ruse get her to fall over the edge of the hole the uprooted tree would leave, and she would fall into the void. When she had fallen, they said, he was to replace the tree and then he would recover his health and his power.

That afternoon he went outside his lodge and pulled up the tree. He peered over the edge of the hole it left, and he could see another world below. He called his wife to come and see it. When she came, he said, "Lean over the edge. You can see another world below." She knelt beside the hole and leaning over the edge, looked down. She saw darkness, and a long way below, she saw blue, a shining blue that seemed filled with promise and delight. She looked at her husband and smiled, eyes dancing with pleasure. "It looks like a beautiful place there," she said. "Who would have thought that the tree of light would be growing over such a place!"

"Yes," her husband agreed. "It surely seems beautiful there." He regarded her for a moment carefully, then said, "I wonder what it is like there. Maybe somebody could go down there and find out."

Astonished, the woman looked at her husband. "But how would someone do that?"

"Jump." The husband said.

"Jump?" She asked, looking down through the opening, trying to calculate the distance. "But it is very far."

"Someone of your courage could do it," he said. "You could jump. Become the wind or a petal from this tree," he indicated the tree lying fallen next to them. "A petal could fall, gently, on the wind it would be carried. You could be a petal in the wind. You could be a butterfly, a downgliding brightbird."

She gazed for a long time at the shining blue below her. "I could jump like that. I could float downward. I could fall into the shining blue world below us."

"Yes," he said. "You could."

For another long moment she knelt gazing downward, then taking a deep breath she stood, and flexing her knees and raising her arms high over her head she leaned into the opening and dove through.

For sometime the sorcerer watched her body as it fell downward through the dark, toward the blue. "She jumped," he finally said to the council as they made their way slowly toward him. "She's gone."

And they raised the tree and placed it back firmly in its place, covering the opening to the other world with its roots.

A Lot Changed After She Fell

When the memory had surfaced it had been a simple image. A small white bird, hovering in the wind. Or a petal, white, floating. Then a tree, covered with pale blossoms. Shining. When Ephanie remembered what had befallen her, she had remembered the story that told it. An ancient story told longago around the motherfires in the lodges far to the east of San Francisco where she sat in the shadows, contemplating the uncertain shafts of sunlight that hovered in the air and sliced brightness onto the floor. That story. About the woman who fell from the sky. Who the skyspirit birds had rescued, had held safe upon their outspread wings until a place could be made to lay her.

She remembered the tale, all of it. The woman who in her arrogance and brightness had taken a fall. From which she had never returned. From which had come the earth.

After she fell, after the birds caught her, after they made land for her, making it secure on the back of the Grandmother Turtle, she had lain, swooning for a time. Then she had awakened and moved around, exploring the land she had caused to come into being. After a time she had given birth to a child, a girl, who, many turns later had also given birth, to twin boys. The daughter had died during labor because one twin would not be born second to his brother, would not be born in the usual way but forced his way into life through his mother's side, killing her. He had lied about it to the grandmother, the woman who fell from the sky, saying his brother had killed their mother, and she had believed him.

Believing him she had taken him with her to her lodge. Had returned for the body of her daughter, leaving the other child, the innocent one, in the forest alone. To live or die as he might. Taking the body of her daughter, she flung the head into the sky, where it became the moon. She hung the body from a tree that stood near her door, and it began to shine, giving the light that in later times would be called the sun. And having done this, she went inside and nursed the baby she had accepted, raising him.

Was it the sorcerer-chief's jealousy, his fear that betrayed her? Or was it her own arrogance, her daring, leading her to leap into the abyss from which there was no return? Ephanie wondered about that, turning the question over and over in her mind. In her mind laying the question against many memories, against the history, against the tales, against the myths. Against her own life. Hours she pondered, slowly growing stronger, more clear, as the light in the room turned to shadows, to twilight, to dark. Still she sat, re membering.

It had been a windswept day. A perfect sharp day. One of the spring days that was filled with joy. With delight. With hovering bright air sprites, laughter, mad plans and hours and hours to fulfill them. Ephanie had gotten up at first light. Had run outdoors to greet the sun. That shone sweetly on the newly budding trees. Across the lot from her house she had seen the appletree, blooming heavily, covered in blossoms, radiant in the early morning light. The windcleared air was sweet on her face, her bare arms and legs. The earth sent a pleasuring chill through her bare feet. She stood a long while at her door, the door whose frame was painted blue like all the doorways in the village. Stood there in the new sun waiting for it to be time to begin the day. For it to be time to go to Elena's house. To gather her into the morning as she gathered her every morning when Ephanie was not at boarding school. Waiting, she let the light and the tree's blossoms flow into her, the song they made together swell into her chest, into her leg muscles and arm muscles. Into her brain. And after a long time she went inside to get ready for the day.

When she came out again water was tumbling through the irrigation ditch that ran alongside the field near her house. On her way to Elena's she stopped for a while to watch it as it made its way along the channel laboriously dug for it, laboriously cleaned each year. The sight of it, the first irrigation of the year, always filled her with joy. There was so little water there, where she lived. It was so precious, so dear. She welcomed it like a relative, a dear one she hadn't seen for a long time. She began dancing in her body, in her mind, dancing to the chant the running water made as it tumbled on its way. She imagined that she could see the short green blades of grass that would soon line the ditch, feeling glad, so glad that it was time for growing things again. When the dancing reached her feet she turned and ran, skipping and hopping, even doing one flip and a handspring, to Elena's. She hoped no one was watching and saw her do them. They would scold. Would say that a twelve year old girl shouldn't be acting that way. That she might get hurt, she might fall and break something. Her neck, maybe. And they would laugh, and she would turn away, angry, unable to reply. But it was too fine a day to worry about that, and she was twelve. She didn't care so much what they said. She felt full of energy, good spirits, life. It was a perfect day and she was going to Elena's and they were going to find all sorts of exciting things to do.

They did. Though not what she had thought. Not what she ever would have thought. How such a perfect day would turn like that. Would turn her life like that. Into something she would not recognize for years.

Innocent it had begun, that day. In peace and high spirits. In beauty it had begun. Filled with hope, with mischief, with delight. With ditches and hearts full of pleasure. She had gotten Elena and soon they had escaped into the warming Saturday sun. Into the light. Freed from adult eyes they had walked along the dirt road, planning their day. They went into the old store, Ephanie leading, Elena hanging back slightly, as they went through the door and into the shadowy building. The long floor was dark with the oil they swept it daily with. Ephanie had done it, used the great pushbroom they had, swept oiled sawdust carefully over the aisles that ran between the darkstained counters. She had pushed the broom over that floor, careful to make certain every board was swept with the shavings. She looked over the floor then with a professional eye, checking to see if Stephen had done the job right the night before.

They sauntered along the aisle, nodding to a couple of customers—an old woman who stood quietly near the counter on the side of the store where the groceries were shelved, her cotton dress carefully pressed, covered with a red and white checkered apron she had crossstitched in red with a rose design, hair carefully wrapped in a bright flowered bandanna. "Guwatzi," Ephanie said to her. "Da'waa'e," the woman replied. "How's your mother?" the woman asked. "Oh, she's fine," Ephanie replied. "She's at home." They smiled at each other, then each went about her business. Stephen came to the counter then and put down the canned peaches, crackers and tin of lard he was carrying. "What else can I get for you, Aunt Susie?" he asked. "That will be all," the woman answered. "But maybe my old man there wants something," she laughed the particular high pitched laugh of the people as she gestured with her chin toward the man standing near the tall kerosene stove at the far end of the room. He looked up as she spoke, then began to make his way slowly toward her. His dark face was lined from sun and wind wearing on it, even beneath the soft tan Stetson he wore. His flannel shirt and levis were pressed carefully. He stopped across the high counter from Stephen and asked for some tobacco. "I need a new harness too," he said.

As Stephen moved away to help the man choose the right harness, Ephanie slipped behind the counter and sauntered down the inner aisle toward the candy counter. Looking over her shoulder to make certain Stephen was occupied and not watching her, she crouched down behind the counter and reached into the case, selecting several candy bars that were favorites of hers and Elena's. Rising quickly she got back around the counter before Stephen returned. On her way she got the tobacco the man had requested. Putting it on the counter with the rest of the order, she said, "Stephen, I got the tobacco for you. I put it with the rest of the things."

Preoccupied, he responded with a nod. "Okay," he said. "Thanks."

Smiling triumphantly, Ephanie gestured to Elena with her head, and they left the store, giggling.

"Let's go and see if we can find a little snake. Maybe there are some around this early," Ephanie said. "Let's get one and put it somewhere Stephen will find it!" Laughing, Elena agreed. They delighted in tormenting Stephen with his fearfulness of certain creatures. Snakes, lizards, mice. He would yelp with fear whenever one accosted him. Once the girls had discovered his fear they made a practice of secreting such creatures in places Stephen was bound to be. Their best endeavor had been planting a large bullsnake in the outhouse. Stephen had gone in at noon, in a hurry because he was working at the store and was late returning from his lunch break. He opened the door of the outhouse and went in without looking around, of course. The small window let in little light, so he was inside a couple of minutes before the snake made her presence known to him. Suddenly the girls, hiding in the shed that stood near the outhouse, heard a frightened cry. The door flew open and Stephen came bolting out, frantically trying to get his levis up over his buttocks as he ran, hollering loudly, almost falling in his headlong flight.

Unable to stifle their laughter, the two girls had been overcome with helpless shrieks of mirth. They were lying on the shed floor holding their sides, tears running down their faces, howling with laughter when the door had been flung open revealing a furious Stephen standing there, redfaced, his hands planted on his hips. "Very funny," he had managed at last to say, almost choking on the words. "I hope you have a good laugh." And stiffly had turned, closing the door of the shed behind him as he went, and throwing the bolt he locked them in.

That had been the summer before, but Ephanie was still filled with the sense of her superior courage. She wasn't afraid of snakes, and was scornful of Stephen for being afraid. She wanted to frighten him again, to tease him, to make him seem less powerful than she and her friend. She hoped they could find a snake today.

She and Elena climbed down the steep sides of the deep arroyo that bordered the eastern edge of the village. It had been carved by years of rampaging waters that thundered down from high in the faraway mountain during summer storms. There was little danger of flashflooding at this time of year, though, and even if it had been July, the usual time for severe thunderstorms, they would have clambered down its sides, heedless of the potential danger. It was one of their favorite places to go, safe from adults and their demands.

They walked along the dry arroyo bed, skirting huge sandstone boulders that were moved downstream by successive floods, searching for a hole that would signal a snake's den. After some time they gave up the search and settled down under a sheltering boulder to eat their candy and talk. As they finished, they heard Stephen calling. Ephanie scrambled out from their hiding place and climbed to the top of the boulder. It was a struggle because its six foot high sides sloped only slightly and offered only a few widely separated hollows to place hands or feet. Elena climbed slowly behind her. When she reached the top, Ephanie whistled sharply, answering Stephen's call. "Over here," she called.

Stephen came into view, stepping to the edge of the arroyo's opposite bank. "Come on," he said. "I have something I want to show you." He disappeared, and the girls jumped across the five foot span that separated the boulder from the high bank. Reaching the bridge upstream from them, they crossed the arroyo and followed Stephen's retreating figure to the apple tree. On the bridge they broke into a run, excited at the prospect of having something to do, and reached the tree at almost the same time Stephen did.

"Look," he said, gesturing at a heavy length of rope that dangled down from one of the branches high up the tree. "I made a jump." He began to climb the tree, reaching for a thick branch above his head then swinging easily up into the tree. He continued to climb, stopping along the way to grab the rope and wrap its end a few times around his hand. He made his way out along a large branch, almost to its end. It bent and swayed under his weight. The rope was stretched taut, its other end secured to a branch almost opposite the one he stood on. He stood silent for a moment then let out a loud whoop and leaped from the branch swinging out away from the tree. At the crest of the leap, he twisted his body so that he faced the tree, and swinging back toward it, stretched his legs in front of him. Just before he collided with the tree his boots struck the upper trunk, sending him swinging outward again. This time as he began his swing back toward the tree he let go of the rope and dropped to the ground, landing lightly on his feet. "Want to try it?" he said.

Hesitating, Ephanie looked at Elena. Elena looked uneasy. "What do you think?" Ephanie asked her friend. Elena looked up at the branch the rope was tied to. She looked at the branch Stephen had jumped from. "I don't know," she said. "Maybe you can do it. But you should be wearing boots and gloves. You could get rope burns, or your hands might slip. And trying to spring off the trunk with bare feet, you might sprain your ankle or something."

"You gonna try it?" Ephanie asked.

Elena looked down. "I don't think so. It looks too hard."

"You can do it, Ephanie," Stephen said. He grinned at her, daring her with his eyes. "You've done harder things."

Ephanie looked at him steadily for a moment, calculating the risk.

If he can do it, I can, she thought. "Give me your gloves," she said. She took the gloves he handed her and put them in the pocket of her levis. Reaching up to grab one of the lower branches, she grasped it with her hands then swung her legs upward, hooking her ankles over the branch. Then, swinging herself sharply upward, she hooked her leg over the branch and was up in the tree. She climbed toward the branch Stephen had stood on, but she had to detour from it because she was not as tall as he was and couldn't reach the hanging rope as easily as he had. She swung around a branch, reaching out to the rope with her right hand as she held to the branch with her left one. Grabbing it, she pulled it toward her. Then she put the gloves on and wrapped the rope end securely around her left hand. The gloves were leather and loose on her, but she thought they'd be all right. Readied, she edged her way out along the branch she had chosen to jump from. It was slightly below and to the side of the one Stephen had used, and was somewhat smaller. But she figured it would hold her lighter weight.

As she reached the place where she thought she could make the jump, she stopped. Steadying herself by holding to a branch above her head, she stood and looked out. She saw the apple blossoms surrounding her, smelled their sweet scent swirling around her, filling her nostrils with perfume.

She stood, calculating the jump, her hold on the rope. Her heart was pounding loudly in her ears, and she was beginning to sweat with nervous anticipation.

"Jump!" Stephen said, loudly enough to jerk her from her trance. "Pretend you're an appleblossom, floating gently to the ground. Just make sure you hold on tight," he added, concern flickering across his upturned face.

"Maybe you shouldn't, Ephanie," Elena said. "It doesn't look safe."

"Oh, go ahead, Ephanie," Stephen said. "Go ahead. Jump."

She heard Elena saying something just as she took off. It sounded like "Fall." Or maybe it was "Don't fall." But she was already falling. Her fingers did not cling tightly enough to the rope within the slippery, loose gloves. Or she let go before she had time to get her balance. Or the branch the rope was tied to snapped with her weight as she plummeted downward when she leaped from her perch. She didn't know what had happened, exactly, only that one moment she stood on the branch, holding the rope and imagining her outward swing through the spring-bright air, and the next she was on her back on the ground, smiling up at the frightened faces of Elena and Stephen. "It's okay," she had groaned. "I'm all right. I just knocked the wind out of myself, that's all. Give me a minute," she said. "I'll be all right."

And later, coming to again, lying on a board that some men were carrying, her father among them, his face gone ashen with fear. And Stephen. Looking like a stranger, eyes gone somewhere beyond her, beyond them there.

They took her to Albuquerque, to the hospital. They said she'd broken two ribs and punctured a lung and it had collapsed. They drained the fluid that had collected there with a longlong needle and a terrifyinghuge syringe. They said soothing things to her. They said she was lucky she didn't break her neck.

She didn't say much except that she was sorry. That she shouldn't have done that. That Elena had said for her not to. That she should have listened to her, to all of them, to their warnings, to their fear, to their complaints. "I guess I am not so tough after all," she had said. Or thought. "I guess I shouldn't do things like that again."

She Knew All About Falling

After she fell everything changed. How she dressed. How she walked. What she thought. Where she went. How she spoke. The old ease with her body was gone. The careless spinning of cowboy dreams. She no longer cavorted along the roads, over the mesas, among the branches of the sheltering trees. No cartwheels. No flying leaps from rooftops to horse's back. No wild handsprings, or flipping head over heels from one spot to the next, diving headfirst into space, through the air to land on her feet, running, shouting, free.

Instead highheels and lipstick. That she suddenly craved, intently. Instead full skirted dresses that she'd scorned only weeks before. Instead sitting demure on a chair, voice quiet, head down. Instead gazing in the mirror, mooning over lacey slips and petticoats. Curling endlessly her stubborn hair. To train it. To tame it. Her. Voice, hands, hair, trained and tamed and safe.

After she fell the sun went out. She went out carefully from then on. She sang long plaintive songs of love, of romance, dreamed of leaving Guadalupe for someplace else. Dreamed of being tall and pretty and dated. Adored. Mated. Housed in some pretty house somewhere far from the dusty mesas of her childhood, somewhere that people lived in safe places and had lawns and plenty of water and spoke in soft voices. Like her mother, like the nuns, had told her about. Like the books had said. Someplace green and soft. Someplace nice. With vacuum cleaners and carpets and drapes. With sofas instead of couches, refrigerators instead of iceboxes, shopping centers instead of general trading stores.

After she fell she gave up teasing her city cousins for being sissies when they were afraid to climb the trees or jump the wide crevices in the high mesas where she had such a short time before leaped and danced from rock to rock. Instead she sat with them and talked about boys and clothes and other girls. Instead she exerted every ounce of intelligence toward learning how they held their heads, their hands, their mouths. And practiced secretly in her room alone. Learned to prance and priss, and did not notice the change, the fear behind it. The rage. And did not ever say aloud, not even in her own mind, what it was all about.

After she fell she had begun rising early to attend morning Mass. Had given up grandiose daydreams for Lent. Had forgotten how to spin dreams, imaginings about her life, her future self, her present delights. Had cut herself off from the sweet spring of her own being. Bless me father for I have sinned. But I won't sin anymore, she vowed. Had learned piety and modesty.

Had studied hard, made good grades. Practiced handwriting, trying to make each letter, each word perfect, like they were in the Palmer Handbook Sister had taught them from when Ephanie was in the fourth grade.

Until now, studying, reading, singing and chanting, thinking the long months through, she finally understood. Mournful, filled with grief for the lie she had learned, had lived, had told, had embedded within every action, every gesture, for all the years since she fell from the tree and forgot who she had meant to be, what she had meant to do.

Until now, some quality of the light, some sound in the wind. Some freshness, perfume on the air, reminded her, brought back the memory she had for all these years held back, refusing to remember, to see. The tree. Stephen. Elena. Falling from so far. Crashing to the ground. Hearing her mother saying, "Don't climb those weak branches, you'll fall." Hearing the nuns say "Don't race around like that. Be a lady." Punishing her when she forgot the rules and ran, yelled, jumped on the beds and broke the slats. Sending her to confession to tell the father her unruly sins. "Bless me Father for I have sinned. I jumped on the bed. I fell from the apple tree."

"All those years," she said to the deep shadows that clung to the room. "All those years, and I never realized what had happened." And now she knew. That what she had begun had never been completed. Because she fell she had turned her back on herself. Had misunderstood thoroughly the significance of the event. Had not even seen that she had been another sort of person before she fell. "I abandoned myself," she said. "I left me." And began to laugh, realizing. To laugh as all the memories came flooding back. Herself cartwheeling through the village. Whooping and hollering as she and Elena galloped their horses along the long dusty road, practicing with their ropes to send the whirling loops sailing over the heads of the placid cows who wandered freely on the reservation lands. I was going to be a hero, before I got sidetracked, she thought. I was going to be full of life and action. I wasn't going to be the one who lived alone, afraid of the world. Elena and I, we were going to do brave things in our lives. And we were going to do them together.

204

And what had happened to all of that? A fall, a serious fall. A conversation a few years later that ended her friendship with Elena. A fear, a running away, an abandonment. But I had already left myself before Elena abandoned me, she thought now. Because I thought I should have been smarter than to listen to Stephen's dare. Because I was hurt. Because I was in the hospital for a few days, alone and scared and feeling so guilty. So guilty I never trusted my own judgment, my own vision again. "Yes, my dear," she said out loud to herself, "you took quite a fall." And felt pure amazement at the long time it had taken before she had finally found again the ground.

And how she had tried over all that time to evade the truth of it. Of her arrogance. Of her bravery. Of her pride. Of her attempts to make Stephen responsible for her sanity, for her children, for her life. Of his misjudgment of her ability. Of his anger and his fear. Of his guilt, that had held him bound to her over all of these years. And of Elena. Of the long buried conviction Ephanie had harbored that Elena had made her fall. Believing that Elena had commanded her to fall when she had shouted that last warning that Ephanie had barely heard and would never forget hearing. All of it flooding through her now, through her mind and through her body. The terrible pain of her chest. The confusion, the fugue she had fallen into for days, for a lifetime, after she fell. She felt them again. And the rope searing her hand as she leapt into the air. And the sharp wrenching of her shoulder as her body jerked against the rope, when the full weight of her jolted along its length. And she heard again the loud snap. The branch split. The branch the rope was tied to had split, spilling her from her height far up in the huge tree onto the ground. Where something had broken, something that had taken her lifetime to mend.

She gasped with the power of the memories sweeping through her. Felt sharp pain as she tried to breathe. Felt her belly tighten, her shoulders hunch, curving around as though to soften the blow. Saw again the rocks she narrowly missed slamming into. Felt again the fear as she realized the height from which she had fallen. That damn Stephen, she thought now, as she must have thought then, "I'll get him for this. Just you wait and see." And filled with the memories and their pain and rage, their fear and fury, she stumbled from the livingroom where she had sat for so many hours and made her way to her bed.

And fell asleep once again feeling her young body's strength, its power after so long. Knowing another turn had been made. A connection mended that so long ago had snapped. Tomorrow I'll write Stephen. Tell him what I've found. Myself. I found me, after all this time.

Kurena. Sunrise

"Sister. Sister. I am here."

Ephanie opened her eyes. Looked around. Saw someone, shadowy, at the bottom of her bed.

"I have come to tell you a story. One that you have long wanted to hear."

Ephanie saw that the shadowy form was a woman whose shape slowly focussed out of the swirl of vapor she was cloaked in. She saw that the woman was small. There was something of a bird, a hawk perhaps, about her. Her eyes gleamed in a particular way, like no shine Ephanie had ever seen. The woman was dressed in the old way and her hair was cut traditionally, so that it fell in a straight line from crown to jaw. The sides formed perfect square corners on either side. Straight bangs fell over her forehead, almost to her eyebrows in the ancient arrangement that signified the arms of the galaxy, the Spider. It was another arrangement of the four corners that composed the Universe, the four days of sacredness that women remembered in their bodies' blood every month.

The woman wore a white, finely woven manta and shawl, each richly embroidered in fine black wool with geometrical patterns that told the story of the galaxy. Ephanie recognized only the spider among the symbols embroidered there. She saw the woman's thick, snowy buckskin leggings, wrapped perfectly around her calves. She raised herself to a sitting position and with her hand made the sign of sunrise, the gesture of taking a pinch of corn pollen between fingers and thumb, then opening them as though to let the pollen free.

The spirit woman began to speak, chanting her words in a way that seemed so familiar, that brought Ephanie near tears.

"In the beginning time, in the place of Sussistinaku, The Spider, Old Woman, placed the bundles that contained her sisters Uretsete and Naotsete, the women who had come with her from the center of the galaxy to this sun. She sang them into life. She established the patterns of this world. The pattern of the singing, of the painting she made to lay the spirit women upon, the pattern of placing the bundles that contained their forms, of the signs that she made, was the pattern she brought with her, in her mind. It is the pattern of the corners, their turning, their multidimensional arrangings. It is the sign and the order of the power that informs this life and leads back to Shipap. Two face outward, two inward, the sign of doubling, of order and balance, of the two, the twins, the doubleminded world in which you have lived," she chanted.

And in the living shadows that swirled around the spirit woman's face, Ephanie saw moving patterns that imaged what the woman was saying. Saw the corners lying flat, like on paper, then taking on dimensions, like in rooms, or on the outside of boxes and buildings, then combining and recombining in all of their dimensions, forming the four-armed cross, ancient symbol of the Milky Way, found on rocks and in drawings of every land. Saw the square of glossy, deeply gleaming blackness that was the door to the place of the Spider. Saw held within it the patterned stars, the whirling suns, the deep, black brilliance of the center of the sun. Saw the perfect creation space from which earth and her seven sisters had sprung at the bidding of the Grandmothers, long ago so far, before time like a clock entered and took hold.

She understood the combinations and recombinations that had so puzzled her, the One and then the Two, the two and then the three, the three becoming the four, the four splitting, becoming two and two, the three of the beginning becoming the three-in-one. One mother, twin sons; two mothers, two sons; one mother, two sons. Each. First there was Sussistinaku, Thinking Woman, then there was She and two more: Uretsete and Naotsete. Then Uretsete became known as the father, Utset, because Naotsete had become pregnant and a mother, because the Christians would not understand and killed what they did not know. And Iyatiku was the name Uretsete was known by, she was Utset, the brother. The woman who was known as father, the Sun. And Utset was another name for both Iyatiku and Uretsete, making three in one. And Naotsete, she with more in her bundle, was the Woman of the Sun, after whom Iyatiku named her first daughter Sun Clan, alien and so the combinations went on, forming, dissolving, doubling, splitting, sometimes one sometimes two, sometimes three, sometimes four, then again two, again one. All of the stories formed those patterns, laid down long before time, so far.

The One was the unity, the source, Shipap, where Naiya Iyatiku lived. The two was the first splitting of the one, the sign of the twins, the doublewoman, the clanmother-generation. From whom came all the forms of spirit and of matter as they appear on earth and in earth's heavens. Which could only come into being in time, the counting, pulsating, repetitive, cycling beat, held in its four coordinating patterns by the power of the three who become seven in all the tales eventually. The forms of flame. The dark flame. The gold flame. The flame of white. The Grandmother flame. The sister flame. The flame of the sun. The fire of flint. The fire of corn. The fire of passion, of desire. The flame of longing. The flame of freedom. The flame of vision, of dream.

In the patterns before her eyes, within her mind, that pulsed and flowed around and through her Ephanie found what she so long had sought. The patterns flowed like the flowings of her life, the coming out and the going in, the entering and the leaving, the meeting and gathering, the divisions and separations, how her life, like the stories, told the tale of all the enterings, all the turning away. Waxing and waning, growing and shrinking, birthing and dying, flowering and withering. The summer people and the winter people, that ancient division of the tribe. The inside priestess and the outside priest. The mother who was the center of their relationship to each other and to the people, the things of the earth. What was within went without. What was without, went within. As Kochinnenako returning home stepped four times up the ladder, each time calling, "I am here." And on the fourth step, at her words, her sister had cried with relief. And Kochinnenako vanished, could not therefore return. Ephanie understood that Kochinnenako was the name of any woman who, in the events being told, was walking in the ancient manner, tracing the pattern of the ancient design.

Ephanie looked at the face of the spirit woman, eyes drawn there with undeniable force, and saw that powerful, gleaming hawk beaked face changing, changing, growing old, old, until it was older than time. The face of Old Woman, of hawk, of butterfly, of bee. The face of wolf and spider. The face of old woman coyote. The face of rock and wind and star. The face of infinite, aching, powerful, beloved darkness, of midnight. The face of dawn. The face of red red flame. The face of distant distant star.

And from that great distance, the voice was saying. In a whisper that held the echo of starlight in its depth. That a certain time was upon them. That Ephanie would receive a song.

"The time of ending is upon the Indian. So few, so few are there left. So many being killed. So many already dead. But do not weep for this. For it is as it should be.

"My sister, my granddaughter. A door is closing upon a world, the world we knew. The world we guide and protect. We have ever guarded it. We ever will protect it. But the door closes now. It is the end of our time. We go on to another place, the sixth world. For that is our duty, and our work.

"But we will leave behind in this fifth world certain things. We go so that the people will live.

"Each spirit has its time and place. And it is a certain spirit, a great one, which calls to us now. We go on. The others come behind us. As we go, they take our place. And when they are ready for the next step, others will replace them. For that is the law of the universe, of the Grandmother. The work that is left is to pass on what we know to those who come after us. It is an old story. One that is often repeated. One that is true.

"It isn't whether you're here or there. Whether the people are what you call alive or dead. Those are just words. What you call dead isn't dead. It is a different way of being. And in some cases, in many, the new place, the new way of looking at reality and yourself, is far more valid, far more real, far more vital than the old way.

"I am not saying we want to die. Only that one way or another we live. And on another earth, just like this one, in almost the same place as the one you are lying in, talking with me, the world where your room is, where the city you call San Francisco is. I am also in San Francisco. But it is a very different version of the place from the version you inhabit.

"Come. See my city. Visit me. I think you will like it here. I think you will be surprised to see that death is not possible. That life and being are the only truth.

"Long ago, so far, the people knew this. That was when they could see the person leave the flesh, like you can see someone take off their clothes. They could see the change. Then old Coyote said there would be death. The people would no longer see the whole of the transformation in its entirety. They would only see the body, first vital, then still. So that they would want to go on from where they were. So they would have reason to think. About what life is, about what their flesh is. So they would learn other ways to know, to see. The katsina withdrew so that you would know their true being in yourself. Iyatiku withdrew so you would put her thoughts into your own hearts, and live them as was intended by All That Moves.

"The story of the people and the spirits, the story of the earth, is the story of what moves, what moves on, what patterns, what dances, what sings, what balances, so life can be felt and known. The story of life is the story of moving. Of moving on.

"Your place in the great circling spiral is to help in that story, in that work. To pass on to those who can understand what you have learned, what you know.

"It is for this reason you have endured. That you have tried to understand. When you give away what is in your basket, when what you have given takes root, when it dances, it sings on the earth. Give it to your sister, Teresa. The one who waits. She is ready to know.

"The stories of the old ones, of Utset, Iyatiku and Naotsete, of corn sister and sun sister and of the Spider, shadow sister, is just that. Each gives over what she has and goes on.

"Pass it on, little one. Pass it on. That is the lesson of the giveaways that all the people honor. That is the story of life here where we are and where you are. It is all the same. Grow, move, give, move. That is why they are always leaving. And always coming home. Why it is so that every going out is a coming in. Why every giving is a getting. Every particle in creation knows this. And only the human beings grieve about it. Because only the human beings have forgotten how to live.

"Jump.

"Fall.

"Little sister, you have jumped. You have fallen. You have been brave, but you have misunderstood. So you have learned. How to jump. How to fall. How to learn. How to understand.

"We are asking you to jump again. To fall into this world like the old one, the one you call Anciena, sky woman, jumped, fell, and began in a world that was new."

And the corners grew endless to fill the room. To surround Ephanie and the woman who sat near her on the bed. They grew larger, somehow brighter but with no more light than before, growing, filled, filling her mind and her eyes, her body and her heart with dreams.

And There Was The Spider

And she dreamed. About the women who had lived, long ago, hame haa. Who had lived near caves, near streams. Who had known magic far beyond the simple charms and spells the moderns knew. Who were the Spider. The Spider Medicine Society. The women who created, the women who directed people upon their true paths. The women who healed. The women who sang.

And she understood. For those women, so long lost to her, who she had longed and wept for, unknowing, were the double women, the women who never married, who held power like the Clanuncle, like the power of the priests, the medicine men. Who were not mothers, but who were sisters, born of the same mind, the same spirit. They called each other sister. They were called Grandmother by those who called on them for aid, for knowledge, for comfort, for care.

Who never used their power to coerce. Who waited patient, weaving, silent. Who acted when called on. Who disappeared. Who never abused. Who never allowed themselves to be abused. Who sang.

And in the dream she opened her eyes. Hearing a bird sing. She looked out of her window. Believing she was home, in Guadalupe, that the golden sun was in the window, that the tall trees were singing to the birds, that the birds were singing to the trees.

She sat up, gazing at the window. From which foggy light streamed. She brushed back her untamed hair with a strong, thin hand. The turquoise ring on her finger shone, dully it gleamed. She saw a white, hand-woven shawl, heavily embroidered with black and white designs lying crumpled on the bottom of the bed. She stared at it for a moment, hearing the birds, hearing a chant in her mind, feeling it throbbing at her throat, feeling the drum resonant and deep in her chest. She leaned forward and reached for the shawl. Wrapped it around her shoulders and chest. She lay back down on the pillow. Eyes wide open she lay. Remembering her dream.

Re membering all the wakings of her life. All the goings to sleep. Re membering, humming quietly to herself, in her throat, in her mind she lay. Understanding at last that everything belonged to the wind.

Knowing that only without interference can the people learn and grow and become what they had within themselves to be. For the measure of her life, of all their lives, was discovering what she, they, were made of. What she, they, could do. And what consequences their doing created, and what they would create of these.

And re membered the voice of the woman, who sat in the shadows and spoke, saying "There are no curses. There are only descriptions of what creations there will be."

And in the silence and the quieting shadows of her room, in her bed surrounded by books and notebooks and silence and dust, she thought. And the spiders in the walls, on the ceiling, in the corners, beneath the bed and under the chair began to gather. Their humming, quiet at first, grew louder, filling all of

212

the spaces of the room. Their presence grew around her. She did not move.

And around her the room filled with shadows. And the shadows became shapes. And the shapes became women singing. Singing and dancing in the ancient steps of the women, the Spider. Singing they stepped, slowly, in careful balance of dignity, of harmony, of respect. They stepped and they sang. And she began to sing with them. With her shawl wrapped around her shoulders in the way of the women since time immemorial, she wrapped her shawl and she joined the dance. She heard the singing. She entered the song.

I am walking   Alive
Where I am   Beautiful

I am still   Alive
In beauty   Walking

I am   Entering
Not alone

Paula Gunn Allen was born in 1939. The daughter of a Laguna Pueblo, Sioux, and Scottish mother and a Lebanese-American father, she was raised in a small New Mexican village bounded by a Laguna Pueblo reservation on one side and an Acoma reservation on another. Spanish, German, Laguna, English, and Arabic were all spoken throughout her upbringing at home. Paula spent eleven years at a convent school—from the age of six to seventeen—yet was strongly influenced by her mother's stories about Native American goddesses and traditions. It was after earning a B.A. in English literature and an M.F.A. in creative writing when Paula seized the opportunity to "return to [her] mother's side, to the sacred hoop of [her] grandmother's ways." Now as one of the country's most visible spokespeople for Native American culture, she is also an award winning writer and a professor of English at U.C.L.A. She was awarded the Native American Prize for Literature in 1990, and that same year her anthology of short stories, *Spider Woman's Granddaughters* was awarded the American Book Award sponsored by the Before Columbus Foundation and the Susan Koppleman Award sponsored by The Women's Caucus of the Popular and American Culture Associations. She received a post-doctoral Minorities Scholars Fellowship from the National Research Council-Ford Foundation for research and was appointed associate fellow for humanities at Stanford University, both in 1984, a post-doctoral fellowship from the Institute of American Cultures, U.C.L.A. in 1981, and a N.E.A. writer's grant in 1978. A major Native American poet, writer, lecturer, and scholar, she's published seven volumes of poetry (most recently *Skins and Bones,* San Francisco/Albuquerque; West End Press, 1988), the novel, *The Woman Who Owned the Shadows* (San Francisco; Aunt Lute, 1983), a collection of her essays, *The Sacred Hoop: Recovering the Feminine in American Indian Traditions* (Boston; Beacon Press, 1986), and two anthologies: *Studies in American Indian Literature* (N.Y.; the Modern Language Association, 1982) and the well-received *Spider Woman's Granddaughters: Native American Women's Traditional and Short Stories* (Beacon Press; 1989 and Columbine/Fawcett; 1990). Her most recent work is *Grandmothers of the Light: A Medicine Woman's Sourcebook* (Beacon Press, 1991). The two volume set *Voice of the Turtle: A Century of American Indian Fiction* (N.Y.; Ballantine) is forthcoming. Her prose and poetry appear widely in anthologies, journals, and scholarly publications.

Photography by Tama Rothschild

aunt lute books is a multi-cultural women's press that has been committed to publishing high quality, culturally diverse literature since 1982. In 1990, the Aunt Lute Foundation was formed as a non-profit corporation to publish and distribute books that reflect the complex truths of women's lives and the possibilities for personal and social change. We seek work that explores the specificities of the very different histories from which we come, and that examines the intersections between the borders we all inhabit.

Please write or phone for a free catalogue of our other books or if you wish to be on our mailing list for future titles. You may buy books directly from us by phoning in a credit card order or mailing a check with the catalogue order form.

Aunt Lute Books
P.O. Box 410687
San Francisco, CA 94141
(415) 826-1300